# TERROR IN DESERT SKIES

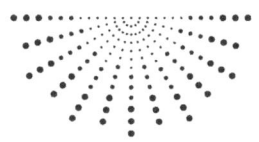

## KATHRYN LANE

*Terror in Desert Skies* is a work of fiction. References to historical events, business establishments, real people, real locations, or other places are used fictionally. Other names, characters, organizations, incidents, events, and locations are the product of the author's imagination, and any resemblance to actual events or locations or persons, living or dead, is entirely coincidental.

Copyright © 2025 by Kathryn Lane

All rights reserved. No part of this book may be used or reproduced or transmitted in any form, including electronic storage and retrieval systems, except by explicit written permission from the publisher. Brief passages excerpted for review purposes are excepted.

ISBN: 979-8-9924223-0-6

eBook ISBN: 978-1-7354638-9-6

Printed and bound in the USA.

Copyright fuels creativity, encourages diverse voices, and promotes free speech—creating a vibrant culture. Thank you for buying an authorized copy of this book. By supporting authors, you are making it possible for writers to continue publishing their works.

Tortuga Publishing, LLC

Bobhurt3@comcast.net

The Woodlands, Texas

Editor: Sandra A. Spicher

Cover Design: Zizi Iryaspraha Subiyarta

Interior Design: Danielle Hartman Acee, authorsassistant.com

Expert Readers: Dr. Joseph Burckhardt, Andrew Mills, and Jorge Lane Terrazas

*For my husband, Bob*

*My son, Philip*

*And in loving memory of my mother, Frances Lane*

# LIST OF CHARACTERS

This list is provided for the reader's benefit. Characters are loosely listed in order of appearance. A few minor characters are omitted.

**Nikki**—private investigator at Security Source, based in Miami.
**Eduardo**—Nikki's husband. He is a neurosurgeon at Mt. Sinai in Miami Beach.
**Keiko**—Eduardo's housekeeper in Colombia, who recently relocated to Miami to live with Nikki and Eduardo.
**Andy**—Nikki's brother, researcher on hibernation for the European Space Agency and a hot-air balloon pilot.
**Cindy**—Andy's wife and Olivia's mother.
**Olivia**—Cindy and Andy's daughter.
**Stan Stevens**—owner of a hot-air balloon scheduled to fly in the mass ascension. He also owns companies that manufacture weather balloons, drones, and communication devices.
**Gustavo Marquez**—chief of the chase crew.
**Derek Brown**—Stan's close friend and consultant for Stan's projects.
**Kenny**—Stan's son from his first marriage to Juanita Rodriguez Stevens.
**Melissa**—Stan's fourth wife.
**Brad Wood**—chase crew member in charge of the burner system.

**Zebras**—name for the launch directors on the field that coordinate balloon flights.
**Sammy Amaya**—offstage character and Andy's friend.
**Celia Hernandez**—witness who saw a small flying object near Andy's hot-air balloon.
**Santiago Cobos**—lead officer from the Albuquerque Police Department.
**Charlotte**—Security Source's office manager and computer geek.
**Floyd**—owner of Security Source, the investigative company where Nikki works.
**Lisa Morales**—a detective with the Albuquerque police department.
**Helen and Harold Smith**—Cindy's parents.
**Dr. Patel**—an intern at the university hospital.
**Dr. Khan**—head neurosurgeon at the university hospital.
**Dr. Raj Sharma**—neurophysiologist supervising the team of intraoperative neuromonitoring specialists.
**Carmen Ruiz**—Dr. Sharma's technologist.
**Mark Edwards**—minority partner in Stan's company.
**Juanita Rodriguez Stevens**—Stan Stevens's first wife and Kenny's mother.
**Maxine Sanchez**—reporter at the Center for Investigative Reporting.
**Carol Peters**—Stan's competitor in the surveillance and weather drone industry.
**Clive Underwood**—CIA operative and Floyd's friend.
**Ramon Estrada**—informant for the reporter Maxine Sanchez.
**Juan Estrada**—Ramon's son.
**Vasquez Medina**—offstage Mexican cartel character.

# CHAPTER ONE

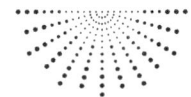

The scent of hot asphalt filled the air as Nikki mounted her rented Harley: a shiny black Street Glide. The Sandia Mountains dominated the skyline to the east. The foreground was all bright orange cones and a blinking road sign that warned traffic of the crew repairing potholes.

The workers, wearing gloves, full-face respirators, hard hats, and coveralls overlaid with high-visibility vests, toiled under the harsh New Mexico sun. An old gray dump truck idled nearby. Its tilted bed carried a load of steaming black asphalt and its door proclaimed the company name Potholes and More. Next to the truck, a hotbox trailer kept the asphalt mixture warm. A crew member used a long-handled shovel to scoop the hot, sticky material into waiting wheelbarrows. Two men moved the wheelbarrows from one pothole to the next, dumping the mixture carefully into the jagged gaps in the pavement. Another man used a tamping tool to press the asphalt into place. A fifth guy rolled a plate compactor over the fresh asphalt fill.

Nikki wondered how they could work in such heavy gear. A sixth man stood idly by the dump truck. She had the urge to ask him for a mask to avoid breathing those fumes. He must have caught her looking at him, for he gave her a wave and a winning smile. She waved back.

Eduardo, oblivious to the road work, revved his rented Ducati Scrambler and grinned at Nikki. "I could get used to this."

Nikki turned to see if Keiko, who had joined them on this trip, was ready to take a ride.

The seventy-year-old Keiko swung her leg over the Honda CB500X and settled into the seat. "Get used to it? I've *missed* this." She ran her hands over the handlebars like an old friend she hadn't seen in years. She turned to Eduardo with a spark in her dark eyes.

"In that case, we'll buy one for you when we return to Miami," Eduardo said.

Keiko had recently moved in with them from Medellin, Colombia, where she'd used a motorcycle to get around that crowded city. Nikki adjusted her gloves and asked Keiko to lead the way to Route 66.

Keiko had studied the map when they'd first arrived to rent the bikes. They were in the university area, and she told them they'd ride toward their hotel in Old Town.

She gave a sharp nod and pulled her visor down. "Follow me."

Engines roaring, they rolled onto the street, carefully skirting the area under repair, and merged into the steady pulse of Albuquerque's late afternoon traffic. The hum of their bikes blended with the purring of passing cars.

Route 66 stretched before them like a ribbon of history. Neon signs cluttered the sides of the street. The signs would flicker to life as soon as twilight set in. They would announce available vacancies at old, faded motels, or light up the windows of retro diners promising the best Hatch green chile burgers, or advertise hip cafés proudly showing they'd been converted from classic gas stations. Nikki felt a rush of adrenaline, and she hoped Eduardo and Keiko were enjoying the sights too.

Nikki's brother Andy and sister-in-law Cindy had invited them to experience the International Balloon Fiesta in Albuquerque. The event would start the next morning before sunrise. They would get up early and drive their rental car to the Balloon Fiesta Park for the mass ascension.

In the meantime, they had rented motorcycles to tour a snippet of Route 66. Called Central Avenue as it traverses the city of Albuquerque, the old road attracts travelers from all over the world who want the mystique of a long-gone era.

Nikki was excited to claim she'd ridden a motorcycle on Route 66. It had been one of the more offbeat items on her bucket list, and now, at last, she could say she'd done it. A modest claim, but one that filled her heart with quiet satisfaction.

She and Eduardo had dreamed of taking a longer trip—just the two of them on this road. Maybe they'd ride all the way to Sky City, the legendary Acoma Pueblo perched high atop a sandstone mesa. If only time weren't always in such short supply. She drifted to another dream still waiting in the wings: to hike the Camino de Santiago in Spain, where the isolation and rough terrain might offer a spiritual recalibration.

A car honked—three short, chirpy beeps as it passed. She glanced over, catching the driver's wave before he sped ahead. A local welcome she figured.

She admired Keiko's skillful riding. Having her with them filled her heart with joy. Eduardo had always thought of Keiko as his second mother. She had no family of her own, so Nikki suggested they invite her to join them in the US. The attorney who handled Eduardo's immigration did all the paperwork for Keiko to relocate to the US.

Another car honked as it passed. An angry driver this time. Nikki felt like a novice rider and was not surprised at the driver's impatience. She watched Keiko negotiate through traffic, zipping past slower vehicles or settling in behind faster ones. She was clearly accustomed to riding in the far more chaotic streets of Medellin.

Nikki allowed herself to drift into thoughts of Keiko's background. She'd been orphaned in Japan as a child. An aunt and uncle, living in Colombia, South America, had brought her to live with them. It was curious to Nikki that she had also lost her parents, though Nikki had been a teenager when her parents died in an auto accident. Her grandparents had taken responsibility for her and her brother.

Eduardo pulled up from the rear and stayed next to Nikki, bringing her thoughts back to the present moment. She turned and smiled at her husband. They both followed Keiko.

Nikki had only ridden since she'd met Eduardo four years ago while on assignment in Colombia. In Medellin, he'd taken her for a ride on his Harley. She'd been so terrified that she hardly breathed the entire time. They had motorcycles in Miami but had been too busy to ride much.

Keiko signaled a right turn, and Nikki thought Keiko was taking them onto a side road to get out of the heavy traffic on Central Avenue.

Within two blocks, she realized Keiko had steered them to the center of Old Town, a cluster of buildings built by the Spanish governor Francisco Cuervo y Valdes in 1706. A parish church, San Felipe de Neri, stood across the plaza. The church's serene adobe façade had set the standard for the architecture in the town square. Keiko stopped her bike and asked Nikki if she wanted to visit the church.

"Another time," Nikki responded. "Right now, we should return the motorcycles and get our rental car. We'll drive to the hotel and see if my brother and his family have arrived."

Nikki was anxious to see her family, especially her niece, the eighteen-month-old Olivia. The toddler reminded Nikki of her son, Robbie. She'd lost her only child in a tragic accident when he was twelve. Nikki would never fully recover.

Keiko would lead them back to the motorcycle rental service even though their hotel was only four blocks from where they were right now. Traffic on the return ride had subsided.

When they pulled into the motorcycle rental lot, Nikki swung off her bike, stretching her arms as she removed her helmet. "Route 66, the Mother Road. That was worth it."

"The city is far more interesting than I'd expected," Eduardo said, waving the attendant over to return the motorcycles.

"I agree," Keiko said. She grinned and, removing her helmet, shook out her hair. "This city has a lot of soul."

---

The hotel parking lot was full of pickups, the majority with gondolas or other hot-air balloon paraphernalia secured in the beds. The vehicles would be used by the chase crews at the balloon fiesta the next day.

"We're the lone sedan in a sea of pickups," Keiko said, gazing out the window.

"This is too crowded. Let's park down the street," Nikki suggested.

"How about taking this place?" Eduardo asked. He took an open spot for their rental car close to the hotel entrance.

"You always find great parking," Nikki said. "You're so lucky."

"I am very lucky." Eduardo leaned over to give her a quick kiss on the lips.

Inside the lobby, Nikki phoned her brother. Andy and Cindy had arrived half an hour before and were settling into their room.

"We'll meet you downstairs for a drink in about five minutes," Andy said.

"If we can find space." Nikki told him the place was overflowing with balloonists.

She informed Eduardo and Keiko that her family would be down soon.

Within minutes an elevator door opened. Olivia ran out on her stiff little legs, like any eighteen-month-old would run. Nikki moved to greet her, but the child rushed back to her mother, overwhelmed by either the crowded lobby or by an aunt she probably didn't remember from the last time they'd been together.

Nikki introduced Keiko to Andy and his wife, Cindy.

While they waited for a table at the patio bar, Andy explained the plan for the next day. His friend, Stan Stevens, owner of a balloon that would fly in the fiesta, was hosting a crew party at the Hacienda Restaurant later that evening. They were all invited.

As they chattered about going or not going to the party, Keiko entertained Olivia with hand games and peekaboo.

"Keiko," Nikki said, "you and Olivia seem to talk the same language."

"They'll be fast friends for life," Eduardo said. "Keiko is a natural with children."

"Even though I never had any of my own, I love children," Keiko added. She glanced at Olivia, who was expecting the next clue in their game.

"You have me," Eduardo retorted, pouting like a child. "I thought I was your adopted son."

Keiko grinned. "Yes, you were my bocchan, as we say in Japanese, my young master. You still are."

The conversation drifted back to planning the evening and the next day. Cindy and Nikki decided they'd stay at the hotel and let the boys have a night out. Keiko also opted to stay in, saying she wanted to get a good night's sleep before the big balloon fiesta opened the next morning.

As soon as Eduardo and her brother left for the crew party, the women called it a day and headed for the elevator.

Nikki wondered who was taking care of the animals that her brother and Cindy worked with as part of the research project they did for The European Space Agency. She knew that Cindy loved the work so much she was always hesitant to leave them.

"Who is feeding your research animals while you're away?" Nikki asked.

"Two fellows from the University of Arizona. They're doing their postdoc research on the impact interplanetary travel may have on sleep and circadian rhythms. They love our chipmunks and kangaroo rats. This winter, they'll work with the hibernating bears."

"Sounds like you're lucky to have them," Nikki said.

The elevator stopped. Nikki and Keiko said goodnight to Cindy and Olivia and headed down the hall toward their rooms. Passing by a window, Nikki caught sight of the late evening sun reflected on the Sandia Mountains. The mountains glowed reddish, an almost watermelon hue. No wonder the early conquistadors had named them the Sandias, the Spanish word for watermelon. Tomorrow, they would all witness a sunrise over the Sandias.

# CHAPTER TWO

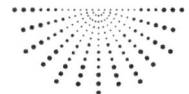

"I'm not part of the chase crew and I don't know the host," Eduardo said. "Are you sure it's okay that I'm here?"

"You're my guest," Andy said, slapping his brother-in-law's shoulder.

A man wearing a crewneck over an Oxford shirt greeted Andy with a bear hug.

"Stan and I have been friends since we met at Stanford," Andy said, introducing his friend to Eduardo.

Stan shook Eduardo's hand. "Glad you're here."

"It's a great party," Eduardo said, thanking his host. Considering the forty or so people attending and the open bar, Eduardo was happy not to be picking up the bill.

Andy worked the room, chatting with people he knew and introducing himself and Eduardo to those he didn't. After a couple of beers, Eduardo partook of the appetizers set out on a long table that staff kept refilling from the kitchen.

Stan walked up to them, asking Andy to step out to the patio for a minute.

When Andy returned, he told Eduardo that Stan had been called away for an urgent business meeting in Washington, DC. "He's asked me to pilot his balloon tomorrow. I'll call Cindy to see if she wants to copilot.

Stan's son also has his license, but he's so young that Stan won't let him fly on his own."

"I remember you and Cindy talked about buying a balloon," Eduardo said. "This is a great chance to participate in the fiesta."

"Stan wants me to keep his travels confidential," Andy said. "Though people will find out tomorrow morning that he's not around to fly."

Another man walked up. Andy introduced Gustavo Marquez, the crew chief for Stan's balloon.

"Are you ready to crew tomorrow?" Andy asked.

"You bet," Gustavo said. "If there were paid positions in the chase crews, that's how I'd earn a living. It'd be a hell of a lot more fun than filling potholes." He laughed.

Andy held up his beer. "I'll drink to that."

"We saw workers repairing potholes on Central Avenue today," Eduardo said. "A company called Potholes and More."

"Yeah, I had some men up that way," Gustavo acknowledged. "I was up there part of the morning too."

"What's the 'more' part of Potholes and More?" Eduardo asked.

Gustavo laughed. "Fun activities, like chasing balloons. Also, I fill potholes the old-fashioned way."

"What does that mean?"

"Only that I use hot asphalt," Gustavo explained, "not the temporary patching material so many companies use now."

Andy excused himself and went to the patio to call Cindy.

When he returned, Eduardo and Gustavo were deep in conversation about motorcycles and hot-air ballooning.

"You guys are acting like you've had too much to drink," Andy joked. He laughed as he asked the bartender for another beer.

"I was merely saying that I prefer motorcycles to balloons," Eduardo said.

"When you crew in New Mexico, you're often chasing balloons across the desert." Gustavo took another chug of beer. "Chasing them in a pickup or an all-terrain vehicle over the bumps, rocks, and arroyos gives you a real feel of power."

"Daredevil power," Eduardo said.

"You got that right." Gustavo held his beer up for a toast.

When another man joined them, Andy introduced him as Stan's close friend and creative genius, Derek Brown.

"Where's Stan?" Derek inquired.

Andy glanced around. "Not sure. Maybe he's outside."

Eduardo did not understand what was so important about keeping Stan's business trip a secret until tomorrow morning, but there must be a reason for Andy to cover for his friend.

"Cindy wants to fly tomorrow," Andy whispered to Eduardo. He helped himself to another round of appetizers. "We'll need to leave the hotel about three-thirty a.m."

"Then we should head back," Eduardo suggested.

Andy glanced out the window. "Wait, I'll be right back."

Eduardo looked out to see what had caught his brother-in-law's attention. A woman was standing by herself under a large cottonwood. Andy stood near her but did not approach her. She seemed to be talking on the phone. That must be why Andy held back.

When Andy returned, he and Eduardo left the party and climbed into Andy's pickup. Andy was quiet and seemed pensive on their way back to the hotel.

"Cindy and I will drive to the balloon park. We need to arrive early to prepare for the launch and to inform the chase crew that we're piloting instead of Stan. That'll give you an extra hour of sleep time," Andy said. "Cindy asked Nikki to take care of Olivia so she can join me as copilot. In fact, Olivia is spending the night in Keiko's room, so we don't awaken you in the morning."

# CHAPTER THREE

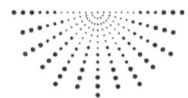

Nikki scanned the crowded Balloon Fiesta Park. Hot-air balloons, in various stages of preparation, billowed gently in the breeze. The 360-acre park on the north side of Albuquerque buzzed with balloon enthusiasts from around the world. Eighty acres were used as the launch field, leaving the rest for parking, vendor booths, a medical tent, ambulances, police, fire engines, and an assortment of specialty tents. Mounted police patrolled the area, keeping their horses at the perimeter of the field. Nikki saw a couple avidly talking to an officer while their three children petted the horse's nose.

In the distance, the Sandia Mountains glowed in the golden rays of dawn. Nikki elbowed her way through a throng of teenagers lining up to watch the mass ascension at the park. She'd promised Cindy to get her daughter to the balloon before they lifted off so they could take pictures. She looked back to check that Keiko, carrying the eighteen-month-old, was following her. She thought of stopping for Keiko and Olivia to admire one of the horses up close, but she had to keep her promise to get Olivia to her mother before their balloon launched.

The opening ceremony had just concluded, and the crowd was moving, vying for the right spot to stake out. The ceremony had included a light show projected from drones in the early morning sky. It had displayed 3-D images of the ubiquitous New Mexican symbols of red and green chilis, aliens from outer space, and the state flag. Immediately following the light show, the Dawn Patrol balloons launched at sunrise, signaling the official opening of the event.

Nikki craned her neck, searching for the balloon her brother and his wife would fly today. She steeled herself against the cool morning breeze and zipped up her leather jacket. With thousands of fans swarming the launch field, Nikki hoped she could find Andy and Cindy before they were airborne.

The colorful fabric envelopes of the balloons covered the dry grass like a patchwork quilt. Other balloons lofted skyward from various sections of the field as she broke through the crowd. Eduardo caught up with her. He placed his arm around her shoulder.

"Magnificent, isn't it?" he said in English, his Colombian accent seemingly more pronounced by the sunrise they'd just witnessed over the Sandias. The sunlight now illuminated the colorful balloons.

She smiled and glanced over her shoulder again to make sure Keiko and Olivia were right behind them. The petite Japanese woman seemed to relish the opportunity to care for the child while the toddler's parents ascended into the sky in a hot-air balloon.

"The balloons remind me of Japanese lanterns," Keiko said, stepping next to Nikki. "They float away in the same manner. But these balloons are bigger and carry people."

Olivia babbled and giggled with excitement as she gaped at the colorful shapes rising into the sky. She pointed to those inflating on the ground as if she understood where they started their journey.

Nikki, stepping out from Eduardo's embrace, caught a whiff of the mouth-watering green chile aroma that the breeze carried in from a nearby vendor selling breakfast burritos.

The hiss of propane burners in the balloons broke the rhythmic hum of the crowd's palpably excited voices. The noise coming from the burners annoyed Nikki in a way she didn't understand. The hiss disturbed the delicate beauty of the vibrant envelopes being inflated on the ground and the balloons already rising into the sky.

Eduardo took photos of the spectacle. He also framed balloons behind Keiko holding the joyful Olivia. The child reached her hands toward the sky as if to catch a balloon.

Nikki checked for text messages and read the latest one Andy had sent. They were still on the ground, waiting for them before launching. She scanned the field, then smiled when she spotted him waving her over. The balloon was tethered to the ground with ropes held by members of the chase crew. Two of them moved in to hold the gondola as the envelope was inflated. Andy and Cindy had been flying for a little more than a year and both had taken balloonist training, including survival techniques in case of an emergency. When Nikki asked about safety, Andy assured her that ballooning was the safest sport in aviation. He'd acquired his commercial certificate, and Cindy had recently passed the private license certification.

The balloon, belonging to Andy's friend Stan, displayed a striking turquoise-blue envelope emblazoned with a black and orange logo. It featured a stylized globe with silver squiggly lines, like lightning, reaching toward the sky from the top of the globe. As the balloon's envelope continued to inflate, black lettering printed in a semicircle under the globe boldly stated CONNECTING THE WORLD, though the name of Stan's company was Omega Satellites.

Andy stood in front of the gondola. To his left was a young man, about sixteen. Andy reached for Cindy and pulled her close. He signaled for Nikki to take pictures. The young man was most likely Stan's son, Kenny, from a prior marriage. Nikki had never met Kenny, or even Stan for that matter. Her sister-in-law had mentioned that Stan was on his fourth marriage and making a special effort to include his teenage son in activities they both enjoyed. Kenny lived with his mother, and apparently, he did not get along with his young stepmother, Melissa. He had passed his balloonist's exam, but his father was understandably nervous about letting him fly on his own.

With Stan being called away at the last minute, Andy would cover as pilot for the entire weekend. Yet the fiesta's program showed Stan flying both Saturday and Sunday.

When Andy asked her to copilot, Cindy had jumped at the chance. It was almost midnight when she called to ask Nikki if she and Keiko could take care of Olivia. She'd sounded so excited about piloting that Nikki immediately agreed.

Nikki hoped Andy was not nursing a hangover this morning. Eduardo didn't drink much, yet he'd had three or four beers at the crew party and was probably feeling them—and the lack of sleep.

Andy introduced Kenny to his family and Keiko when they approached the balloon.

"Mama, mama," Olivia said, stretching her arms toward her mother.

Keiko handed the child over to Cindy.

Cindy pointed out different balloons to her daughter, like the one depicting a rat with huge eyes. Olivia seemed most excited over a pink elephant, complete with a trunk and big ears, that had just launched.

Andy called the head of the chase crew, Gustavo Marquez, to meet his sister and Keiko. Gustavo held up his hand signaling he'd be right over, apparently needing to give orders to the volunteers that were helping to inflate the envelope.

As soon as he was introduced, Gustavo's captivating smile won Nikki's approval. She peppered him with questions about the chase crew responsibilities.

Andy glanced around as if looking for details that needed attention. At one point, he walked straight to a nearby balloon that was preparing to launch. He engaged in conversation with a man and a woman, but Nikki didn't pay much attention. She was fascinated by the work carried out by the crew members.

Gustavo briefly explained the duties of the other members of the crew, stating that his experienced guy, Brad Wood, was helping with the burner system and inflating the envelope while the younger ones, holding the balloon to the ground, were recent recruits to crewing, though in real life, they worked at his company.

"What kind of real-life work?" Nikki asked.

With a laugh, he said they filled potholes.

"Gustavo was the supervisor on the pothole repairs we saw yesterday," Eduardo said.

"Really?" Nikki asked. "You must have been the one standing by the dump truck." She had almost said he was the man with the great smile, but she'd caught herself in time and kept it to herself.

"That would've been me," Gustavo said, "the one standing around doing nothing." He grinned again and excused himself to help the balloon crew with the setup.

The volunteers holding the ropes kept the balloon from flying off without a pilot. Nikki shivered to think a complete novice might be inside a gondola that could take off unexpectedly. What would happen in a case like that? How could an inexperienced person be rescued from a runaway balloon?

Andy returned, looking too serious for someone presumably enjoying the activity. Nikki walked over to him to ask if he was okay.

"It's just something I need to tell Stan," he mumbled. "It'll wait until I see him."

An hour and a half had elapsed since the mass ascension had started. The flight time for Andy and his copilots was coming up.

"The ascension is a series of controlled launches that takes almost two hours to complete," Andy explained to his sister. "It's a methodical process to avoid accidents or injuries."

Nikki saw the airspace over the field was full of balloons. Most were drifting south toward the city of Albuquerque, though a few floated toward the mesa on the west side. The sight was beautiful yet terrifying.

"How can you know if there are balloons above you if you cannot see through the envelope?" Nikki asked. "I think it'd be dangerous to fly into one."

"That's the role the zebras play, those men wearing the black and white striped shirts," Andy said, pointing to a man directing a launch not too far from them. "They're the launch directors. Think of them as air traffic controllers. Gustavo has notified that guy that we're ready, so he'll come over and tell us when we can fly."

Kenny climbed into the gondola. Andy moved near the balloon and instructed Kenny to check the burner system in preparation for takeoff. Cindy returned her daughter to Keiko. Andy helped his wife aboard.

Nikki gave Olivia a kiss on the forehead and told Keiko to let her know if she needed help taking care of the toddler.

"I love having a child to watch," Keiko said. She smiled and added, "I'm pretending she's my magomusume, my granddaughter."

The zebra signaled Andy that they were cleared for flight. Nikki appreciated the appropriate nickname. They were easily visible in their black-and-white shirts.

Nikki held her breath as the balloon left the ground. With her fear of heights, there was no way she would fly in an open gondola.

Eduardo snapped more pictures. Keiko nestled Olivia in her arms and spoke to her in Spanish, though the child seemed oblivious as she reached her arms toward her mother. Kenny was working the burner while Andy supervised him. Cindy spoke into her mouthpiece, probably touching base with the chase crew. Theirs was one of the last balloons to lift off.

With graceful ease, the gondola swayed as it rose further into the air. Its occupants leaned over the edge to wave at them. Cindy's hair, coming loose from a ponytail, whipped in the breeze. She blew kisses to Olivia, and Keiko urged the child to return the gesture.

The colorful sky must have had close to six hundred balloons gracefully drifting southbound. Nikki forgot her apprehension and allowed herself to relax into the moment and imagined the sights that Andy and Cindy were seeing now that they'd gained altitude.

Nikki reached for her phone and snapped photos of the turquoise-blue balloon as it ascended, the sunlight catching the vibrant fabric and making it glow.

As it rose in the sky, Eduardo suggested they track down the vendor making the breakfast burritos. He grabbed Nikki's hand and turned toward the Hatch Shack on Main Street in the park.

Nikki didn't budge. "I can't leave. This is too beautiful. Look how splendid the colors are, how softly the balloons are drifting away. It's magical."

"We can watch them as we walk to breakfast."

"Look!" Nikki gripped Eduardo's hand. "What's that flying next to Andy's balloon?"

"I don't see anything," he said, craning his head.

"It must be a drone, the way the sunlight's hitting it." Nikki glanced at Eduardo.

Without warning, a sharp crack split the air.

Nikki's head whipped back to her brother's balloon. The gondola jerked violently. Flames bounced from it and rose into the envelope. Gasps rippled through the crowd as the balloon's envelope shriveled and drooped. It reinflated as flames poured over the gondola and cascaded down its side.

"Oh my God," Nikki whispered desperately. "Please, no."

A teenager taking photos bumped into Nikki. She wanted to scream. She wanted to run. Her loved ones were in danger and all people could do was take pictures.

"They're in trouble," Eduardo said. "They're losing altitude."

Flames engulfed the envelope. The balloon plummeted toward the ground in a terrifying arc.

# CHAPTER FOUR

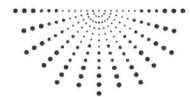

The balloon crashed with a deafening thud into the cabin of a pickup truck. The gondola rolled off the hood and toppled onto the ground, throwing Andy and Cindy onto the field. It rolled over Kenny, trapping him. The envelope fell into a tangled heap of burned fabric, covering the pickup. Without the wind to fuel them, the flames quickly abated.

"Get Olivia out of here," Eduardo commanded, handing the keys to Keiko. "Wait for us at the rental car."

Screams erupted from the crowd. People ran, some toward safety, others to get a morbid view of the accident, taking videos and photos.

Nikki shrieked. "Not my family. Please God, save them."

Eduardo grabbed her arm, and they ran toward the crash site.

The acrid smell of propane filled the air.

Bystanders were already gathering by the gondola. A few were pulling the partially burnt envelope off the pickup and away from the burner assembly.

"Andy," Nikki cried as she dropped to her knees beside him. His hair was charred, blood streamed from a deep gash on his head, and his face was patchy with burns.

Eduardo surveyed the scene. He yelled at bystanders pulling Kenny's trapped body out from under the gondola to wait for the medics to move the injured. A few feet away, Cindy was sprawled on the ground, motionless.

"Call 911 and tell them to get three ambulances over here," Eduardo hollered at a bystander. He remembered seeing emergency vehicles parked at the edge of the field.

---

Nikki's trembling fingers fumbled to find a pulse in Andy's neck, feeling as if her action were done in slow motion. It was as if the accident caused the world to freeze. Or maybe her mind had slowed down to grapple with the unfolding tragedy. Movement across the field caught her attention. A man racing toward the balloon seemed unnatural in the world she was experiencing. She watched him. As he ran, he pulled up a red kerchief from his neck to cover his face, leaving it just below his sunglasses, covering his nose. He approached the gondola, crouched beside it for a moment, and then leaned in, angling his face for a better look at the damage inside. Dazed, she watched as he put on gloves and crawled partially under the gondola. With a sigh of relief, she realized he had probably turned off the gas escaping from the burner.

The noise of the crowd was replaced by Nikki's pounding heart. The familiar sound of sirens filled the air. She looked up and the kerchiefed man was walking away. Why? Was he an angel saving those around the balloon from injury if the propane tank ignited? Or was there a sinister reason he'd been there? Could she be too jaded from her years as an investigator to trust someone at a crime scene trying to help? She snapped several pictures, but the man was disappearing into the crowd, his back toward her.

Eduardo knelt at Andy's side, assessing his injury. Andy opened his eyes briefly and closed them again. "He's alive," Eduardo said, "but we need urgent help to stabilize him." He stood and waved the paramedics over.

The next few minutes became a blur as Nikki watched the EMTs place her brother on a stretcher. The event security personnel scattered about, trying to control the onlookers snapping pictures as if they were watching a circus. Tears rolled down Nikki's face. She pounded the earth and sobbed.

The roar of a helicopter filled the air. It was flying in from the north side of the field, avoiding all the balloons drifting south and west. She glanced at Eduardo who was helping the security guards try to control the crowd. They asked them to move away so the chopper could land.

Nikki ran to Cindy.

Cindy's eyes fluttered. Nikki fell to her knees next to her mangled body. She touched Cindy's shoulder to avoid the burned skin on her face and arms.

"Thank God, you're alive."

Cindy whispered. "Olivia . . . take care . . . of Olivia."

"You're going to make it," Nikki said. "Medics are here."

Cindy's eyes closed.

Nikki reached for Cindy's shoulder again. "Stay awake, please Cindy, stay here with us. We need you. You must stay here for Olivia's sake."

A second chopper landed not far from where medical personnel were securing Andy's stretcher inside the first one.

The wail of the ambulance sirens had hardly faded when the first police vehicles pulled up to the chaotic crash site. Two marked squad cars screeched to a halt. Uniformed officers stepped out, talking into their radios as they assessed the scene. Fire engines, two of them, were close behind. One stopped closer to the balloon and two men jumped out to survey the damage.

The lead officer, a tall man with a firm jawline and reflective sunglasses, stood next to his vehicle and spoke into a long-range acoustic device. "Alright, folks, back up. For your own safety, we need everyone to stay behind the perimeter."

The noise from the crowd soon quieted to a murmur, though bystanders still recorded every detail of the accident with their phones.

Nausea struck Nikki as she watched Cindy. She moved away to allow the medics better access. One of them took Cindy's pulse at the carotid artery. He moved on to Kenny, on the ground nearby. Another medic carried beige blankets from the ambulance to where she lay. He used a blanket to cover Cindy, including her face.

Nikki froze. This could not be happening. Cindy had spoken to her. Cindy couldn't be gone. No, this could not be real.

The medic approached Nikki and asked if she was a relative.

She nodded.

"I'm afraid they're both gone. I'm sorry. A doctor is on the way, but there's nothing we can do."

How could this have happened? Nikki's stomach clenched tight. Olivia would grow up without her mother.

A police officer asked her to move outside the perimeter, but when he learned she was a relative, he backed away, only asking her to be careful.

Eduardo appeared beside Nikki, telling her to meet Keiko at their rental car. "That's where she'll wait for you. I'm going to the hospital. Andy's in critical condition."

Nikki looked at her husband in disbelief. "Cindy and Kenny didn't make it."

"I know," he said. "You should call Cindy's parents. And Stan."

"Keep me informed. I'll take care of Keiko and Olivia." She told him she'd look around the crash site first.

"Be careful," Eduardo admonished. "This may not have been an accident. You don't suppose this is related to Andy's friend, Sammy Amaya?"

Nikki looked at the crumpled remains of the gondola and wiped tears from her cheek. "That drone I saw. It could have caused this. I hope it's not revenge or sabotage. Related to Sammy? I don't see why it would be. Only time will tell. But if someone caused this tragedy, I'll find them."

Eduardo, already racing to the medevac helicopter, had not heard her. He jumped aboard and the helicopter lifted off. Nikki closed her eyes to say a prayer.

When she opened her eyes again, two officers were unspooling yellow police tape, cordoning off the area as a third officer moved to further assist the event personnel directing the crowd to get farther back. On this side of the large field, the festive energy of the balloon fiesta had turned into somber silence, punctuated by murmured speculation and the crackle of police radios.

# CHAPTER FIVE

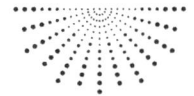

Still in shock, Nikki slipped into autopilot. Her first investigative task was to take photos of the crash scene. She would find out if this had been an accident or, God forbid, something worse. If the latter, she wouldn't rest until she brought the culprits to justice.

Getting a grip on her emotions, she surveyed the area. The pickup cab that the gondola had initially hit was crushed to the seat level, with only a slight bump visible where the steering wheel had held the weight of the gondola. Apparently, the pickup belonged to another chase crew, and the owner was speaking with police officers. He must be getting the information needed to file a claim. Nikki was struck by the surreal thought that the world was nothing but financial issues. Even in Andy's case, the hospital and doctors would be glad to learn he had good medical coverage.

A bystander, behind the cordoned off area, waved persistently at Nikki. In a daze, she walked over to speak with the person. A woman, short and stout, stepped forward eagerly. Her large brown eyes darted from side to side.

"Is there something you want to tell me?" Nikki asked.

"I-I don't know. It happened so fast . . . but—" She broke off, glancing around as though afraid someone might overhear.

"But what?" Nikki pressed, her voice calm but firm.

"I saw something flying . . . like a dish. At first, I thought it was a large bird, but it wasn't." She looked at Nikki, her eyes focusing for the first time. "It hovered close to the balloon for a minute or so. Then there was a flash, and the balloon caught on fire."

Nikki's stomach churned. "Did you see where it went?"

"No," the woman said, her eyes darting around again. "It disappeared. But I swear I saw it. I'm not crazy."

Nikki paused for a second. "Can you describe it?"

"Black, maybe gray. A red blinking light underneath. The light was just a pinhead. It flew right up to the balloon," the woman said in an agitated voice, as if not caring now if anyone else heard.

"Did you see it after the explosion? After the fire started?" Nikki asked.

"Definitely before," she said, sounding more confident. "Now that I think about it, maybe it set off the explosion."

"Where were you standing when you saw it?" Nikki worked to keep her emotions under control.

The woman pointed toward the center of the field. "I was about thirty yards in that direction. The balloon was high, and from that angle, I could hardly make out the world logo. That's when I saw the little thing fly in from the east and hover around the balloon. Then the fire started in the gondola," she said. "From where I stood, looking at the balloon, the Sandias were clearly in the background. That's why I say it flew in from the east."

Nikki had also thought she'd seen a drone even though Eduardo had not seen it. The woman's account confirmed that something had flown near the hot-air balloon. Its flight had to be from the east or northeast, since the balloons were all heading south and west. Nikki asked the woman for her name and requested her phone number in case she wanted to reach her later. The woman, Celia Hernandez, shared her contact details.

"Are you willing to tell the police what you've just told me?" Nikki asked.

Celia nodded.

"Please wait here," Nikki said. She headed toward the officer who appeared to be in charge. On the way, she took more photos of the crash site with the mountains in the background. She wanted to get the angle Celia had mentioned when the balloon gondola caught fire.

Nikki felt her adrenaline kicking in. Her mind raced through the scenario of the balloon on the ground, the liftoff, the members of the chase crew jumping into the truck. Her knuckles turned white from gripping her phone.

The photos of the wreckage, debris, and the angle from where Celia had stood were still fresh on the screen. She approached the officer to report Celia's information.

"I'm Nikki Garcia," she said, her voice steady despite the whirlwind of emotions. "My brother and his wife were in that balloon."

The officer paused, his stern demeanor softening. "I'm sorry to hear that, ma'am. Are you okay?"

"Not really, but my brother was airlifted to the hospital. I hope he makes it. My sister-in-law"—Nikki swallowed hard—"my sister-in-law didn't survive." She stopped to take a breath and added in a hoarse whisper, "This crash may not have been an accident."

The officer's brow furrowed. "What makes you say that?"

"That woman over there. Please talk to her. She saw a drone near my brother's balloon before the small explosion that caused the fire. I also saw it, but I wasn't sure what I'd seen."

The officer told Nikki he'd report what she'd informed him. He stepped aside to make a phone call. When he finished, he headed toward the drone witness. Nikki followed him. The woman's large brown eyes darted from her to the officer.

Turning toward Nikki, the officer asked her to move further back so he could interview the witness privately. "I've called a detective to follow up on your allegations. She'll be in contact with you to get your testimony," he said, handing his card to Nikki.

Officer Santiago Cobos, Nikki read from the business card. She put the card into her pants pocket and jogged to the area Celia had pointed out. As she slowed to a walk, she mentally plotted out a circle within which she would look for clues. It was worth a try.

She covered the area slowly, searching the ground for anything unusual. The dirt was covered with buffalo grass and desert weeds that had been crushed by people, trucks, and balloons. Concentrating on her task, she caught the glint of a small metallic object in the sunlight. Kneeling, she carefully extracted a charred device embedded in the dirt.

It was a compact circuit board encased in partially melted plastic, with what looked like a broken piece of a miniature camera lens protruding from one side. She wrapped it in a tissue and pocketed it. After walking the area a second time, she found no further pieces of evidence. Cigarette butts covered the ground, despite the rule against smoking around propane.

Nikki headed toward the fire engines that were still on the field, though they had not really done anything. A tall, lanky man introduced himself and asked if he could be of assistance.

She asked if he or any of the firefighters had inspected the burner system on the crashed balloon.

"That's not really our job," he said. "That's for the police or the NTSB, the National Transportation Safety Board."

"How would anyone know if the burner or the propane tank had been tampered with?" Nikki asked.

"You should direct your questions to the police or the NTSB."

Nikki pulled her private investigator license out to show the firefighter.

"I'm sorry, ma'am, I can't answer your questions. I'm not being difficult. It's just not my place."

Another vehicle roared up.

"That's most likely the forensic personnel. Ask them, if you wish," the man said.

The forensic technician surveyed the scene and began photographing the wreckage while a couple of others searched the ground, looking for evidence or fragments of any sort. They were bagging a few items, but Nikki could not see what they'd found. The forensic technician also took pictures of the damage to the truck where the balloon had fallen.

Next, he asked the ambulance personnel to uncover the bodies so he could record them too. Nikki's stomach churned and she thought she'd faint, but she knew she must watch to make sure she'd catch anything unusual.

Once he was done, Nikki explained she was related to the victims and asked if he'd seen any evidence of wrongdoing. He responded that if he'd found something suspicious, he would not be able to discuss it with her even if she was related to the victims. The labs would evaluate the evidence and render an opinion.

Another car pulled up. The man who stepped out, wearing a white coat, appeared to be a doctor who had come to examine the bodies. Nikki walked up to him. He introduced himself and asked if she was a relative. When she nodded, he told her she could remain there while they moved the bodies, or she could move away if she preferred. He instructed the medics to prepare the remains for transport to the morgue.

Nikki remembered that she needed to call Cindy's parents. The call went to voicemail, and she left a message for Cindy's mother to call her back.

Flashes of traumatic memories of the day she'd lost Robbie flooded Nikki's mind. Losing a loved one was the toughest part of living. Her emotions overpowered her, and she started to cry. The doctor asked if she wanted to say farewell to her sister-in-law before they took her to the morgue. Nikki glanced up at the man and wiped her tears. She reminded herself to remain calm and alert so she could work for justice.

She had an important message for her sister-in-law before they took her away. Nikki kneeled and gently touched Cindy's shoulder.

"Eduardo and I will take care of your daughter if Andy is unable to do it," she whispered as tears flooded her eyes. "We'll be there for her." She leaned over and kissed an unburned spot on Cindy's forehead.

Seeing Cindy bundled into the ambulance that would take her body and Kenny's to the morgue tore at Nikki's heart. Olivia had lost her mother. Nikki prayed that Andy would make it for his daughter's sake.

# CHAPTER SIX

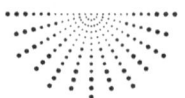

Watching the ambulance as it left for the morgue, Nikki said a silent prayer of thanks that Keiko was taking care of Olivia and that they were safely at the rental car. She glanced at a text from Eduardo. He sent the hospital address and told her preliminary tests on Andy showed he'd need brain surgery.

She in turn texted Keiko that she'd meet her at the car soon. They would drive to the hospital where Andy would probably undergo surgery.

Nikki snapped several photos of the compact circuit board with its broken lens in the burnt plastic casing and put it back into her pocket. Then she forwarded the pictures to Charlotte, Security Source's office manager and tech whiz, asking her to investigate the piece.

She also shared news of the crash—Cindy's death, Andy's head injury, and the death of young Kenny Stevens. She asked Charlotte to inform Floyd, their boss and owner of Security Source.

No sooner had she hit the send button than Charlotte called. Upon hearing her voice, Nikki started sobbing. Charlotte offered to fly out and help, but Nikki told her she could help most by staying in Miami where she could do research from her office.

Nikki cleared her throat. She named several people for Charlotte to begin investigating: Stanley Stevens; his current wife, Melissa Stevens; his son from his first marriage, Kenny Stevens. "There's a chase crew and I don't know their names, except for Gustavo Marquez. There's a crew member named Brad. You can find rosters naming pilots, chase crews, launch directors, and sponsors. You'll have to access the balloon fiesta online to get the data."

"I'll start immediately," Charlotte said, "and don't hesitate to call me day or night if you need something."

"Add Stan's first three wives to your research. See if anyone has a vendetta strong enough to want to kill him. He was the pilot named in the program to fly today, but he had to leave town for a business trip. And most importantly, check out Stan's businesses, especially Omega Satellites." Nikki thanked Charlotte and they ended the call.

---

Andy's chase crew pulled their truck up as close to the crash site as possible. Gustavo jumped out, wearing a baseball cap with the world logo. The other three crew members stayed in the truck. Nikki was glad he'd arrived. Maybe he could help her scour the area for further clues.

"Nikki!" Gustavo called out, jogging over to her. His expression was grim. "We heard the emergency call. What happened? Is everyone okay?"

Nikki's voice cracked, "Andy's alive, but badly hurt. Eduardo went with him to the hospital." She gestured toward the wreckage. "But Cindy didn't make it. Neither did Kenny. They've been taken to the morgue."

Gustavo's jaw dropped, and he nodded, eyeing the scene. "What can we do to help?"

"Stan," Nikki said. "You can call Stan and give him the awful news. I'll wait."

Gustavo paced as he spoke on his mobile phone. He returned to inform Nikki that the police had already notified Stan of the tragedy.

She nodded. "I've scanned the area over there," she said, pointing to where she'd found the broken piece, "but with you here, why don't we widen the search to see if we find anything suspicious. The only thing is that we must stay outside the perimeter."

Gustavo swallowed hard, his Adam's apple visibly moving. "Suspicious? Do you mean this was not an accident?"

"It could be sabotage. Do you know who might be after Stan?"

He looked at the crash site. "I've only known Stan for about a year.

And I only met Andy and Cindy a few months ago. But I've been handling balloons forever, so I'll start with the wreckage and the burner system."

"If that officer will let you," she said, signaling the direction of the officer with her eyes. "If you go inside the police barrier, you'll be trespassing."

"As the crew chief, I should be able to inspect the balloon. I'll talk to him."

Nikki shook her head. "He won't budge, believe me."

"Then can you distract him?" Gustavo asked in a soft voice. "That way I can crawl in to get a closer look at that propane system."

Nikki agreed it was worth a try. Yet she felt uncomfortable trying to divert the officer's attention. What if she got caught colluding in evidence tampering? She'd be asked to leave, for sure. Looking around, she recognized a perfect opportunity. A camera crew had arrived near the crash site and was setting up to film the mangled balloon and pickup. Bystanders crowded the yellow tape, and more were gathering to watch the filming.

"Why don't you move away and give me a minute. Once I wave to you, get in and take pictures," she said. She stepped with deliberate determination toward the officer guarding the scene.

As she approached, Nikki raised her phone as if in frustration. "Officer, I'm sorry to bother you, but there's a group of people over there. Looks like a television crew taking pictures of the crash site. Isn't that illegal? I'm going over to tell them to stop."

The officer frowned and walked part way around the pickup to see what she was describing. "Let me handle it. I'll ask them to stay further back."

The officer moved toward the camera crew, leaving Nikki alone. She waved Gustavo on. He slipped under the tape and crouched near the wreckage, examining the burner assembly. Nikki positioned herself to keep an eye on the officer, the crew chief, and the surrounding area.

Impatiently, she tapped her fingers against her pant legs. Gustavo was taking too long to examine the burner. After a couple of minutes, he got out his phone and it looked like he was taking pictures or a video. Her pulse jumped when she saw the officer returning to her side of the accident scene. He was talking on the phone and didn't seem to notice Gustavo. At least, not yet.

She coughed to get his attention as she walked up to him.

"Can't you get those people to leave?" she asked.

"Wait a second," he said into his mobile phone, putting it against his chest. He glanced at Nikki. "It's the media and they have a right to take videos. As long as the crowd stands further back."

"In that case, can you introduce me to the head of the news team? I'd like to make sure they know that one pilot is in critical shape and two passengers died. Maybe they can ask the viewing public for prayers."

"Let me call you back," he said, cutting his call. He turned to Nikki. "Follow me."

---

Gustavo thanked her for distracting the officer. "I got a couple of good pictures."

"I'm glad it worked out," Nikki said. "I spoke to the TV reporter and asked the viewing public to pray for the two passengers who lost their lives." Nikki choked up and cleared her throat before she continued. "And to pray for my brother, who needs brain surgery."

Gustavo showed Nikki a picture. He explained that the coupling, the permanent hose that connects the fuel tanks to the burner, looked intact. "But see here," he said, pointing to a closeup shot of the safety valve, "this is angled all wrong."

Nikki swallowed hard. "And what does that mean?"

"It may have caused a slow leak. It might be the reason the envelope caught fire. I don't know why it was bowed."

Nikki's pulse quickened. "Could it be deliberate?"

"The valve is bent, but it could have happened during the crash," Gustavo said.

"My gut tells me it was done on purpose. The question is when, and who could have tampered with it? Can you airdrop those pictures to my phone?" Nikki asked, pulling her mobile out and setting it up to receive the photos.

Gustavo blinked repeatedly before speaking. "It couldn't have been tampered with beforehand because I was there . . . unless someone loosened it after it was unloaded this morning. It could have happened when I moved the truck out of the way."

"That's scary," she said. "Means someone from the chase team tampered with it."

Gustavo shook his head lightly, as though he were thinking. "Nobody on the team would do something like that. At least not on purpose."

"Where was the balloon kept before being brought here?" she asked, recalling all the balloon equipment tied down on truck beds at their hotel. Had Stan's balloon been out in the open where anyone could access it?

"In Stan's garage. I picked the truck and balloon up at two a.m. and brought them here."

"Did you know Stan was not flying?" she asked.

"Not till Andy told us this morning."

"How did you get the truck and balloon?" Nikki asked.

"Stan gave me the passcode to get into his garage. I figured he was sleeping in for another hour, especially after last night's party."

The next picture showed a fragment of melted material hanging from the hose connection.

"What about that?" Nikki considered showing him the fragment of circuit board and camera she'd picked up but decided against it for now.

"I assume the fire caused it," he said, airdropping the pictures to Nikki's phone.

A woman strode up to them.

"I'm Lisa Morales, a detective with the Albuquerque police, Northwest Area Command," she said.

The detective's large dark eyes, enhanced with lash extensions, stared directly at Nikki. Wisps of black hair cascaded onto her shoulders. Her immaculate white blouse was buttoned to the top, giving the impression this woman didn't tolerate nonsense.

"I'm here to question the witness, Nikki Garcia."

"That's me," Nikki said, "I'm Andy Garcia's sister. My brother is the pilot from the balloon that crashed. He's been airlifted to the hospital in critical condition. And my sister-in-law didn't survive the accident. What do you want to know?"

Gustavo glanced at Nikki for guidance, and she gave him a slight nod as if asking for him to stay close.

"Officer Cobos said you thought the crash was due to sabotage. I hear you've been making some bold claims. Care to elaborate?" the detective commanded.

"Absolutely. First, I found this fragment of a circuit board near the wreckage. If you notice, it's attached to a fractured lens. I think it comes from a drone." Keeping it in the tissue, Nikki handed the piece to the investigator.

The detective's brow furrowed as she studied it from several angles. "People fly their drones here all year long, except when there's a big event like the balloon fiesta. On the weekends, you'll see them out here with their dogs, their kids, their drones."

"But this one is burnt." Nikki was quick with her response. "Like it was impacted by the fire. I saw something flying just above the gondola right before the accident."

"Let me remind you that you should not tamper with the crime scene." Detective Morales bagged the fragment. "I'll take this."

"Wait, I'd like a picture." Nikki snapped a photo of the detective's hands as she sealed the plastic bag. "I picked it up outside the yellow tape, so I wasn't tampering. A witness told me she saw a drone or something fly in. That confirmed what I saw too. I walked to the area where the balloon was flying right before the crash and found the fragment."

Morales straightened. "A witness?"

Nikki gestured toward the cluster of bystanders. "Her name is Celia Hernandez. She called me over because she saw what she thought was a drone flying next to the balloon just before it went down. It looked as if it had targeted the burner."

The detective scribbled on a notepad. "Your brother was the pilot. What experience does he have?"

"He has a license. You can check that out. The others, my sister-in-law and the balloon owner's son, were also pilots. Both were killed."

Detective Morales frowned. "More than one pilot in a hot-air balloon." She looked straight into Nikki's eyes. "It's like overloading the circuit, with them crowding each other in the controls. Most accidents are caused by pilot errors. A few by equipment failure."

"Too many pilots overload the circuit?" Nikki asked, aghast. She shook her head, trying to keep her composure. She wanted to scream. How could this woman be so callous?

"You're convinced it was sabotage. Is that correct?" the detective asked.

"Yes," Nikki's jaw tightened as she answered. She opened her camera app and brought up the photos of the man in the kerchief that had approached the balloon gondola. "This man jogged out of nowhere to the balloon before the police arrived. He tied the kerchief around his face, put gloves on, and bent into the gondola. I think he turned off the gas, but I don't know for sure. Initially I was thankful he'd done that to prevent an explosion. Then it occurred to me he might have been covering his or someone else's tracks."

Detective Morales tapped her fingers against her notepad, as if she were weighing Nikki's words. "Do you know who he was?"

Nikki shook her head, explaining that it'd happened so soon after the accident that she wasn't thinking. Otherwise, she would have followed him.

"Alright," Morales said. "I'll talk to Ms. Hernandez myself. But I'll need your contact data first. And the photos of that man."

The two women exchanged phone numbers and Nikki airdropped the pictures.

Morales nodded curtly. "I'll see what our forensics team can make of it. But Ms. Garcia, if you're going to keep investigating on your own, I suggest you tread carefully. This isn't a playground."

Nikki felt her expression harden. "I know it's not a playground—it's my family's lives. I'm not going to stop until I find out who did this."

Morales held her gaze for a long moment before stepping back. "Fair enough. Just don't step on my toes."

As Morales walked away, Nikki motioned to Gustavo, who had been standing off to the side.

"What now?" he asked, his voice low.

"Now," Nikki said, glancing in the direction the detective had gone, "we let her do her job—but we keep digging on our own. Those photos you took of the burner valve, the police detective will want them."

Gustavo told Nikki he could provide them, or she could since she also had them now.

"Someone wanted that balloon to crash," Nikki said, "and I'm going to find out why."

# CHAPTER SEVEN

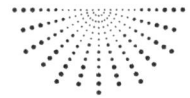

Nikki retrieved her purse from the trunk of the rental while Keiko secured Olivia in the child's safety seat. Nikki always carried her baby Glock in the large purse that Floyd had given her years ago when they worked a fraud case together in Medellin. For domestic airline flights, she'd check the gun in a special locked case. With a child around, she had to be extra careful.

Climbing into the car, Nikki strapped herself into the driver's seat and waited for Keiko to get into the passenger side.

As Nikki waited, she thought about Keiko's life and her own. Both had lost their parents when they were young and had emigrated from their home countries to their adopted countries, Colombia for Keiko and the US for Nikki. It was not unusual for a Mexican teenager to move north, but it was for a Japanese child to move to Colombia. An aunt and uncle living in Medellin took Keiko in, and she remained in her adopted country even after she was an adult. She'd chosen to stay in South America because she'd found a wonderful family to work with—Eduardo's parents. She had been a devoted housekeeper for Eduardo's mother and then for Eduardo after his mother had died. Keiko felt that the Duartes were her family, and Eduardo fully reciprocated the feeling. Having attended school in Colombia, Keiko spoke fluent Spanish and reasonable

English, though she felt she was losing her fluency in Japanese for lack of speaking it.

Nikki had met Keiko in Colombia when she met Eduardo. That was four years ago now, and Nikki had loved the diminutive woman from the day they met. Just as she had fallen in love with Eduardo at what she'd thought was her first sight of him.

Yet, she and Eduardo later discovered they had met years earlier, as children, in Barcelona. Eduardo insisted he'd fallen in love with her when he first saw Nikki on the rooftop of one of the city's top attractions, Gaudí's Garden of Warriors at Casa Mila.

Reflecting on the serendipity of that rooftop encounter and rediscovering each other in Medellin as adults calmed Nikki. Fate had conspired to bring them together.

Keiko belted herself in. Nikki gave her a quick update and thanked her for taking care of her niece. With the GPS on, Nikki took off for the University of New Mexico Hospital.

Slow traffic caused by balloon enthusiasts coming and going from the park made Nikki jittery. She drove on the shoulder to pass the line of vehicles. Once on Interstate 25, the route was a straight run until the GPS alerted her to take the Lomas Boulevard exit. From there, it was about a mile to the hospital.

Nikki rushed through the automatic doors of the hospital's main entrance, stopping inside to wait for Keiko and Olivia. The sterile brightness of the lobby overwhelmed her senses. She approached the reception desk, her voice clipped but controlled.

"I'm here for Andrew Garcia. I'm his sister. He was brought in by air ambulance."

The receptionist glanced at her computer screen. "Room 403, Trauma Ward. Take the elevator to the fourth floor."

Nikki nodded and turned toward the elevators with Keiko and Olivia trailing, but the receptionist called out to her.

"Ma'am, children under twelve aren't allowed in the trauma ward. Your child will need to stay here."

"She's my niece. It's her father we're here to see before he enters surgery," Nikki clarified quickly, her frustration mounting. "Can you grant me an exception?"

"I'm sorry," the receptionist said sympathetically. "It's hospital policy. Someone will need to stay with her in the lobby."

Nikki exhaled sharply to calm her nerves as she turned to Keiko. "Can you stay here with Olivia?"

Keiko nodded immediately, adjusting the toddler on her hip. "Of course. Go take care of your brother. We'll go to the cafeteria to get something to eat."

Nikki leaned closer to Olivia, her voice softening despite the urgency in her tone. "I'll be back soon, sweetheart. Stay with Keiko, okay?"

The child stared at her with wide, curious eyes but didn't cry. Nikki gave her a quick kiss on the forehead before straightening up again and heading toward the elevator, her resolve hardening with each step. Alone in the elevator, Nikki took several deep breaths and let them out slowly. The doors opened and she stepped into the hallway and followed the sign toward the trauma ward. She saw Eduardo through a glass door. His face was tight with concern as he spoke to a young woman in a white coat who barely looked old enough to be a medical student.

---

"You've called my hospital to verify my credentials." Eduardo's voice was firm. "Are you waiting for my brother-in-law to die before you give me clearance?"

"What's going on?" Nikki asked, joining Eduardo as he argued with Dr. Patel.

Eduardo felt relief for a brief moment when he saw Nikki. He touched her arm. "There's no surgeon available to operate on Andy," he said, feeling his face turn hot.

"I thought he'd already be in the OR," Nikki said.

Dr. Patel cleared her throat. "It's complicated. I'm an intern. I need one of the more experienced surgeons to be there."

Eduardo glanced at Andy lying in a bed, surrounded by monitors. He turned back toward Nikki and scoffed. "I've offered to assist because the other neurosurgeon, Dr. Khan, is in a six-hour surgery that started about half an hour before we arrived. It's also a critical case."

Nikki glanced at her watch. "Isn't another surgeon available?"

"The other two neurosurgeons are out of town," Dr. Patel answered.

"One of the world's best brain surgeons is standing right here," Nikki said. "Go operate, both of you, before my brother dies."

Dr. Patel hesitated. "There's a gap in your practice. You graduated from Harvard, interned at Mt. Sinai in New York, and practiced neurosurgery in Colombia. Then you didn't perform surgeries for three years. Six months ago, you started working at Mt. Sinai Medical Center in Miami Beach."

"I took a sabbatical to study for the board exams in the US. I've performed over two dozen complicated surgeries since I've been working in Miami Beach. You verified that already." Eduardo was exasperated.

"What's the issue?" Nikki asked.

The intern, a slender woman with dark penetrating eyes, bit her lip, clearly torn. "Liability. If something goes wrong—"

"There will be a liability if you don't perform the surgery he needs. Let's go. Now!" Eduardo said. "My wife will sign off that we won't sue you or the hospital."

"Hospital regulations call for—"

"Dr. Patel," Eduardo said, "if my brother-in-law dies because you won't agree for me to assist, my wife will sue the hospital. And you too!"

The young intern was taken aback. "The surgical team is standing by to assist, but even as a monitoring neurosurgeon, Dr. Duarte, you must sign some papers. I'd prefer to wait until our senior surgeon finishes his current surgery before proceeding." Her voice sounded scared.

"Wait?" Nikki's voice rose. "Andy doesn't have time to wait!"

Eduardo interrupted. "You must use me as the monitoring neurosurgeon," he said firmly. "I may not be licensed in New Mexico, but I have the expertise to guide you through the operation if necessary."

Dr. Patel hesitated, glancing between them. "It's against protocol to—"

"Protocols won't matter if he dies!" Nikki snapped. She looked as if her frustration was boiling over.

"Under dire circumstances, like in this situation," Eduardo said, "medical ethics and the law permit exceptions to state licensing rules, especially in life-threatening emergencies. Let's see an administrator and get the paperwork signed." He glanced through the window at the monitors hooked to his brother-in-law. "He's going to die unless we act now."

Dr. Patel exhaled shakily. "Fine," she said at last. "Go scrub in."

"First I need to see the pre-op scans," Eduardo said. "And we need them loaded to the monitor in the OR."

Dr. Patel nodded. "The CT scan shows a subdural hematoma. It's huge. There's also a hematoma forming under the skull."

"Obviously too big to heal on its own, but what about a burr hole procedure?" Eduardo asked.

The intern shook her head. "It's beyond a burr hole. Besides, there are a couple of clots, like arms, stretching out from it. That's why I concluded he needs a craniotomy."

"Any skull fractures?"

Dr. Patel bit her lip. "Neither the MRI nor the scans reveal any."

"The envelope obviously slowed the balloon's freefall, even though they fell something like eighty or ninety feet. I need to see the MRI to confirm the hematoma's location," Eduardo said, "so let's get to it."

Dr. Patel said the MRI identified the precise area with the buildup of blood that could be life threatening. "It also shows inflammation building up in the brain."

"And what about oxygen and liver function?" he asked.

"Liver function is good and so was the oxygen." She turned to a nearby nurse. "Call the attorney to come with the emergency consent forms. Prep OR-3 while I review the pre-op scans with Dr. Duarte and tell the rest of the surgical team to get ready."

# CHAPTER EIGHT

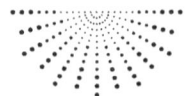

Nikki stretched and exhaled to relax. In the private room where Andy lay, the beeping that the ICU-grade monitoring equipment emitted made her dizzy. She felt like retching. Andy's charred hair had been shaven in preparation for surgery. His face and neck had been washed, and the burns did not look as bad as Nikki had feared, given his appearance following the crash, though his face was now covered with a mask delivering the critical flow of oxygen he needed. For the first time, she saw that his hands were also burned.

Nikki was anxious about the beeping of the heart monitor until she realized it was relatively rhythmic. She felt every second that passed as if it were an eternity. Full of emotion, she stood near Andy's bedside, taking in her brother's burned, unconscious face. Then she studied the screen displaying his heart and respiratory rates, his blood pressure, oxygen saturation, and the $CO_2$ levels Andy was exhaling.

Eduardo, Dr. Patel, and the other seven members of the surgical team —including the anesthesiologist, his assistant, the two OR nurses, and the intraoperative neuromonitoring specialists—were in final preparation for the emergency surgery. Eduardo had explained many times to Nikki how a patient's electrical signals from the brain, spinal cord, and peripheral nerves were carefully monitored during brain surgery to prevent damage to that all-important organ.

Suddenly, the monitor emitted a sharp, rapid alarm—a piercing sound that cut through the sterile air of the trauma ward like a knife.

Nikki's heart lurched as she glanced at the screen. The once-regular heart rate line was now erratic, the numbers fluctuating wildly. The oxygen saturation percentage dropped sharply, from a stable 96% to a perilous 83%, its corresponding number flashing red.

"What's happening?" Nikki's voice was a mix of panic and urgency as she turned to the nurse at the bedside.

"His oxygen levels are plummeting," the nurse said, her tone professional but tense. She quickly adjusted the flow of oxygen through the mask covering Andy's face. "BP is dropping, too, 85 over 50 and falling."

---

Eduardo, pulling on surgical gloves, stepped into the room. The young intern, her eyes wide, appeared at the doorway behind him as the alarm continued its relentless blare. Dr. Patel grabbed the stethoscope from around her neck and moved to Andy's bedside.

"We're out of time," Eduardo said firmly, his voice carrying the authority of his years in the operating room. "He's decompensating. The pressure on his brain is worsening."

Dr. Patel hesitated, her gaze flicking between the monitor and Eduardo. "I . . . I don't know if we're ready—"

Eduardo interrupted, his voice rising. "The hemorrhage is causing a midline shift. If we don't relieve the pressure now, his brain can herniate. We can't risk that!"

He told the nurse that he'd push the hospital bed to the OR, and he ordered her to step in beside him with the monitoring equipment.

"I can't do this," Dr. Patel said, pleading in a hoarse whisper. "I'm not ready. You do the surgery, and I'll assist you." She helped push the bed down the hallway.

In the bright, sterile environment of the operating room, a team of medical professionals surrounded the patient, each with a crucial role in the high-stakes brain surgery. Near the far corner of the room, just beyond the surgical table, the intraoperative neuromonitoring team set up their equipment with meticulous care.

Dr. Patel introduced them quickly as Eduardo positioned himself to take the lead in the surgery. "This is Dr. Raj Sharma, our supervising neurophysiologist, and his technologist, Carmen Ruiz. They'll be monitoring your brother-in-law's brain activity."

"I'm glad you're all here," Eduardo said. "Now let's save this man's life."

# CHAPTER NINE

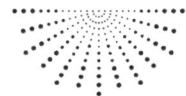

Nikki paced the hall of the trauma ward attempting to focus on a prayer for her brother's surgery. She reflected on the fragility of life. One minute everything is happy and bright and, in a flash, something awful, something unchangeable alters its course. Olivia would grow up without her mother. Nikki couldn't help but think of that tragic day when she lost her son, Robbie. Death was so cold, so permanent, so final. Her brother was undergoing risky emergency surgery. "Please live," she whispered, hoping her words would permeate his brain waves. "For Olivia's sake, you must live."

She needed to check on Olivia and she wanted to continue praying for her brother, but her mind behaved like a caged animal. Feeling frozen, she was unable to organize her thoughts to pray or to walk downstairs to check on her niece either. Life couldn't be so cruel as to take Andy, too. Or could it?

What if she left the trauma ward to run downstairs and Eduardo needed her? How would he find her? Did he have his mobile phone with him or was it tucked away in a locker with his street clothes? How would he communicate if she took the elevator to the first floor?

Finally, her resolve returned, and she asked the nurse on duty to take her phone number and call her if her husband, Dr. Duarte in OR-3, came looking for her.

"My eighteen-month-old niece is downstairs, and I need to make sure she's doing okay."

The nurse agreed.

Nikki, her mind a whirlwind of conflicting thoughts, hurried to the elevators. When she emerged on the first floor, she couldn't find Keiko or Olivia anywhere. When Eduardo had wheeled her brother toward the operating room, his calm demeanor had done little to ease her own nerves. Eduardo was in full control of himself, and she knew she had to follow his example.

Instead, panic took over and she rushed to the bathroom, calling Keiko's name. Getting no response, she hurried to the registration desk. Terrifying thoughts assaulted her the entire way. Could the person who sabotaged the balloon have kidnapped Keiko and Olivia?

Nikki approached the receptionist. She told Nikki that the Japanese woman had taken the child outside to cut flowers. "I loaned her a pair of scissors and an empty vase. The two of them headed to the side of the building."

Nikki managed a faint smile as she thanked her.

The weight of the day pressed on her chest as she navigated the bustling hospital lobby. When she pushed through the door, her senses were assaulted by the hum of traffic. The air outside was crisp, and the sky had a few scattered clouds. She turned the corner to see Keiko and Olivia on a concrete bench set in a garden with a miniature waterfall in the shade of six large Siberian elms. Away from the chaos of the street, the small flower garden provided a restful escape.

Keiko deftly arranged an assortment of greenery, goldenrod, and asters she'd apparently foraged from the edges of the garden beds. She spoke to Olivia in soft, soothing tones. The child had a piece of greenery in one hand and a sunflower in the other. Nikki gazed on, immediately feeling the calmness Keiko imparted.

Olivia giggled and waved the sunflower when she saw Nikki. Her infectious laughter lifted Nikki's heart.

"What are you doing?" Nikki asked softly.

Keiko looked up with a serene smile. "Ikebana," she said, gesturing to the delicate arrangement she was crafting in the vase balanced on the bench. "It helps calm the mind."

"The day I met you in Colombia, you'd made an Ikebana arrangement for me. Harmony, you called it."

"I remember that, but I think the motif was love. I knew Eduardo had fallen in love with you. I wanted to encourage the two of you."

Nikki crouched beside her, studying the arrangement. The asters stood tall and colorful, their purple petals vivid against the goldenrod's cheerful yellow. The greenery framed the arrangement in a way that seemed deliberate yet effortless.

Nikki sat on the empty end of the bench. Olivia immediately scrambled down.

"Tia Ki, Tia Ki," she said, her baby talk for Tia Nikki, Aunt Nikki. Waving the sunflower, she toddled over, continuing her chatter as she handed the flower to Nikki. Nikki caressed Olivia's soft auburn curls.

"Thank you for taking such good care of her." Nikki pulled some money out of her purse and placed it in Keiko's hand. "For whatever you purchased in the cafeteria."

"It's too much," Keiko protested, handing it back.

"Please keep it. For spending money as you take care of Olivia."

Keiko nodded. "Olivia is a strong little girl, just like you. How is your brother?"

"In surgery. It'll take several hours. The hospital's head neurosurgeon isn't available, so Eduardo will perform the surgery with an intern working alongside him."

Keiko's expression grew thoughtful as she placed the final sprig in her arrangement. "Eduardo will do what's necessary. Trust him."

Nikki glanced at Olivia, who was now babbling happily to herself. "It's hard to feel in control when everything is falling apart."

Keiko rested her hand on Nikki's arm. "You're in control, Nikki. Even when things seem impossible, you always find a way. Eduardo's told me that."

For a moment, the weight on Nikki's chest felt lighter. She stood, brushing dust from her pants. "Thank you, Keiko. I needed to hear that."

Feeling a glimmer of hope for the first time since the crash, Nikki bent down to kiss Olivia's cheek. "I must go back up, but I'll return later to check on you. Call me if you need me. Okay?"

Olivia waved at her aunt.

Keiko nodded. "We'll be here, finding peace with the flowers."

# CHAPTER TEN

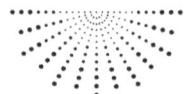

The heart monitor beeped steadily in the cold and silent operating room, the only sound beyond the shuffle of doctors, nurses, and technicians. Eduardo's mind was clear and sharp—just as it always had to be when lives hung in the balance.

"I'm ready to start," Eduardo said, looking at Dr. Sharma. "Alert me of the slightest concern."

He glanced from the electrodes Carmen had placed on Andy's scalp to the screen displaying a series of rhythmic waves—Andy's brain activity in real time.

Eduardo, gloved and masked, wore surgical eye loupes that would magnify the brain and aid in the precise work he was about to do. Though surgeons usually avoid operating on relatives, in this situation, Eduardo was the only choice. He was prepared for this delicate surgery—a craniotomy. His fingers hovered over the instruments laid out on the sterile tray, choosing a craniotomy saw designed for precision. It was the size of a scalpel but far sharper, its thin, metal blade designed specifically to cut through skull without causing excessive trauma to the surrounding tissue.

Dr. Sharma's low-pitched voice was reassuring. "Baseline EEG looks stable. No abnormalities are detected."

Eduardo leaned over Andy's head. He'd already marked the incision site in blue ink, an exacting map of where he would expose the brain. His hands steady, he gently placed the blade against the thin skull. He supported his right hand with his left to make certain he did not penetrate too deeply, though the saw itself had safeguards built into it to prevent penetrating the underlying tissue.

The blade cut through bone with a high-pitched whine. Eduardo felt the fine vibration. His grip tightened on the saw slightly as he carefully guided it along the blue line at a slight angle, his eyes never leaving the area of incision. The out-sloping angle would help to hold the bone flap in place once glued back into its location at the end of the surgery. The air was thick with tension. Eduardo was an unknown entity to this team, but his focus did not waver.

Once the cut was completed, Eduardo switched to a bone flap elevator, an instrument used to gently lift the bone from the skull. He worked quickly but cautiously, carefully detaching the piece of skull. He cradled the fragile and priceless piece of bone.

The nurse handed him a sterile container filled with disinfectant solution. With steady hands, Eduardo placed the bone in the solution, ensuring it was fully submerged. The liquid would preserve the bone, keeping it free of contamination so it could be reattached later. The container would be placed in the small medical grade freezer in the room until the bone flap was needed again. The procedure was familiar to him. He had performed more than two thousand brain surgeries, but he was always awed upon seeing the human skull separated, even temporarily, from the brain beneath. A moment of raw vulnerability—a reminder of the fragility of life.

He glanced at the monitor once more. Andy's vitals were stable, for now. The true test would come when the hemorrhage and hematomas were dealt with. The pressure the bleeding caused would be relieved, though the surrounding tissue would be swollen from the trauma. In the pre-op MRI, Eduardo had seen enough bleeding that he thought a third hematoma might have formed.

Eduardo looked up at Dr. Patel, Dr. Sharma, and the rest of the team. "We've got to relieve the pressure, fast," he said, speaking with authority.

# CHAPTER ELEVEN

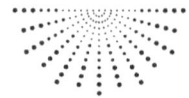

Nikki's phone vibrated. Charlotte, her research guru, was calling. When she answered, both Floyd and Charlotte were on the other end. She left the trauma center and stepped into the hallway.

"Has your brother had surgery yet?" Floyd asked.

"Eduardo is operating on him right now."

"Eduardo? Really? Don't they have neurosurgeons in New Mexico?" Floyd asked.

"Long story. The head of the department was already in surgery with a car accident victim. The other two neurosurgeons are away on vacation. Only an intern was available when Andy was brought in. She's assisting Eduardo."

"Tell me what you need. You know we're here for you," Floyd said.

Nikki choked up. "Olivia's lost her mother. I pray my brother makes it through the operation."

There was total silence on the call.

"If you need more time off," Floyd said, "you know you can take all the time you want."

"Thank God for Keiko," Nikki said, stopping for a deep breath. "She's taking care of my niece and she's doing a better job than I could do at the moment."

"Charlotte told me you think the balloon was sabotaged."

"That's right," Nikki said, relating the reasons for her suspicion.

Floyd asked if the police were investigating.

"They are," Nikki said, "and I've had an initial interview with the detective, Lisa Morales. I have a feeling she thinks I'm making wild accusations."

Charlotte told Nikki she had preliminary findings on some of the people Nikki had asked her to check. "Kenny had a few minor offenses—speeding tickets and a DWI."

"DWI?" Nikki repeated. "He was only sixteen."

"I noticed," Charlotte said. "Stan, his dad, is an important player in the weather balloon, drone, and communication fields. So far, I've found that he has a couple of lucrative government contracts. But I haven't had time to dig deeper."

"Send me details on the contracts, large or small," Nikki said.

"One is with the Chinese government," Charlotte said. "That's a big one."

"Check to make certain those sales have complied with US export laws."

"I already did and everything looks fine," Charlotte responded.

"What about the three ex-wives and the current one, Melissa?" Nikki asked.

"Melissa seems to be the trophy wife. She's a model, for *Vogue* no less. She and Stan have two children. But get this, they've used a surrogate both times, though Melissa contributed the eggs and Stan gave the sperm. She's only twenty-eight and she's gorgeous."

Floyd chuckled. "A model can't go ruining her figure by getting pregnant, right?"

"But there's more. And this is the most serious," Charlotte said. "It's about Gustavo. He's a felon. And a former certified public accountant. Though he's lost his license."

Nikki gasped. "Are you sure? He seems like such a nice guy. What'd he do?"

"He embezzled funds at a large auto dealership in Denver. Head of the finance department, he'd built quite a scheme falsifying invoices on deliveries and returns on auto parts used by the repair shop. The chief mechanic coordinated with him. Gustavo moved to Albuquerque when he was released eighteen months ago," Charlotte said.

"I assume the chief mechanic also served time. Is he out now?" Nikki asked, thinking about the fellow she'd photographed running across the field.

When Charlotte confirmed that the man, Manuel Quezada, had been released, Nikki asked her to get information on him along with full-body photos. "And please compare them to the picture I sent you."

She could hear Charlotte keying away, getting information on the man.

"Here it is," Charlotte said. "He moved to California. Still lives out there. Works at a food distribution company."

More keying sounds.

"I'm on his Facebook page. He's short. I don't think he's involved, but I'll double-check the airlines for any flights he may have taken recently. If I find something, I'll let you know."

"What other stuff have you uncovered?" Nikki asked.

"Stan's balloon and drone business has a minority owner, Mark Edwards. Don't have info about him yet. Kenny's mother is Juanita Rodriguez Stevens, a real estate agent in Albuquerque, though she has offices all over the state, including the ski resorts in Taos and Angel Fire. Stan is a silent partner in her business."

"Maybe he put up money for her company as part of their divorce agreement," Floyd said.

"Could be. I'll research that," Charlotte said. "And I'll look into the other two ex-wives."

"Are you planning to check with the medical examiner or the morgue about the autopsies?" Floyd asked.

"Yes, I'll follow up," Nikki said. "And I'll go to Kenny's funeral if I can, but that's at least a week or so away." She asked Charlotte if she'd been able to find anything out about the mini circuit board in the picture she'd sent.

"Not yet. If I don't come up with something, I'll ask my husband to research it. You know he's a genius with IT stuff, right?"

"Wouldn't you agree that Charlotte is a genius too?" Floyd asked Nikki.

Before being able to respond, Nikki had an incoming call and told them she had to take it. She swallowed hard before answering. It was Cindy's mother. She glanced at her watch. It had taken the Smiths three hours to return her call.

"Hello, Mrs. Smith. Thanks for calling back. I have sad news that I need to share with you." Nikki paused.

"I don't understand. What are you talking about?"

"There's been an accident," Nikki said. "Andy and Cindy were in a hot-air balloon this morning—"

"Is Cindy okay?" Helen Smith asked, anxiety already in her voice.

"I'm terribly sorry. Cindy's injuries were severe, and she passed away."

There was total silence for a few seconds.

"I'm so sorry," Nikki said.

"Where's Olivia?" Helen managed to choke out the words.

"She's safe. She's with me. Olivia was not in the accident."

Helen sounded as if she were crying. Nikki heard her call out for Harold, her husband. A minute later, Cindy's father was on the phone.

"Is this some kind of joke?" he demanded in an angry voice.

When Nikki explained about the accident, he asked what they'd done with Cindy's body. "The medical examiner will perform an autopsy. It will go to a funeral home and then the body can be released."

"What about Andy?" he asked.

"He's in critical condition and is undergoing brain surgery."

Harold scoffed. "So, he made it, but not my daughter. Figures. First, he put her in danger around hibernating bears, and now the damn balloons . . ." his voice trailed off to a whisper.

Nikki could hear Helen crying in the background. "I'll stay in touch. Contact me if there's anything you want me to do. Please know how much we loved your daughter. I'm so terribly sorry about this tragic accident."

# CHAPTER TWELVE

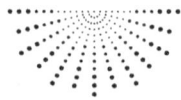

Nikki's phone buzzed. Thinking that it could be Cindy's parents again, her stomach flipped as she answered without checking the caller's ID. She was surprised when it was the nurses' station telling her a woman by the name of Maxine Sanchez wanted to speak to her about the balloon accident. She was in the lobby.

Nikki thought it could be another eyewitness, and she rushed downstairs. A heavy-set woman in her mid-forties with salt-and-pepper hair walked toward her as she exited the elevator.

"I'm Maxine Sanchez, an Albuquerque based reporter at the Center for Investigative Reporting." She extended her hand. "I'm investigating the accident and would like to interview you."

"Maxine, as you know, tragedy has stricken my family. I'm waiting for my brother to come out of brain surgery. Please forgive me, but it's not a good time."

"Just call me Max," the woman said. "Did you know that Stan Stevens was the intended target, not your brother and his wife?"

Nikki's investigative antennae immediately lit up.

"What do you mean?" she asked, realizing too late that she'd fallen for the reporter's ploy.

"Stan's made a lot of money, and a lot of enemies. Important enemies.

Omega Satellites has had several contracts with foreign governments, but its proprietary drone communication systems are subject to EAR and reserved for US use alone."

Nikki thought for a second before she responded. Export Administration Regulations control exports. They restrict licensing and sales for technology patents that can be used for both military and civilian purposes. She'd already discussed that with Charlotte.

"There's nothing wrong with that practice," Nikki said, taking a breath before continuing. "Companies like Lockheed Martin and General Atomics sell their best and most innovative products to US agencies and sell downgraded products to foreign governments. Even computer and software companies do that."

"You are correct," Max said. "But countries like China, North Korea, and Russia would stop at nothing to get the latest technology in fighter jets, computers, drones, you name it. Plus, I received an insider tip about a new technology invented by Stan's company that will revolutionize communications."

Nikki was stunned.

"I'll tell you what," Nikki said. "I'll work with you to uncover what's going on. I'd like to learn the truth behind this accident, but you need to agree to my conditions."

Maxine asked what Nikki wanted.

"First of all, anonymity. You cannot use my name. If I'm going to get useful information for you, my name can't be published in written, oral, or in any other format."

Maxine agreed and asked what more she wanted.

"You share leads and information with me. You can't keep anything from me if we're going to work together."

"Are you looking for credit on whatever I eventually publish on this case?" Maxine asked.

"Not at all. You can take all the credit," Nikki assured her, thinking that she needed to have Charlotte research this reporter. "But if at any point I think you're not being honest with me, I'll pull the plug."

Maxine said she understood and agreed to Nikki's conditions.

"Have you spoken to Lisa Morales, the detective?" Nikki asked.

"Not yet," Maxine said. "She'll give me the usual police spiel about not being able to discuss an ongoing investigation. She's a good professional, tough and honest, but she's horribly overworked."

"What else did your tipster say about Stan's innovative technology?"

"Only that patents are pending on a breakthrough communication discovery that was a game changer. It's subject to ITAR, the International Traffic in Arms Regulations," Maxine explained.

Nikki felt dizzy. An advanced military application? "Do you realize that could put people investigating the accident in danger?"

"Danger?" Maxine repeated. "Like retaliation from foreign governments or their agents?"

"Like you and I could be in danger if an enemy is trying to steal the technology. They would stop at nothing to get what they want or to conceal their secret."

"Does that scare you?"

"Not for myself," Nikki said, thinking out loud, "but I must think about my niece. She's eighteen months old and she just lost her mother. Her father is undergoing brain surgery as we speak. She will need me. At least until her father recovers."

"I'll understand if you want to step away from this. Maybe think about it and get back to me?"

"I'm in for now," Nikki said, "but I reserve the right to pull out at any time. If you agree to this, I'll help."

"It's a deal," Maxine said.

Nikki looked around the lobby. "How did you find me?"

"That was easy," Maxine said. "I listen to the news, I talk to people, I have informants."

Nikki raised an eyebrow and studied the reporter briefly. "I have two ideas to follow up on. If they're promising, I'll share the data with you. And I need to know how your tipster knew that Stan was the intended target."

"The person said Stan was supposed to be piloting this morning."

"That was in the official schedule, but Stan got called away on business," Nikki said. "Seems to me that those behind the plot to kill Stan would have known he was called to DC late yesterday."

Maxine agreed, but she noted that the online schedule still showed Stan piloting at the mass ascension. "Usually, the online pilot list reflects the latest changes, so maybe Stan never notified the Fiesta of the last-minute substitution."

Or he left it that way on purpose, Nikki thought. "Can you share the name of the person who provided the tip?"

"Just as you've asked for anonymity, I must protect my sources."

"And if I need the name to continue my end of the bargain," Nikki said, "you will have to trust me."

# CHAPTER THIRTEEN

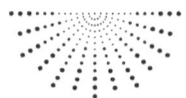

Eduardo worked quickly and deliberately, his hands steady despite his brother-in-law's perilous situation. He checked the monitor that tracked Andy's vital signs—his blood pressure was still low, but the oxygen levels were stable. The real threat, Eduardo knew, was the subdural hematoma that lay beneath the surface. The force of the crash had caused a blood clot to form between Andy's brain and the outer layer of the protective covering, putting pressure on the delicate tissues of his brain.

"Scalpel," Eduardo requested, his voice firm yet controlled. A nurse placed the instrument in his hand, and he carefully made an incision along the dura to access the clot.

Eduardo was thankful his brother-in-law was in the sterile environment of the operating room. This moment—this focused, clinical precision—was the only thing that Eduardo focused on now.

Dr. Sharma interrupted. "There's a slight drop in amplitude on motor invoked potentials. It may be a positional false alarm." He ordered Carmen to recheck all connections.

Eduardo paused, tightening his grip on the scalpel.

After a few tense moments, the signal stabilized.

"False alarm. You may proceed," Dr. Sharma said in a steady and reassuring voice.

Eduardo inhaled and exhaled slowly before continuing. Grabbing a suction device, Eduardo gently cleared away the blood that had pooled around the clot, taking great care not to disturb the surrounding brain tissue. The hematoma was sizable. Slowly, he separated the clot from the brain, suctioning the remaining blood from the area, giving the brain the room it desperately needed to return to its natural size.

"Get the coagulation tool ready," Eduardo said softly. The nurse prepped the Aquamantys system.

"How does it all look?" Eduardo asked Dr. Sharma.

He assured Eduardo that the patient's brain waves continued within their desired limits.

With the last of the clot removed, Eduardo used the Aquamantys system to cauterize minor vessels, stopping them from bleeding that might threaten another clot.

Eduardo allowed himself a moment of relief and pushed the goggles with microscope loupes to his forehead. He checked the surface of Andy's brain and then repositioned the loupes over his eyes to ensure that no further blood was accumulating. The pressure had been relieved in the brain. The danger of permanent damage was lessened.

"Looks good," he murmured. He was amazed that the skull had not been fractured, making the surgery so much easier.

Eduardo now turned his attention to the dura, the brain's protective outer layer. He carefully stitched the membrane back together, ensuring there would be no leaks of cerebrospinal fluid.

The next delicate part of the procedure was replacing the bone flap. He indicated he was ready to insert it. The nurse had already removed the container with the skull flap from the freezer and warmed it to room temperature. Dr. Patel held the surgical adhesive and sealant so Eduardo could use them to prepare the open skull ridges and apply them to the edges of the flap before inserting it into the skull.

Eduardo held the flap with surgical forceps, inspecting the edges before applying the adhesive and then the sealant, aligning it back into the cavity. It slid into place like the final piece of a puzzle. He checked that the bone was secure and that it aligned with the surrounding cranium. He worked methodically, making sure the bone would stay in its proper position as the body healed.

Once the bone was securely reattached, the scalp would need to be closed. Eduardo turned to Dr. Patel and asked if she'd like to put the stitches in. She thanked him, saying he was doing fine and should finish the procedure himself. The surgical assistant handed him a needle and thread. Using a precise, delicate motion, he sutured the skin along the incision, closing the wound in layers. The stitches were tight, but not too tight, a balance between securing the tissue and avoiding excess pressure on the brain.

After a few more quick sutures, the last layer of skin was sealed, and the incision was closed. Only the small hole where Eduardo had inserted a drain tube to clear out any postoperative bleeding remained unstitched. He stepped back for a moment, assessing the work. Andy's skull had been restored, his brain now free from the pressure that had threatened his life just hours before.

"Finished," Eduardo said quietly. He allowed himself a small exhale, but there was no room for celebration yet. The hardest part was done, but Andy's recovery would be long and uncertain. He thanked the team, turned to Dr Patel, and asked her to supervise the patient in his post-op recovery. "Don't forget to prepare for any complications. I'm going to inform the next of kin."

# CHAPTER FOURTEEN

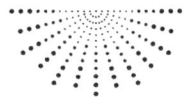

Eduardo glanced at a clock. The surgery had lasted five and a half hours. On his way to update Nikki, he realized he could use a cup of coffee. He hadn't eaten breakfast and now it was past his normal lunch hour.

Nikki was sitting in the room where she'd met Dr. Patel. She smiled when Eduardo approached. He figured she'd seen his expression and knew the operation had gone well. She threw her arms around him. He whispered that Andy was in recovery, and she would soon be able to see him.

"Let me remind you," he said, looking into her eyes, "Andy's not out of the woods yet."

"The worst part is behind us, isn't it?" she asked.

Eduardo nodded and sat on the love seat. "He'll be in intensive care for maybe five or six days, if all goes well. As soon as we can move him, I'd like to take him to Miami Beach for his full recovery."

Nikki sat next to him. She told Eduardo she'd already started the investigation into the accident. "It seems they may have been after Stan. My head is spinning from all the people who may have had motives to kill him."

"You think that's who they were after? Not your brother?"

"Stan was the pilot named in the program. A reporter I spoke to told me that the official one online still shows him as the pilot."

"A reporter?" That worried Eduardo. "Are you sure it's a good idea to speak with a reporter?"

"Maxine Sanchez, that's her name, came to see me. She claims a tipster told her Stan was the intended target. I've suspected that too, though it's too early to prove it."

Eduardo reached for her hand. "I know you want to solve this case, but please be careful. You should keep what you discover to yourself. Reporters are in the business of sharing their findings."

Nikki looked pensive. "I'm exercising caution," she assured her husband.

"What about Olivia?" he asked, not convinced. "Seems like she'll need a home. She needs you. We can bring her to live with us until Andy recovers. And I know Keiko will be indispensable in taking care of her. She loves kids."

Nikki grimaced. "She's already been so helpful that I feel guilty. I've left her alone, taking care of Olivia."

Eduardo smiled. "She's happy to do it, I'm sure." Standing, he told her he needed nourishment. "And coffee. We didn't eat breakfast. Remember?"

Nikki led her husband, still in scrubs, to the cafeteria on the first floor. On the way, she told him about Gustavo, the chase crew's chief.

"A felon? Wouldn't that keep him off the team?"

"It's volunteer work, so I doubt they did a background check. Gustavo is a CPA, or he was until his embezzlement was discovered. Plus, he had a lot of experience in ballooning. He'd even been a pilot himself before he was sent to prison."

Eduardo shook his head. "It's amazing how people think they can get away with white collar crime."

"Unfortunately, fraud can pay handsomely."

"Until they're caught." Eduardo laughed. "And even then, they may offend again, if they get the opportunity."

"What brought that up?" Nikki stared at him.

"Just thinking about people who commit fraud. Getting caught won't change them." He picked up a tray and put two plates on it.

Nikki grabbed flatware and added it to the tray. "I watched the news while I waited in the lobby. The balloon crash made the national news. It was the report they filmed while I was at the field. They mentioned Stan's name and his balloon company."

Eduardo looked at the woman behind the counter and pointed to the chicken on the food line, holding up two fingers. Turning to Nikki, he told her that once they sat down to eat, he wanted to hear about other leads she was pursuing.

When the server put a thigh and a drumstick on his plate, he pointed to the mashed potatoes. She added a heaping mound. Again, he indicated a double serving, and she plopped another big spoonful on his plate.

Nikki asked for one piece of chicken and waited for the salad selection further down the food line.

"How long do I have until I can see Andy?" she asked.

"In half an hour he should be regaining consciousness." Eduardo picked up the drumstick and bit into it savagely.

Nikki laughed. "You *are* hungry, aren't you?"

Eduardo swallowed the chicken. Salty, but moist. "Hey, I've worked hard today."

# CHAPTER FIFTEEN

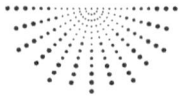

Nikki's mobile buzzed. She hesitated to answer and did so only after the fifth ring. The caller identified himself as Stan Stevens and asked to speak to Nikki Garcia.

"Speaking," she said.

He explained that his crew chief had given him her number. "I'm so sorry about Cindy. How is your brother?"

"Out of surgery. I'll see him in recovery as soon as they let me in. I met Kenny this morning. Let me extend my condolences." Nikki's eyes became moist. "Is there anything I can do for you or your family?"

"Thank you." Stan sniffled. "Juanita, that's Kenny's mother, is beyond shattered. Kenny was her only child." He cleared his throat and asked if she'd spoken to the police.

Eduardo had finished eating and gulped his remaining coffee. He signaled to her that he was returning upstairs.

"I talked to them about six hours ago at the crash site," Nikki said.

"Why?"

"No reason," Stan said. "It's just that they notified me of the accident. I'm in Denver to pick up my business partner. We'll depart for Albuquerque shortly. In the meantime, if you learn anything from the police, would you mind calling me?"

Nikki agreed. She ended the call, cleared their tray and dirty dishes from the cafeteria table, and rushed to the elevators.

She found Eduardo sitting next to Andy's bed. He'd been moved to a private room in the intensive care unit. Monitors behind his bed were beeping, blinking, and graphing his heart rate. He was receiving oxygen in his nostrils. Bandages covered the burns on his face and hands.

Eduardo, seemingly relaxed, extended his hand to take hers. "He's doing well."

Nikki appreciated her husband's calming presence amid the chaos of her own mind. "Can we talk?"

Eduardo nodded.

"Stan asked me to relay anything the police tell me. Don't you think that's odd?"

Eduardo shrugged. "Not really. He's probably stressed out and may be groping for reasons this happened. After all, his son died. Or he may be concerned about the impact on his business. You said the incident made the national news, and the newscaster mentioned Stan by name as the manufacturer of the balloon that went down."

"Maybe. Somehow . . . something about his conversation felt calculated. Like he was fishing for information."

"Do you think he's hiding something?" Eduardo asked.

"I'm not sure, but my antennae went up."

Eduardo was about to respond, but a soft groan from the bed caught their attention.

Andy seemed to be trying to talk, but it was unintelligible. Nikki's heart skipped a beat. She looked anxiously at Eduardo.

Andy's eyelids fluttered. His gaze seemed unfocused.

Eduardo spoke to him softly, asking him how he felt.

The words Andy uttered were impossible to understand, but it was clear he was trying to speak. His expression was dazed. He closed his eyes and reopened them.

"What . . . what happened? Where am I?" he finally whispered.

"In the hospital. You were in an accident." Eduardo gently placed his hand on Andy's shoulder. "You're going to be fine."

"The balloon?"

"Yes," Eduardo said, "the balloon crashed."

"Where's Cindy?" Andy asked. He turned slightly as if he were attempting to get out of bed.

"Don't move." Nikki placed her hand on his forearm, over the tubing that was taped there, urging him to remain in bed.

"I have to find Cindy," Andy said.

Nikki took his hand. "Cindy didn't make it." Her throat tightened and she glanced at her husband.

"No . . . no, this can't be," Andy said. His expression changed and he looked as if his life had been swept away.

With a lump in her throat, Nikki told him he must live for Olivia's sake.

Andy gripped his sister's hand. "You . . . you're right. My daughter needs me. But I need Cindy. We both need Cindy."

# CHAPTER SIXTEEN

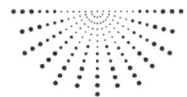

Eduardo pulled Nikki into an embrace. "I'm so glad it's all looking good. Operating on your brother stressed me before I went into the OR. But I had to do it. When I took the scalpel in my hand, I became fully focused. It's the first time I've operated on a family member."

"You saved Andy's life," Nikki said, looking at her brother, who had fallen asleep. "I'm so thankful."

Dr. Patel marched into the room, interrupting them. She was followed by a short, stout man in his fifties.

"This is Dr. Kahn, head neurosurgeon," Dr. Patel said.

He and Eduardo shook hands. Dr. Kahn stepped to Andy's bed. "I understand it was touch and go for a while. I've gone over the patient's chart, and it all looks good. I want to thank you for filling in."

Eduardo acknowledged his remark with a nod.

"I've arranged for you to continue supervising the patient, if that's okay with you," Dr. Kahn said. "Of course, I'll be in every day to check on him. Report any incidents directly to me. Special requests must come through Dr. Patel or me."

"I appreciate that," Eduardo said.

"Call me if you need anything," Dr. Kahn said over his shoulder as he left the room.

Nikki waited until the head neurosurgeon was out of hearing range. "That was short and sweet."

"Hey, everything's working out. It must be difficult for Dr. Kahn to admit to any shortfalls within his department," Eduardo said.

Nikki told her husband that she would drive Keiko and Olivia to the hotel and get them settled for the rest of the afternoon. "Afterward, I'll drive to the field. I'd like to see the crash site when there are fewer people around. Want to come with me?"

Eduardo hesitated for a second. "I've arranged with the head nurse for me to sleep in the sofa bed in Andy's room tonight. I won't be comfortable if I stay at the hotel. Or if I get too far from the hospital." He took Nikki's chin in his hand and looked into her eyes. "Why do you want to return to the crash site?"

"To see if I can find anything out of the ordinary. I may have missed something this morning."

"Be careful and call me afterward." Eduardo kissed her lightly on the lips.

---

In the main lobby, Nikki passed the receptionist. A vase with beautifully arranged asters and goldenrod sat on the desk behind the counter. The receptionist waved and told her that Keiko and the little girl were still outside in the garden.

After dropping Keiko and her niece at the hotel, Nikki drove toward the balloon fiesta field. The late afternoon sun cast a golden hue over the sagebrush, in full bloom, in the desert and the foothills of the mountains. She parked the rental and walked toward the crash site. That side of the launch field was eerily quiet compared to the chaos from earlier that day. An event was taking place at the opposite end of the field, but there was no one around the crash area. Even the yellow tape was gone. The pickup truck it had hit had been hauled away. Yet she could still detect the impact site in the crushed buffalo grass.

Nikki took a deep breath and gazed toward the Sandias. The sunset reflected off the limestone mountains, bathing them in watermelon pink.

When she turned back toward the crash site, a man was crouching there, seemingly inspecting the ground. Where had he come from? He stood and walked toward her. Nikki's pulse quickened. He reminded her of the man she'd taken a picture of earlier, the one who had run to the balloon after the crash and turned off the burner. She aimed her phone toward him and snapped two photos from waist height, hoping the man would not realize she'd taken them.

Adjusting her leather jacket, she strode over to meet him halfway. He was stuffing something into his pocket and gave her a friendly smile.

"Hi, if you're here for the twilight glow, it's at the other end of the field."

"Not really," she said. "I'm having a look at this morning's accident site. It looks as if you are too."

"By any chance are you Nikki Garcia?" he asked. "Andy Garcia's sister?"

Nikki froze for a split second, then masked her surprise with a smile. "That's me. And you are . . . ?"

"Oh, sorry, I'm Derek Brown. A friend of Stan's," he said, extending his hand.

She found that he had a firm grip.

"Nice to meet you, Derek. And what brings you out here?"

"Stan called. He was on his way to Albuquerque but got delayed in Denver. He owns his own plane, you know. He had something to do as soon as he landed in Albuquerque. I think he was going to see Kenny's mother. Stan's first wife, Juanita. I thought I'd look around. I mean, it's tough. You know, after what happened here today. Losing his son. That's tough."

"Didn't I see you earlier today?" Nikki asked.

"Me? Here? No, no, I was on the other side of the field."

Nikki studied him closely in the half-light of the sunset. "You do know that my brother's wife was killed in the accident?"

Derek looked at the ground. "Stan told me. I'm sorry. And he told me Andy's in the hospital. If there's anything I can do . . ." his voice trailed off.

Nikki thanked him and asked how he knew Stan.

"Stan and me, we go way back. I've consulted on several projects over the years."

"Projects?" Nikki raised an eyebrow. "You mean like drone and balloon manufacturing?"

"More the communications end. Mostly research on drone systems. Stan's a good guy and runs a tight shop. He's made investments in several interesting ventures. And that's where I come in."

Nikki bit her lip. "I could swear I saw you shortly after the balloon crashed."

Derek hesitated. His friendly demeanor became serious. "I was close, but not here."

"You ran across the field," Nikki said. "I saw you."

He shook his head. "I don't think so."

"I even took a picture of you," she said.

"Oh, yeah, that's right." Derek shook his head slightly as if to recall the incident. "I came running to see if I could help. I was so horrified that I left. There was nothing for me to do."

"Did you call Stan?" Nikki asked.

"I spoke with the police. I gave them Stan's phone number. They were the ones who called him."

"Must be the stress of it all, but I remember seeing you turn the burner off."

Derek's jaw tightened. "It's all a blur. In a crisis, my instincts kick in. I do things that I can't remember later. It gets scrambled in my brain."

"But you do remember running to confirm that it was Stan's balloon that came down. Is that right?"

He stuttered unintelligibly.

"And now you're here to find evidence the police did not detect. Did you find something? Like what you stuffed in your pocket?"

Derek acted as if he were going to respond, but the headlights of a car, driving on the field, headed toward them.

"That's—that's probably Stan," he stuttered. "I—I'd better meet up with him."

Nikki sensed Derek's relief at being off the hook. "Before you leave," she said, "did Stan tell you what might have caused the accident?"

"No, just said he's determined to figure it out." Derek jogged away.

Nikki's mind buzzed with questions.

## CHAPTER SEVENTEEN

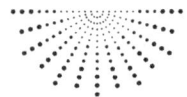

Nikki expected the car to leave the field after Derek jumped in the passenger seat. Instead, it dimmed its lights and rolled toward her.

The driver stopped and stepped out, leaving the dimmers on.

"I'm Stan," he said, giving Nikki a slight embrace. "I'm saddened by today's events. I don't understand what happened and I'm determined to find out why my balloon crashed."

"It's been a hard day for all of us," Nikki said.

"Hard doesn't begin to describe it. I'm thankful Andy's made it. Thanks for giving me the update when I called earlier."

"He still has an uphill battle, but the worst is behind him."

With twilight upon them, it was difficult for Nikki to pick up on any facial clues, but she kept asking questions. "What kind of malfunction could have caused the crash?"

"It was my balloon, my equipment. Less than a year old. I need to find out if it was equipment failure, pilot error, or God forbid, something worse."

"Something worse?" Nikki asked. "Like what?"

Stan cleared his throat. "A detective called me, a couple of hours after the police informed me about the accident. She said the police are investigating witnesses' allegations of the accident being caused by a drone. In other words, sabotage. Then I called you to find out about Andy and to know if the detective had contacted you."

"Sabotage?" Nikki repeated. "What do you think?"

"I wouldn't have considered something so sinister if the detective hadn't mentioned it. The real question is who was the intended victim? Me or my company?"

"What makes you think someone was after you? You don't think Andy was the target?"

"Well, I was supposed to be flying the balloon. And I manufacture weather balloons. Sort of obvious, isn't it?"

A chill went down Nikki's spine. The police were taking the idea of sabotage seriously, despite the detective's cavalier attitude earlier in the day.

"I'm meeting with Detective Morales as soon as I can, maybe tomorrow," Stan continued. "Has she set up an appointment with you?"

"I spoke with her briefly on the field, after the accident," Nikki said, "but I'm sure she'll want an in-depth interview."

"After you speak with her, let's talk," Stan said. "I want to get to the bottom of this. And there's a reporter who contacted me—Maxine Sanchez. She's always out to get juicy gossip. Her methods can be reckless. If she contacts you, watch out."

Nikki let it pass. She didn't want to reveal that Maxine had already been in touch. "Does Derek work for you?"

"Yes, contractual work. Plus, he's a childhood friend. He's brilliant but has difficulties working on a team, so I use him on pieces of projects where he can basically work on his own."

"Did you send him out here to look around?"

Stan told her Derek had come out on his own but had called to inform him he'd be at the crash site. "So I told him I'd come out and meet up with him. I'd better get going. Let me know if there's anything I can do for Andy."

Nikki watched Stan's silhouette against the dim lights of his car as he walked away. She wanted to cry, but the tears wouldn't come. Jumbled thoughts bounced in her brain and kept her from focusing.

As she drove back to the hotel in Old Town, she put Eduardo on speaker. After asking about her brother's condition, she told her husband about her visit to the crash site.

"I don't have a good feeling about Stan. He seems to be digging for information. He lost a son in this crash and yet his biggest concern seems to be that either he or his company may have been the intended target in the balloon crash."

"Your intuitions have served you well in the past, but you'd best remain objective until you get a few more facts," Eduardo cautioned. "We never know how people react when they've lost a close family member."

"Meeting Derek only made me more suspicious. The guy was crawling on the ground, and he pocketed something when he saw me. He was a little weird and super nervous. When I asked questions, he lied or didn't answer directly. The last thing he told me was that Stan is determined to find out what happened."

"More than anything, my beautiful private eye, keep yourself safe. If there was sabotage, those people could come after you if they think you're a threat."

Nikki sighed. "I'm going to miss you tonight. Don't know if I can sleep without you next to me."

"Call if you want to talk." Eduardo told her he loved her and sent a kiss over the phone.

# CHAPTER EIGHTEEN

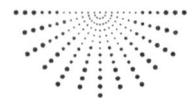

By the time Nikki arrived at the hotel, Olivia was asleep. Keiko told her that she and Olivia played hide-and-seek, and that she'd also taken her for a short walk to the plaza in the center of Old Town, four blocks from where they were staying.

"I enjoyed the adobe Pueblo style of the buildings. Very minimalist. We went into a couple of stores. At one, they told me there's a Japanese garden at the Albuquerque Bio Park. If you're okay with it, I'd like to take Olivia there tomorrow. It's not too far from here."

Nikki gave her permission for them to visit the Japanese garden. She wanted to tell Keiko to be extra careful and avoid isolated spots in case of an emergency, but she didn't want to scare her. Besides, Keiko had already shown she was vigilant. It was Nikki who feared the worst, given that there were so many questions about the crash. "Call an Uber to drop you off and pick you up when you're finished."

"I found a bookstore that sold crayons and coloring books. We colored for the last hour before Olivia fell asleep. She'd had a busy day." Keiko smiled, her eyes crinkling as they always did when she smiled. "She only asked for her mother once."

Nikki shook her head. "How are we going to explain to an eighteen-month-old that her mother is not coming back?"

"Focus on today and don't worry about the future," Keiko said. "You will figure it out."

Nikki leaned over the bed to kiss Olivia's curly hair. Her mobile buzzed and she told Keiko she'd take it in her own room, adjoining the one Keiko and Olivia shared. "We'll leave the door open," she said, stepping through to the next bedroom.

"Hi, Max, what's up?" Nikki asked when she saw the reporter's ID show up on the screen.

Maxine's voice was low and urgent. "I contacted Carol Peters. Said she'd heard a rumor about Stan being in negotiations with a foreign government over surveillance drones. Apparently, the deal went sour."

"Who's Carol Peters?"

"Owner of a drone company. She's still a small player in that field. Her company makes recreational drones, but she's branched out into weather and surveillance equipment. She hears industry secrets, so to speak. It's a lead you might want to follow up on, though it may not go anywhere."

"Aren't you in a better position to do that?" Nikki asked.

"You're the PI, I'm just a reporter." Maxine's voice became almost whiny. "You can meet with her while I look into other things."

"Did she mention which foreign government?" Nikki asked.

"China," Maxine replied. "She didn't know any details, but she was clear that Stan was involved."

Nikki's mind raced. Surveillance drone sales to the Chinese government? Sounded like a high-stakes situation with powerful players involved. Stan was successful, but had he overstepped his boundaries and violated US export laws? Nikki also suspected Maxine was not being completely transparent about what she knew.

"Has this deal gone sour recently?" Nikki asked.

"It has," Maxine said. Her voice picked up in pitch. "That makes the timing of the balloon fiasco quite ominous, don't you think?"

"What about Melissa, Stan's wife?" Nikki asked.

"I don't think she'd have anything to do with this. She's too busy modeling."

"I understand she didn't get along with Kenny."

"But that doesn't mean she'd kill him," Maxine said. "Besides, how could she organize bringing a balloon down at the last minute when she learned her husband wasn't piloting after all?"

"True," Nikki said. She sighed before continuing. "Let me sleep on all this and I'll see what I should do." She ended the call and dialed Charlotte's mobile.

When Charlotte answered, Nikki apologized for calling her at home. "I realize it's a couple of hours later in Miami, but I'd really appreciate it if you can check out Maxine Sanchez, a reporter at the Center for Investigative Reporting, and Carol Peters, a manufacturer of surveillance drones."

"Right, sounds like you need this pronto. I'll do a quick search and send you an email on my findings."

Nikki told her not to spend too much time on it tonight, but to work on it the next day at the office if she found information worth pursuing. She thanked Charlotte and asked her to send an email if she found anything of interest on either one.

Nikki returned to the adjacent room to remind Keiko to wake her up if she needed anything or if Olivia awakened. She also told her she was going to take a shower and then go to bed.

In the shower, Nikki thought about the details of the crash and what Celia, the witness, had said about the drone that had flown near the balloon before it crashed. She did not want to jump to any conclusions, but Carol Peters owned a company that also manufactured drones. There was also the possibility that the Chinese government had been in negotiations with Stan. Could they have sent a killer drone in to bring the balloon down? And what about Derek, Stan's friend, who had rushed in to turn off the burner? None of this made sense.

The warm water running over Nikki's body was the only relaxing activity she'd experienced that day. The warmth felt comforting, and it made her think of Eduardo. She wished he could be with her this evening, yet it was more important that he remain at the hospital in case Andy needed a doctor during the night. What better physician to have there than Eduardo?

Her thoughts jumped from one topic to another like lightning flashes. They reminded her of the silver squiggly lines from the stylized globe logo on Stan's balloon. The slogan boldly declared Connecting the World. Except that her thoughts were not connecting at all. Rather than continue theorizing, she decided to check out Derek Brown online. She did not want to burden Charlotte at this hour.

She stepped onto the bathmat, toweled off, and put a robe on, tying the waistband as she walked toward the desk. Turning on her laptop, Nikki made sure all the security was activated. She brought up an InPrivate page before searching for the name of Stan's odd friend.

After a few minutes, she found Derek's picture. Though it was not really a picture. It was a mug shot.

# CHAPTER NINETEEN

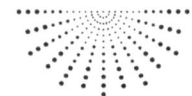

The heart monitor's rhythmic beeping changed to a higher-pitched alert, awakening Eduardo. He jumped from the sofa bed to Andy's side, touched his forehead, and glanced at the monitors behind the bed. The patient's blood pressure was high. Movement and a low groan from the hospital bed alerted him that Andy was awake and trying to sit up.

Instinctively Eduardo reached for the kidney-shaped basin on the bed table and placed it under Andy's mouth just in time to catch his vomit.

"It's alright," Eduardo said calmly.

A nurse came flying in and Eduardo asked her for emesis bags.

His mind raced through possible scenarios. Could the vomiting be caused by the anesthesia or the painkillers? Or was it coming from swelling in the brain? Had he reattached the bone flap too soon? Brain surgery disrupts the electrical activity of the brain, which can result in seizures. Had Andy suffered a seizure? Or heaven forbid, could it be a new bleed?

The nurse opened the top drawer on the nightstand and handed him a stack of bags. As he took one to Andy's mouth, the nurse took the basin to clean it. Andy retched violently this time. Eduardo tossed it in the trash bin and opened another bag in preparation for the next round.

"Could be seizure-induced vomiting," Eduardo mumbled to the nurse. "Grab the bag and hold it for him."

Eduardo checked his vitals. Andy was not only his patient, but he was also family.

Without warning, Andy's body twitched and convulsed.

Eduardo counted the seconds. Under twenty. That was a good sign.

"I need a portable MRI right now. Set it up. Then bring me an anti-epileptic med. Levetiracetam if you have it," he ordered. "And a syringe of steroids, just in case."

The nurse rushed out to call for the portable MRI technician and to gather the requested medication.

"You're going to be fine," he said to Andy. "You've had major surgery. Your brain and body need to readjust. I'll give you something to stop the seizures and keep you from vomiting."

With that, Andy retched again.

When the nurse returned, the MRI technician had already set up the low-field equipment. The 3-D representation of Andy's brain tissue was projected onto the monitor that Eduardo was studying. She placed the medications on the bed table.

"That's really good," Eduardo said as he watched the screen. He asked the nurse to administer the Levetiracetam as soon as the MRI was complete.

"You're going to heal just fine," Eduardo said. Then he thanked the nurse and the technician for their help.

"Can I see Olivia?" Andy asked.

"Hospital regulations don't allow children to visit ICU," the nurse said. Glancing at Eduardo, she asked the child's age.

"A toddler. Tomorrow morning I'll ask my wife to set up a call by speaker phone."

# CHAPTER TWENTY

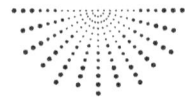

Nikki slept fitfully. Each time she awakened, she pondered the role of every person in the events surrounding the balloon accident. Exhaustion had finally won, and she was sleeping soundly when Olivia's cries awakened her.

Keiko rushed to close the connecting door. Nikki glanced at the clock. It was time to follow up on some leads. Her stomach rumbled, reminding her that she had skipped dinner the night before.

Opening the door to the adjacent room, she found Keiko sitting cross-legged on the floor next to Olivia, showing her how to tear colored paper, apply glue, and stick the pieces on a sheet of white paper. Nikki watched in silent admiration at Keiko's patience.

The woman repeatedly cleaned Olivia's hands to wipe off the glue so the collage could progress. She seemed to be telling the child a story as they worked together.

Olivia giggled and asked, "Where's Mommie?"

With the spell broken, Nikki greeted them. Olivia stood and ran on her stiff little legs toward her and repeated the question: "Where's Mommie?"

"She's gone, sweetie. She's gone."

Nikki's mobile buzzed. It was her husband calling. She forced herself to sound upbeat when she answered.

Eduardo told her that Andy had a complicated night but was stable this morning and feeling much better. He asked about her plans for the day, and she told him she'd found several leads to investigate. She'd visit the hospital later in the day.

"I'll stay at the hospital again tonight. I'd appreciate a change of clothes when you come this way," Eduardo said. "And I promised Andy you would put Olivia on a video call."

Preparing the phone for Olivia to see her father took a few seconds. It took much longer to get Olivia to pay attention to the image on the screen. She held a scrap of paper and kept trying to stick it on the phone. When she heard her father's voice, she glanced at Nikki with a huge smile and said, "Daddy, Daddy."

Once Olivia had finally looked at the screen, she seemed confused by the image of her father. Maybe it was his current appearance, or maybe she was unaccustomed to seeing her father on the phone. Andy told her he loved her and would see her in a few days. He blew kisses and she mimicked him, not just blowing kisses to her father's face on the phone but also tossing kisses around the room.

# CHAPTER TWENTY-ONE

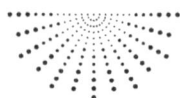

Nikki opened her laptop and sent Charlotte the article with the mug shot of Derek Brown, explaining that he was Stan's lifelong friend. She asked Charlotte to check him out, like what he's been involved in, his prison time, and the like.

An incoming email contained information Charlotte had dug up on Maxine Sanchez and Carol Peters. Nikki wanted to learn more about the reporter she'd teamed up with and she opened the file on Maxine first.

Charlotte had sent her a huge amount of detail about the reporter. Nikki skimmed through mundane data such as Max's being born and raised in Albuquerque and graduating summa cum laude in journalism from the University of New Mexico. That bit confirmed Nikki's assessment of the reporter's smarts.

The file noted various jobs Maxine had held, even a stint as a TV anchor. Her brand of telling it as it is got her removed from the newscaster position. Her reputation as a tough, no-nonsense journalist who sought the truth regardless of the consequences had backfired on her more than once. What took Nikki by surprise was that she'd authored a couple of nonfiction books. The first was an exposé on state legislators in Santa Fe, revealing the author's penchant for uncovering wrongdoing or corruption.

The second book held Nikki's attention. The true story of a cartel boss that Maxine had investigated detailed much of his drug smuggling and human trafficking activities, including sex trafficking of minors. Surely that had made her a few enemies, including the man her work had helped to put behind bars.

Nikki scanned her brain for any connections a cartel boss might have with her brother's buddy, Sammy Amaya, the CIA spy. Sammy had surely dealt with cartels in his undercover persona. Was there any connection between this cartel boss and Sammy? The subject of Maxine's book was Mexican, not Cuban as with Sammy's foes. And Sammy was American, having come here as a kid when his parents left Cuba to settle in the US. Yet Nikki couldn't help but worry about one of Sammy's so-called past connections who might be out to exact revenge by hurting Sammy's close friend—her brother. Andy had helped Sammy escape when Cuban agents abducted him from the mountains near the village of Peñasco, where Andy lived.

Chinese agents wanting Stan killed made far more sense, if the intel that Stan's recent negotiations had soured was correct. Yet she couldn't dismiss the worry that Sammy's enemies could be after her brother.

A knock on the door interrupted her work. Keiko rushed to open it, but Nikki stopped her. "We need to check the peephole."

Keiko had ordered coffee and breakfast. With her trusting nature, she would have opened the door without checking. Nikki made a mental note to work with Keiko on safety and security. Right now, though, she'd take a break from her online research to join Keiko at breakfast, especially since the sweet soul had remembered Nikki's penchant for eggs Benedict over salmon.

After eating, Nikki took coffee to her desk and reopened the files Charlotte had sent. Reading the rest of the findings on Maxine, she was convinced that it was okay to work with the reporter. She had a gnawing feeling that Max was not telling her everything, but she herself only disclosed what was necessary. She had to cut Maxine some slack.

Nikki closed that file and started the one on Carol Peters. She loved the way Charlotte used emoji on her reports. This one had a red heart at the opening sentence and a broken heart at the end of the paragraph. Carol had dated Stan during their years at Stanford. Then they broke up.

Carol had an engineering degree from Stanford's aeronautics and astronautics program. Afterward, she'd gone to Harvard for an MBA. The woman was overqualified for manufacturing hot-air balloons. She could compete with companies building spacecraft. Nikki lingered on that thought. Perhaps Carol was in business to prove to her old fling that she could build a better weather balloon and more advanced drones than he could. The name of her company, Drones over Mars, might indicate her eventual ambition—to participate in the exploration of that planet.

Was there vicious rivalry between the former lovers? Carol's work history before venturing into entrepreneurship included SpaceX in Texas. In fact, she'd been a rising star there.

All the information Charlotte had compiled led her to call Drones over Mars, a California company, to set up an interview with its principal.

Nikki worked through the voice menus to reach a live person. She stated her reason for calling was to speak to Ms. Peters. The person connected her to the company spokesperson. When Nikki insisted on interviewing Carol Peters, he said that was impossible, but he'd be happy to answer her questions.

"I have questions that go all the way back to her Stanford days, and they are rather personal. I don't believe Ms. Peters wants me to discuss them with anyone else." Nikki asked him to relay her message to Carol Peters.

"I'll try, but Ms. Peters is a very private person," he said.

Nikki added that she was in Albuquerque. They could meet wherever Ms. Peters wanted or they could speak by phone. She gave him her contact information.

After finishing the call, she decided that if her tactic did not work, then she'd call Maxine to figure out how to contact Carol.

# CHAPTER TWENTY-TWO

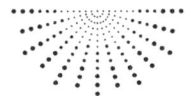

Nikki grabbed a change of clothes for Eduardo, placing the bundle in a laundry bag on the bed. She opened her laptop and was responding to Charlotte's latest email when her mobile buzzed.

Surprise! It was Carol Peters calling.

After introducing herself, Carol asked Nikki what was so sensitive.

"I want a candid opinion of what could have gone wrong with Stan Stevens's balloon," Nikki said.

"Human error. That's what causes most crashes. The other possibility could be equipment failure. For that, you must speak with Mr. Stevens."

Nikki noted that Carol's company competed with his. "As such, I'd like to go into more depth in my interview. Where can we meet?"

"It wasn't my balloon that crashed. You should speak with the owner." Carol's answers were courteous, but her attitude had become curt.

"I think we should meet to discuss—"

"I don't grant interviews in person."

"Look," Nikki said, "I'm trying to understand why my sister-in-law was killed in this accident. My brother's fighting for his life after brain surgery. I need answers."

"I've told you all I know, Ms. Garcia."

"If I don't get a full interview, I might get an article published about your romance with Mr. Stevens during your college days at Stanford. You may not want that to come out. Could make you a suspect in the balloon crash."

"That's called blackmail," Carol said, clipping her words.

"Where shall we meet? And what time?" Nikki asked. "I understand that you're in Albuquerque."

"Three p.m. at the Red Chile Boutique Hotel. Don't bring anyone else with you. I'll text you the gate passcode."

"I'll be there," Nikki said.

Nikki returned to Charlotte's email and praised her for the details about Carol Peters's personal life. The information had already proven to be very useful. Before sending it, she asked her to forward any information on Derek's background. Take a deep dive into this guy, she wrote.

Next, she researched the Red Chile, where she'd meet Carol later. It was on private property and fully gated. She felt a twinge of concern about being in such an isolated location. She'd mention it to Eduardo when she stopped by the hospital.

Before venturing out, she grabbed her purse from the top shelf of the closet, where it was safe from Olivia. She put the strap over her shoulder and made certain the baby Glock inside was secure. Then she asked Keiko to sit down with her for a few basic safety instructions. If Carol had anything to do with the balloon crash, she would not hesitate to retaliate against Nikki. After all, Nikki had practically extorted the woman into meeting with her.

# CHAPTER TWENTY-THREE

Nikki threw her arms around Eduardo and kissed him. She placed the laundry bag with his clean clothes on the sofa.

From the hospital bed, Andy managed to smile. He looked pale, nearly the same color as the bandages over his burns. A tube, probably a drain, protruded from his head. It was so obvious that she didn't know how she could have missed it the day before.

Andy reached his hand out in greeting, even though his arm had other tubes taped to it. Nikki touched his fingers and told him he looked great.

Two young women arrived, saying they were there to help Andy get out of bed. Nikki sat on the sofa, out of their way. One of them glanced at Eduardo and asked if he was the doctor in charge. He nodded and gave them a quick rundown of Andy's condition.

"I've been giving him neurological assessments since he awakened yesterday afternoon," Eduardo said. "He's ready to walk."

Eduardo stood at the edge of the bed as the two therapists detached the monitors from Andy. The lead therapist asked Andy several questions, including what type of surgery he'd had, what day it was, and to name several words that started with the letter of the alphabet that she gave him. She also assessed whether he had any tremors as he extended his arms and legs.

When she completed the assessment, she draped the loose medical cords through a contraption that went over his neck and rested on his chest. She asked Andy to sit up on the edge of the bed. The other therapist moved closer. They each held one of his arms, and the lead therapist instructed him to put his feet on the floor. He wobbled a bit as he stood but was soon able to take a couple of steps.

"You're doing great," she said.

They held him as he slowly walked around the room.

"Can you manage a few steps on your own?" the lead asked. "We'll be right by your side."

Andy nodded. He took about ten steps before he wobbled enough that both therapists grabbed him. They worked with him for half an hour. The lead therapist said he'd done well and that they'd return the next day.

Nikki sat back in amazement at the patience each therapist exhibited during the session. Even though she would miss him on assignments, she was glad Eduardo had returned to his surgical practice.

Eduardo interrupted her musings and confirmed that he'd be spending another night with Andy in the hospital. "He's coming along so well that I'm tempted to sleep at the hotel, but if even a minor incident happens, I want to be right here."

"I understand," Nikki said. "I'm off to meet with one of Stan's competitors, Carol Peters, at three p.m. today."

"Care to say where?"

"At the Red Chile Boutique Hotel in the North Valley. It's on private property, gated."

"Can't you arrange for a more public location?"

"I had to threaten her with bad publicity if she didn't grant me an interview. She picked the venue."

Eduardo took his wife in his arms and whispered in her ear. "I've missed you so much. Sleeping here without you next to me is miserable."

"I know," Nikki said. "I hate it too, but we'll share the same bed again soon. I should return to the hotel to see the latest information Charlotte has sent me."

Andy asked her to give Olivia a kiss from him. She gave him a thumbs up.

Nikki gazed into Eduardo's eyes. "Andy is so lucky to have a world-class neurosurgeon taking care of him."

She waved at Andy and kissed Eduardo again before leaving to take the elevator.

# CHAPTER TWENTY-FOUR

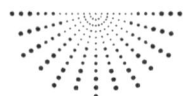

Nikki was driving back to the hotel when Stan's call came. He was leaving the police department after his interview with Lisa Morales, and he wanted to talk.

She agreed. Charlotte's latest research could wait. Speaking with Stan was more important. He'd pick her brain. And she could do the same. Stopping for a red light, she set the GPS for Stan's choice—Blackbird Coffee House in Old Town.

Establishments in Old Town adhered to the adobe Pueblo style exterior, but the warm and welcoming interior took Nikki's breath away. Paintings and small sculptures depicted blackbirds in both stylized and representational settings. The quaint New Mexico décor exuded an air of the traditional accented with whimsical details. Nikki almost forgot why she was there when Stan greeted her and escorted her to the brightly colored, open-air patio.

"I thought we could have more privacy out here," he said. "How's Andy doing?"

The question hit Nikki with a thud. She said he was better. "He knows Cindy didn't make it. Therapists were helping him walk this morning."

Stan raised an eyebrow. "He can't walk on his own?"

"He had *brain* surgery," Nikki said. "Learning to walk again is normal, like a computer resetting itself after being turned off. Last night he had a couple of seizures. His injury was extremely serious."

"I'm sorry. I should have realized he'd need therapy to get going again. Please forgive me, but I must ask if his mental capacity will fully recover. Andy and I have been friends since Stanford. It should be me lying in that hospital bed."

"My husband is cautiously optimistic that he'll fully recover." Nikki looked around the patio at a couple more sculptured blackbirds. "You chose an appropriate place for lunch."

"How's that?"

"Blackbirds symbolize the mystery and mayhem of life, don't they?"

"If it bothers you, we can go elsewhere. There's a ton of places to eat in Old Town."

"No, no," Nikki said, "I'm being philosophical. After all, what are the chances you join a balloon fiesta and end up losing your wife and undergoing brain surgery?"

"I get it," Stan said in a serious tone, "the mayhem."

"And the mystery: Who did it?" Nikki added. "That brings me to ask about your meeting with Lisa Morales."

Stan took a long inhale and let it out with a sigh. He looked into Nikki's eyes. "She asked me a bunch of questions. Told me she'd interviewed several people, including a witness that claims to have seen a drone near the balloon before it crashed."

"What does she think about the witness's account?"

"She didn't say, but I got the gist she thought the woman was unreliable. Said something about the woman's eyes darting around as she gave her statement," Stan said. "I guess the detective thought the witness was lying."

A server approached to take their order. Nikki had lost her appetite.

"The Hatch chile quiche is my favorite," the server said in a chirpy voice.

"Just coffee, black," Nikki said.

Stan followed Nikki's request and added two croissants to the order.

"What's your opinion?" Nikki asked. "Accident or sabotage?"

Stan squirmed in his chair and looked across the patio. "I don't know. I've asked the police chief to release the balloon to me so I can have my guys go over it to determine if it was equipment failure."

"What did the chief say?"

"They'll notify me later if I can take it, after their own investigators perform a thorough inspection," Stan said.

"You've been concerned about the implications to you or your company," Nikki said. "To establish credibility, it needs to be an independent evaluation."

He came to his defense, telling her there weren't many people qualified to do that kind of review. "It takes a balloon manufacturer to detect any issues."

"How about asking Carol Peters? I assume you know her since she also makes hot-air balloons."

The server set the coffee cups and a plate with croissants on the table. Stan took a gulp of coffee.

"She's a competitor." His eyes blinked in rapid succession for a few seconds. "I don't know if she'd be objective."

"Surely, there's someone else in the industry that you'd trust. If you want me to find someone—"

"You wouldn't know anyone." Stan handed her a croissant on a napkin. "These are the best croissants I've ever eaten. You must try one."

She put the napkin and crescent-shaped roll on the table. "That's true, but I know people at the FBI who can help."

Stan dropped his croissant back on the plate. "No way. Not the FBI."

"Then how about NTSB?"

"My guess is that they are already involved," Stan said. "But balloons are not exactly their area of expertise. I want my engineers to do the work."

"Did you know that Derek Brown ran across the field after the accident to turn off the burner?"

"Derek? He never mentioned it." Stan tore off a bit of croissant and ate it.

Nikki asked him why Derek would do that.

"I suppose for safety reasons. To avoid an explosion," he said, chewing.

Nikki told him an explosion had already happened. "It was small, like a firecracker. That's what brought the balloon down. Was Derek removing evidence of some sort?"

"Am I under interrogation?"

"You'd said you wanted to uncover why the accident happened," Nikki said. "I thought you wanted to talk about it and strategize."

"It just sounds so one-sided."

"Then it's your turn to interrogate me," Nikki said, smiling for the first time.

"What does your gut tell you about the balloon coming down?" he asked.

"It was sabotage," Nikki said without hesitation. "You told me that someone might be out to hurt you or your company. Can you think of anyone? A competitor? An enemy?"

Stan stared at the table, shaking his head.

"What about Derek? Do you trust him?" she asked.

Stan glanced at Nikki with surprise. "He's like a brother to me."

"And he's a felon." Nikki savored the effect of her words.

Stan glared at her.

"That was a long time ago. He was nineteen and fell in with a gang that held up convenience stores. At one place, a man pulled a gun on them. It got ugly, with both sides shooting their weapons. But he's served his time and has been totally clean for the last twenty years."

Nikki nodded. Was Stan trying to cover up details behind the crash? Or maybe he was just naïve. But how can a successful businessperson like Stan be so trusting?

"What about your business partner?" she asked.

Stan glanced at her with another surprised expression. "You've really been digging into my friends and associates, haven't you? You'd make a good investigator."

"I am one," Nikki said.

"FBI?"

"Private," Nikki said. "Which brings me to your business partner."

"Mark? Surely you don't suspect him?"

"It's a matter of talking to people to gather as much information as possible before compiling a list of suspects," Nikki said. "I'd like to talk with him, and I'd appreciate it if you'd make an appointment for me."

Stan pursed his lips. "I don't recall hiring you."

"You haven't. My family's been deeply affected by this crash. Cindy's dead and my brother's in the ICU. My niece lost her mother, and we need to see if her father will fully recover. That's why I'm looking into this."

Stan texted his business partner. He immediately got a response and forwarded it to Nikki.

"What about your foreign sales?" she asked, glancing at the text message on her watch.

Stan's eyes slashed anger for a split second. "I have sold equipment to other countries, but it's all in line with US export laws. Are you accusing me of wrongdoing?"

"I want to know what caused that balloon to crash," Nikki said.

Stan stood to leave. "I did not cause that accident."

# CHAPTER TWENTY-FIVE

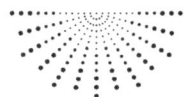

Nikki left the Blackbird Coffee House and parked on a side street. First, she texted Mark to request an appointment. After that, she added a couple of notes from her conversation with Stan into a file on her mobile. She regretted not getting contact information for Melissa, but Stan had been angry enough without questions about his wife. Nikki would find a different way to meet her.

She also needed to refocus her thoughts. If Eduardo were not taking care of Andy at the hospital, she'd call him. Not wanting to disturb him, she called Floyd instead.

After updating her boss on Andy's condition, Nikki told him she wanted to discuss her findings and the motives the various players might have in causing the balloon to fail.

"If Stan's son had not been in that balloon, I'd place him at the top of my suspect list."

"Does he have anything to gain from losing his son?" Floyd asked. "Like an insurance policy?"

"I hadn't thought of that."

Floyd offered to have Charlotte check it out.

"Rumor has it he may have had a deal gone sour with the Chinese government," Nikki said. "I asked about his foreign sales. He got testy, saying they were all in line with US export laws. Charlotte has already confirmed that Omega Satellites has a contract with Beijing."

Floyd said he'd investigate. "I'm in a better position than you to make inquiries about export violations."

"Also, he wants his own engineers to test for possible equipment failure," Nikki said. "He deflects from the tragedy and claims someone is out to hurt him or damage his company, like he didn't lose a son or good friend in the accident. Plus, he's already asked the chief of police to release the balloon to him so his people can examine it. Makes me wonder if he's bribing officials to conceal evidence."

"Do you have other suspects?"

"From the info Charlotte sent, I'd say that both Stan's friend Derek Brown and the chief of the chase crew, Gustavo Marquez, could be suspects."

"Does either one harbor a motive?" Floyd asked.

"I don't know. They both served time. Derek is a strange guy, and I thought he was covering something up after the crash when he rushed over to the gondola. Who knows what he was really doing? Plus, he was at the site of the accident the evening I returned to the park."

"If this guy Derek is hiding evidence, could he be working for an adversary of Stan's?"

"Derek is a consulting engineer, so he might take projects from other companies. That brings me to a competitor, Carol Peters. I'm interviewing her in an hour. She dated Stan at Stanford. They broke up after graduation. It's possible that Derek has worked for her. He'd certainly have knowledge that would benefit her company."

Floyd asked what type of competition Carol was in against Stan.

"Her company competes directly with him in weather balloons, drones, and communications."

It was time to leave for her next appointment. Nikki thanked Floyd for his help.

---

Nikki's stomach churned as she turned onto Rio Grande Place and pulled up to the gate. She input the code that Carol had texted her. A voice asked for her name and her reason for visiting.

The gate opened and Nikki drove through, accessing a road lined with large cottonwoods on both sides. Despite the beautiful setting, she felt uneasy about this meeting. Uneasy enough to think of opening the secret compartment of her purse.

After parking, she arranged her purse for easy access to her gun. Taking a winding pathway defined by daisies, she noticed fields of chile and pumpkins waiting to be harvested. Inside the lobby, a petite and attractive woman stood and greeted Nikki.

"You made it." She introduced herself as Carol Peters.

"It's a lovely place." Nikki shook the woman's hand lightly and looked around.

"A gem. You should stay here sometime. It has a great spa. The food is all organic, the fruit and vegetables come from their own garden." Carol asked Nikki to follow her to an open patio. "I stay in that first casita on the left," she said, pointing out a row of six stand-alone, pueblo-style casitas.

Nikki noticed a BMW with California plates parked near the front door of the casita.

The woman was charming and friendly, not at all the unfeeling, hardcore businessperson Nikki had conjured in her mind. A server arrived wearing a cute apron extolling the hotel's organic lavender. Carol asked for a glass of prosecco and Nikki ordered coffee.

Nikki thanked Carol for meeting with her. "As you've probably seen on the news, the balloon crash yesterday killed two people—Stan's son and Cindy Garcia, my sister-in-law." Nikki's voice cracked. She cleared her throat, getting her emotions under control.

"I'm sorry," Carol said, touching Nikki's arm. "It must be so hard. And your brother is in the university hospital, is that correct?"

"Yes, and he's not out of the woods yet, though we hope for a full recovery."

"I'll keep him in my prayers," Carol said. "Who is taking care of your brother's child? I understand he has a daughter."

Nikki was taken aback. "We are. Until my brother can do it."

"That's nice that you can help that way."

"I don't want to take more of your time than necessary," Nikki said. "Were you at the balloon fiesta yesterday?"

Carol shook her head. "I stay in this lovely place to avoid the crowds.

The balloons drifted by my casita and I got an excellent view of them. The wind currents usually take them south or southwest. I even got a glimpse of my own balloon. You do know I'm a sponsor of the balloon fiesta?"

"You don't fly your own?"

"I go up every chance I get, but not in big events like this. It's kind of scary to see so many balloons flying at the same time. Call me a coward, but a mass ascension is asking for accidents like the one your brother was in."

"I've come to you because I suspect the crash may have been caused by sabotage."

Carol gave Nikki a shocked look. "I can't imagine anyone would use the balloon fiesta that way."

"You'd hope not, but I heard that Stan Stevens's negotiations with the Chinese government have turned sour. Like maybe he reneged on the deal. I know it's a long shot, but I was wondering if there was a chance anyone from that country wanted revenge and shot down the balloon."

"I've heard the same rumor, but I have no way of knowing if it's true," Carol said, sipping the prosecco the server had just placed on the coffee table between the two women. "I mentioned it to my friend Maxine Sanchez, but I really should have kept my mouth shut because it was only hearsay. You should contact her. She's a reporter and she'd love to hear from you."

Carol was all but admitting she was the source of this rumor. Did she know that Maxine had talked to Nikki? Not letting Carol evade the issue, Nikki took a sip of coffee. "Would you know anyone who might have the inside scoop?"

"I heard about it at a business meeting in Washington, DC. I don't remember who mentioned it."

Nikki changed the topic and asked if she could describe Stan.

"Me? Describe Stan?"

"You dated him for a few years, and now you're his direct competitor," Nikki said, smiling.

"That was a long time ago. At Stanford. He was a wonderful guy. I think your brother can attest to that. They've remained friends after college, whereas Stan and I broke off our engagement. A good decision, I think, since he's on his fourth wife now."

"If he'd married you, you might still be together," Nikki said, maintaining her smile. "Maybe he hasn't found anyone that lives up to your qualities."

Carol looked stunned. "I'd never thought of it that way." She gazed at the Sandia Mountains in the distance, beyond the pumpkin field.

"Can you think of a name or two in the industry who might have knowledge of Stan's exports?"

Carol turned back to face Nikki. "Mark Edwards is Stan's business partner. Minority interest, I believe. Mark would like a bigger cut of Stan's business, and I don't mean just the weather balloons, but also the drone and communication sides."

Nikki didn't let on that she'd already asked to meet with Mark. "If you think of someone from that DC meeting, please send me their phone numbers." Taking another sip of coffee, Nikki asked how Carol had started her business.

"All the way back to our Stanford days, Stan and I had plans to build better weather balloons. We knew that computing and communication technologies would improve dramatically and we wanted to ride the wave of upward momentum, so to speak."

Carol took another sip of prosecco.

"The US experimented with balloons that carried sensing devices and transmission systems starting in 1970. That year, the NASA Nimbus-4 meteorological satellite captured the first transmitted weather data from a balloon. Systems continued to improve over the years. Better collection methods and communication systems are still under development."

"Hmm," Nikki said, thinking. "So that's the wave you've been riding. Interesting. Would you and Stan ever consider merging your two companies?"

Carol laughed. "Why would we marry our companies when we ourselves didn't tie the knot? Besides, my company is near Stanford. His is out here."

"You'd have the advantage of size, an all-important factor in business."

"I prefer independence. Being CEO of a tech company brings me satisfaction. Plus, I'll have a bigger, better company than Stan four to five years out," Carol said, glancing at her watch. "Oh, I must go. I have a Zoom conference in a few minutes." She drank the rest of her prosecco and stood.

Nikki thanked her and said she'd be in touch if she needed to ask anything further. Stopping in the lobby, Nikki asked the server to bring the check.

"Ms. Peters instructed me to put it on her tab," the server in the cute outfit said.

---

Nikki returned to the car and took a few seconds to rearrange the flap that concealed her gun. Her unease about Carol had vanished almost as soon as she met her. The woman was charming and more open than Nikki expected. Her only real surprise was the woman's knowledge of Olivia.

Carol was also adept at evading questions. If she had heard about Stan's export deal going sour, she would have remembered who told her. Nikki bet that Carol forgot very little of what she heard about Stan. Carol seemed like a woman capable of taking revenge on a former beau. But killing someone? Nikki doubted that Carol would be capable.

Nikki's mobile buzzed. Carol had sent Mark's information. She drove out of the private property and parked on the gravel shoulder before reaching Rio Grande Boulevard.

She called Eduardo to update him about her meeting, telling him she'd been terrified about meeting Carol, yet she had turned out to be a charming person. Her only concern was that Carol knew where Andy was hospitalized and that he had a little girl. She thought that was unusual.

Eduardo talked for a bit about Andy's continued progress and Nikki told him she'd return to the hotel and spend the rest of the afternoon and evening with Keiko and Olivia.

Before leaving, she made notes of her conversation with Carol. With that task complete, she called Mark to set up an appointment. Again, it went to voicemail.

---

Still parked at the gravel shoulder near Rio Grande Boulevard, she dialed Gustavo.

He picked up on the second ring.

Nikki asked if he had news of any sort.

"I was asked to head up a crew for an English balloonist. His crew chief came with him from England, but the man ate some hot Hatch chile and can't be away from a bathroom." Gustavo laughed. "Changing the subject, how is Andy doing?"

Nikki updated him on Andy's condition.

"I wanted to go by and see him," Gustavo said, "but the talk around the crew members is that he's in intensive care and no one but family is allowed in."

"Give him a couple more days. Then if you want to see him, ask for my husband. He'll give you permission to see him for ten minutes."

"Your husband must have a lot of pull," Gustavo said.

"He's the surgeon who operated on Andy," Nikki explained.

"Ahh, I didn't know," Gustavo said, surprised. "Your husband is a surgeon here in Albuquerque?"

"No, but there was no one else to operate on him, so the hospital made an exception."

Gustavo expressed amazement.

"Is there any talk about the accident?" Nikki asked. "Like speculation who might have done it?"

"The Brit I'm helping has mentioned that the two competitors, meaning Stan and Carol Peters, might have been warring over customers and brought their fight to the field. Most people, though, think it was either pilot error or equipment malfunction."

"And the balloon fiesta goes on as if nothing happened," Nikki said, sadness in her voice.

"There's talk about a vigil to honor those killed. And to pray for Kenny, Cindy, and your brother."

"I had not heard," Nikki said.

"I planned to call you as soon as I had complete information. Seems it will take place Friday night, two nights before the fiesta ends, somewhere at Balloon Fiesta Park. I'll call when I have a definite place and time."

"Please contact me if you hear anything about the accident." She thanked him and ended the call.

Nikki thought about attending the vigil. Would she be able to hold up for such an event? Losing Cindy, the uncertainty of Andy's recovery, and Olivia growing up without her mother. It all got to her. She felt exhausted.

She started the car and headed back to the hotel.

# CHAPTER TWENTY-SIX

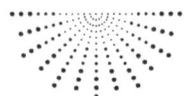

Nikki turned from Rio Grande Boulevard into the hotel parking lot. She was looking forward to relaxing for the rest of the afternoon with Keiko and Olivia, if time spent around a toddler could be called relaxation. In the evening, she would touch base with Eduardo. Her mobile buzzed as she stepped out of the rental. Maxine wanted to meet her a bit later for a drink at the hotel so they could follow up on what each had accomplished and to strategize on their next moves.

When Nikki opened the door to her hotel room, it was eerily quiet. A lump formed in her throat. She called for Keiko. The only sound she heard was the thumping of her own heart. She ran to Keiko's room. Everything was in perfect order. Nikki reached for her mobile and dialed Keiko.

Keiko answered in her usual serene voice. Nikki felt such relief, she would have hugged anyone. An Uber was taking them from the Japanese garden to the hotel, Keiko told her.

Nikki, anxious to see her niece, went downstairs and stood at the hotel entrance. Keiko took the toddler in her car seat out of the car. Once Olivia saw her aunt, she squirmed to get out. Keiko released her and she ran a few steps to where Nikki stood, babbling the words *koi, koi*.

Nikki was so thrilled to see her niece after the scare of not finding her in the room that tears of joy formed in her eyes. She regained her composure before Keiko could notice.

"We saw koi swimming in elegant ponds at the Sasebo Japanese Garden. I taught her to say *koi* instead of *carpas japonesas*, as we say in Spanish," Keiko said. "*Koi* is much easier."

"I can tell she had a great time," Nikki said, "Thank you so much for taking care of her."

On the elevator to their floor, Keiko described the lush green foliage and wooden bridges over ponds where orange, white, and yellow koi swam. "A lovely waterfall fills the ponds and keeps the water crystal clear for viewing the fish."

Nikki called room service and ordered dinner. Olivia played hide-and-seek with her aunt until the food arrived. Then the three of them sat on the floor around the coffee table where Nikki had the server leave the tray of food. After they finished dinner, Keiko filled the bathtub and gave Olivia a bath before putting her to bed.

---

Maxine stood to greet Nikki as she approached the reporter's booth in the hotel bar.

She spoke excitedly as soon as Nikki sat down.

"Wait, Max," Nikki said, "can you repeat that?"

"Derek Brown has worked for Carol. On projects like those he's done for Stan's company."

"How did you find out?"

"By talking to him. He readily agreed to meet with me, even though it's Sunday. Said he's designed drones for her, particularly the component parts of cameras and transmission systems."

"Interesting," Nikki said. "I wonder if Stan knows that?"

"According to Derek he accepted the project only after he'd asked Stan if he'd be okay with him working for a competitor. When I returned home after my meeting with Derek, I called Stan to get his input, and he sounded shocked that his friend had worked for Carol. I think he felt betrayed."

"So one of them is lying," Nikki said, impressed by Maxine's work.

"You got it."

Maxine had already ordered a bottle of red wine. Her glass was half full and she poured some for Nikki, pushing the glass toward her.

Nikki updated Maxine on her meeting with Carol. "She's not only Stan's competitor, but I think she could be out for revenge."

"That business is cutthroat. I wouldn't be surprised if she wants to discredit his company to her advantage."

"I mean revenge for ditching her after they graduated from Stanford," Nikki said, swirling the wine in her glass.

"Oh, the plot thickens," Maxine said, raising an eyebrow. "Sounds like a soap opera."

"Unfortunately, the deaths are not make-believe." Nikki choked up as she said it.

Maxine apologized, saying she had not intended to be insensitive.

Nikki changed the subject, telling Max that Stan and Carol had been engaged when they were students at Stanford.

Maxine almost leaped out of the booth. "How'd you find out?"

"I researched them," Nikki said. "When they were engaged, they'd anticipated the huge demand for weather balloons and their accompanying instrumentation, and they'd planned to open a business together. Until Stan called the engagement off."

"Hmm, that makes Carol a prime suspect in my books," Maxine said. "I wonder if the police know?"

Nikki shrugged and took a sip of wine. "How well do you know Stan?" she asked.

"I don't," Maxine said. "But I interviewed Carol last year at the balloon fiesta. It made the national news. I featured her as a female entrepreneur on a network special. Ever since then, I hear from her periodically."

Nikki considered her next statement before saying it. "Carol told me that her company would overtake Stan's in the next four to five years. I hope the crash wasn't part of her growth strategy."

"What's your opinion on the crash? Was it done on purpose?"

"I hope it wasn't sabotage, but I want to find out what happened." She glanced back at Max. "If someone did it, I want them to pay for it."

"Who's on your suspect list?" Maxine asked.

Nikki took a sip of her wine. "Carol said she couldn't remember who told her that Stan reneged on an export to the Chinese government. It might only be a rumor. You and I have already discussed that this requires abiding by US government regs protecting this type of technology, which can easily be converted to spy equipment. How many times in the past couple of years has the news reported on unknown drones and balloons flying near military bases and nuclear facilities?"

"Are you saying that you don't suspect Stan?" Maxine asked.

"If his son Kenny hadn't died in the crash, Stan would be at the top of my list. But what father would risk his son?" Nikki shook her head. "Stan couldn't have done it."

"When Carol called me to say she was in town," Maxine said, "the first topic she brought up was Stan's foreign deal going sour, implying it was clandestine. I pressed her to name the foreign country. That's when she said they were Chinese and may have been behind the crash."

Nikki winced. "She put it that way? Maybe setting his company up for the fall?"

"Before you told me about Stan dumping her a few years back, I wouldn't have suspected her. Now, I'd hate to think she'd be capable of such a heinous act, but I can't rule her out."

"A mastermind is behind the crash, in my opinion," Nikki said. "It could be Chinese agents, a competitor, or a low-level person with a beef against him, but someone was out to get Stan."

"Even a genuine export deal sanctioned by the government could have gone wrong," Maxine said, refilling her wine glass and swirling it before taking a sip. "However, my gut tells me that if foreigners are involved, the game was to smuggle the goods out."

"What about Stan's wife?" Nikki asked, serving herself more wine.

"Melissa?" Maxine scoffed. "The perfect trophy wife. She could be the only one who knew that Kenny would be flying instead of his father. Even if she wanted to get rid of the kid, would she risk going to jail instead of Hollywood? I don't think so."

"It's too early to tell," Nikki said.

Maxine looked bewildered. "You mentioned a low-level person might be the mastermind. I had not considered that angle. If that were the case, who do you suspect?"

"The felons around Stan." Nikki had seen Maxine show her emotion when she mentioned Stan and Carol's relationship in college, but now shock flickered in the reporter's eyes.

"Felons?" Maxine shifted in her seat.

"The chief of the chase crew, Gustavo Marquez, is one. The other one is Stan's friend Derek Brown."

"I totally missed it. I was too swayed, I guess, by Carol's accusations to do basic research," Maxine said. "That's stupid of me."

Nikki noticed that Maxine was not quite as self-confident as she had originally been.

"We sound like we're running the investigation when the police and possibly the FBI are the ones at the helm." Nikki laughed.

Maxine downed the rest of her wine before speaking. "I respect Lisa Morales, the detective in charge. But she's so overworked with cartel issues and the city's high crime rate. You don't seriously think she'll give this case much attention, do you?"

Nikki thought about Floyd following up with the FBI and the CIA. She was not about to mention that to the reporter.

"It's Sunday evening," Nikki said. "By tomorrow we should really start to dig up stuff."

Maxine looked directly into Nikki's eyes. "I had an informant, kind of a scary guy, when I wrote a book on a cartel boss. Maybe I should see if he knows anything. If the man's still alive."

"Like he was a cartel guy himself?" Nikki asked. "That's scary."

"I'm not sure if he was a member, but he knew a lot about the cartels. Maybe he's heard something about a plot to get Stan's technology illegally."

"A plot involving cartels and foreign governments? Seems like a long shot to me," Nikki said.

"I'm sorry about your sister-in-law, and I hate to bring this up. Is there any possibility anyone would want her dead? Or your brother?" Maxine asked.

"Since they were not officially on the roster to fly that day, I doubt it." Nikki gazed into the wine glass. "If anyone was out to get either one of them, I don't know who it could be. Only Stan, my brother, and my sister-in-law knew that Stan would not be flying. Even the chase crew only found out that morning, about an hour and a half before the launch. My brother does sleep research for the European Space Agency. Hardly stuff that would motivate anyone to knock him off."

"What about your sister-in-law?"

"She assisted her husband with his research. I can't imagine she'd be anyone's target."

"Has your brother given you any useful info about the crash?"

Nikki shook her head. "He had brain surgery. The less thinking he does, the better. In a few days perhaps I can question him."

Then Nikki thought again of Andy's good friend Sammy Amaya, or whatever name the CIA operative was using now. It was not as if she could call him. The CIA took Sammy to an undisclosed location after he'd been discovered in New Mexico by Cuban spies. Could those who had been after Sammy now be coming for Andy? After all, Andy had helped save his friend when the Cubans captured Sammy. If that were the case, they certainly managed to kill Cindy.

# CHAPTER TWENTY-SEVEN

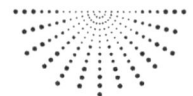

Eduardo couldn't sleep. The beeping of the monitors behind Andy's bed kept him awake and mulling the reasons behind the accident. If he could ask his brother-in-law who could have caused the balloon to crash, he would, but Andy's brain needed to heal before discussing issues like that.

It was two a.m. Eduardo closed his eyes and meditated on his breath, the way Nikki had taught him. He usually found it so relaxing he'd doze off whenever he and Nikki practiced Zen meditation. Relaxation was not taking over tonight. Nikki wasn't with him, and he missed not having her next to him in bed. The sofa bed was uncomfortable. How spoiled he'd become, he mused, going back to his years as an intern in New York's Mt. Sinai Hospital when getting a few winks was important, whether it had been on the floor or in a chair.

A rustling sound troubled his meditation. Expecting to see a nurse checking on Andy, Eduardo opened one eye and saw a tall figure in a nurse's uniform looming near Andy's IV pole. No light had been turned on in the room. Only the glow emanating from the hall made it possible to see the dark form.

"Can I help you?" Eduardo asked, getting up and switching the light on.

The person turned. He was wearing a hoodie, partially covering his face. Eduardo could see only a full dark beard.

Eduardo moved toward him.

The man pushed Eduardo out of the way, causing him to fall against the hospital bed. Eduardo, struggling to keep his balance, leaned into the bed and grabbed the man's arm. The intruder dropped something that clattered to the floor. His height gave him an advantage, and using his free arm, he landed an overhand punch on Eduardo's face. Eduardo pulled harder on the intruder. The man yanked out of Eduardo's grasp and struck him in the chest with a downward elbow.

"What's going on?" Andy asked in a confused tone.

The man pulled the hoodie tighter over his head and ran out the door. Eduardo, catching his breath after the powerful pummeling he'd received, followed. The man had a head start. He sprinted down the hall and into the elevator before Eduardo could do anything.

Eduardo yelled at him before the door closed. Glancing over his shoulder at the nurses' station to seek help, he saw it was empty. The nurses were elsewhere on the floor. He returned to the room and pressed the call button.

Andy was awake and asked about the man with the hoodie.

"I don't know, but I intend to find out." Eduardo searched for the object that had clanked on the floor. It was a syringe. He picked it up with a paper towel. He pressed the call button a second time.

A nurse rushed in. "What's happening?"

"A tall, thin, bearded man carrying this came in," Eduardo held the paper towel in a way that part of the syringe could be seen.

"I don't think the patient required any medication," she said, checking his chart.

"Is there a tall, thin, male nurse working here tonight?" he asked. "One with a full beard?"

The nurse shook her head. "Not on this floor."

"The guy was wearing a hoodie over white scrubs, but when I got out of bed, he punched me in the face and dropped the syringe. Then he bolted out of the room, ran down the hall, and entered the elevator. I followed part of the way but at that point, I returned to the room. I didn't want to leave Andy unprotected in case the guy had brought accomplices with him."

"Hoodie? That's weird," she said. "I'll check who's working the night shift to see if anyone fits your description."

"While you're looking into the staff, inquire if anyone let a tall, thin man with a full beard through the security door into ICU."

She walked to the nurses' station, a few steps away from Andy's room, with Eduardo following her.

"What did the syringe contain?" she asked.

Eduardo held it up. It was a syringe with an off-white liquid with no label. "I'll call the FBI. Their forensic lab will identify the contents."

"Why would anyone want to hurt Mr. Garcia?" the nurse asked, handing Eduardo a plastic bag she took from a drawer in the nurses' station. "I thought he'd been in a balloon accident at the fiesta."

"The crash may have been on purpose, and the perpetrator is attempting to hide his tracks," Eduardo told her.

"That's scary," she said. "In all my years here, no one has ever tried to hurt someone, especially not in ICU. Should police be stationed at his door?"

"Let's first see what the lab says about the contents of the syringe," Eduardo said.

He watched as the nurse sent a message to her staff inquiring if anyone had let a man into the ICU ward that fit the man's description. She received three denials, but the fourth person said a new nurse had followed her through after she entered the code to open the door.

"It's not my hospital, but you should notify security. They should order all personnel to be careful of intruders pretending to be nursing or hospital staff," Eduardo said. "Now if you will excuse me, I'd like to call my wife."

Eduardo returned to the room, checked on Andy, and dialed Nikki's mobile.

"Is everything okay?" Nikki asked. Not surprisingly, she sounded like she'd been asleep.

Eduardo cleared his throat. "I hate to tell you that someone may have intended to harm Andy. Fortunately, I was awake when he came in and I scared the guy off. You need to double down on your security at the hotel. Barricade the doors."

"Wait, I don't understand. Someone tried to harm Andy?"

"Correct. I fought briefly with the intruder, and he dropped a syringe before he could inject Andy, assuming that was his intention. Can you arrange for the FBI to analyze it? They can come and get it tomorrow."

Eduardo heard Nikki try to talk but her words didn't come out.

"I want you and Keiko to be on the alert. In fact, why don't we all pack up and leave once Andy can be air-ambulanced to Miami."

"Are you okay?" she asked.

"I'm fine," Eduardo said. "Did you hear me? We all need to leave."

"You and Andy, Keiko, and Olivia should leave as soon as possible," Nikki said. "I'll ask Floyd to join me. Or one of the other PIs from the office can come out and help with the investigation."

"It's the FBI or the police who must investigate, not you, my love," Eduardo said. "If I go back, you should too so you can supervise Keiko and Olivia."

"Wait a minute," Nikki said, "anyone trying to shut Andy up means he knows something. I need to question him tomorrow. If that's okay with you."

Eduardo told Nikki he'd prefer to wait before questioning Andy, but under the circumstances, he would let her. "You must bring an official investigator with you, though. The police or the FBI, your choice."

# CHAPTER TWENTY-EIGHT

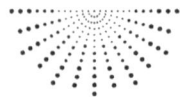

Nikki barricaded the doors to the hallway in both hotel rooms and made certain the windows were locked. She texted Floyd, asking him to call as soon as he could the next morning. She willed herself to sleep, knowing a hectic day was in store for her as soon as the sun rose.

She'd expected Floyd's call to awaken her, but it was Olivia crawling into bed that woke her. Olivia was babbling the word *koi* repeatedly, probably asking to be taken to the Japanese garden again.

"Koi, koi, Tia Ki," Olivia said.

Nikki felt her heart swell with love, just as it had when her son was alive. Olivia reminded her of Robbie in both her physical appearance and her personality. Nikki ached for Robbie. He'd been taken far too soon.

Olivia crawled to her aunt and stood on the bed, holding onto Nikki's shoulders. She jumped up and down as if the bed were a trampoline. Nikki laughed and took Olivia into her arms and went into Keiko's room.

"Oh, I'm sorry," Keiko said. "I took a quick shower. Olivia awakened and I'm afraid she woke you up too."

Nikki said that it was all okay. Even though it was not yet six a.m., she would stay up. "Eduardo caught an intruder in my brother's room last night."

Keiko's hand went to her mouth in shock. "He's in the hospital. How can that be?"

"We think someone may be trying to keep Andy from talking."

"You and Eduardo could be in danger," Keiko said, concern evident in her voice.

Nikki nodded. "You and Olivia too. I hate for you to be cooped up in the room all day, but you must stay safe."

"I was surprised to see the barricaded doors this morning, but I didn't think it'd be such bad news," Keiko said. "Don't worry, I won't let anyone take Olivia."

"I'm so thankful for your help," Nikki said, touching Keiko's hand.

Nikki's mobile buzzed. She was glad to see that Floyd was calling.

"What's up?" he asked.

"Someone may have tried to harm Andy at the hospital. If not for Eduardo, my brother could have been killed." Nikki took a deep breath and detailed what she knew about the incident. She also mentioned that the syringe the intruder had dropped needed to be sent to the FBI lab to identify its contents.

"It's not that I don't trust the Albuquerque police, but I'd like to turn the syringe over to the FBI. Can you arrange that?"

Floyd said he'd see what he could do. He was already in contact with the FBI office responsible for the Albuquerque area. "By the way, Charlotte's done that deep dive you requested into Derek Brown. Other than the armed robbery when he was nineteen, there's nothing else." Before ending the call, he advised Nikki to exercise extreme caution.

---

Nikki had ordered breakfast to be delivered to their rooms when her mobile buzzed again. Lisa Morales identified herself and asked if Nikki had time to talk.

"Me and my partner worked all day yesterday." Morales started talking as soon as Nikki replied. "We interviewed several people, we examined the evidence, including what you provided, and the police department deems the accident was caused by pilot error."

"You can't be serious," Nikki said, biting her tongue to keep from swearing. "You haven't even had time to interview witnesses or investigate people who might benefit from this accident."

"Look Ms. Garcia, the department is officially closing this investigation."

"Before you call it quits," Nikki said, choosing her words with care, "has your forensic department investigated where the broken lens came from? With some luck, you should be able to identify the manufacturer. There was a partial identifying number on it."

"The National Transportation Safety Board has been involved since Saturday. They've declared it pilot error."

Nikki scoffed so loudly that she coughed. "This is incompetence."

"The NTSB determine probable cause and report the facts and circumstances of air accidents," Morales said in a biting tone. "They've looked at the material and the equipment and believe there's not enough evidence to be considered a criminal case."

"I get it," Nikki blurted in anger and surprise, "attempts to kill people continue to be made in this case and you're closing it? Someone tried to kill my brother, the pilot, last night. And yet the case is being closed?"

Morales hesitated. "Your brother? The one in the hospital?"

"That's correct. Someone tried to inject him with something, but my husband fought him off. I know you're shorthanded and overworked, but it's a mistake to say this case is closed." Nikki heard keyboard clatter over the phone.

"I don't see where the police answered any calls at the university hospital," Morales said.

"That's correct. My husband wants the FBI to handle the new developments."

"It's in our jurisdiction," Morales said. "I'll go there myself with a couple of officers."

Breakfast had been delivered to Keiko's room by the time Nikki ended the call with the detective. Rolling her green chile omelet up in a flour tortilla, like an egg burrito, she took big bites and helped it down with gulps of coffee. Then she jumped in the shower.

Once she finished dressing, she sat down with Keiko to explain a few more aspects of security. She asked her to call at the slightest incident, no matter how insignificant.

# CHAPTER TWENTY-NINE

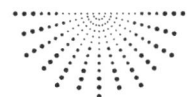

Nikki sprinted toward the hospital entrance and rushed through the lobby to the elevators. Waiting for what seemed like an eternity, she anxiously glanced at the floor indicator to see where the elevators were. The doors on the nearest elevator opened. She took a calming breath, stepped in, and pushed the button to the ICU floor.

"Your eye!" Nikki gasped at seeing her husband. "Have you seen that bruise?"

Eduardo embraced his wife and kissed her lightly on the lips. "The guy slammed his fist into my face. The bruising will fade away in a few days."

Nikki examined Eduardo's eye once more, shaking her head. "Was he acting alone?"

"As far as I know. If he had companions, I didn't see any. We need to return to Miami."

Nikki asked if the police had arrived.

"That could be them now." The elevator had just stopped again on their floor.

Nikki looked at the trio who emerged. Detective Lisa Morales looked like any middle-aged Latina woman in plain clothes. She was accompanied by a male officer in uniform, and they were escorted by a hospital volunteer. Morales introduced herself to Eduardo and asked if he was the surgeon who had operated on the victim of the balloon crash.

"That's correct." Eduardo turned to introduce Nikki.

"We've already met," Morales said, nodding curtly. "And this is Officer Santiago Cobos."

The volunteer addressed Eduardo. "Dr. Duarte, "my supervisor said that since you're Mr. Garcia's surgeon, you're the one authorized to give the police permission to speak with your patient."

"Under the circumstances, you can interview him. Please keep it brief. The patient is recovering from brain surgery."

"Understood," the detective said.

Eduardo led the way to Andy's room, with Nikki and the police following. The volunteer returned to the elevator.

"You look so much better this morning," Nikki said to her brother cheerfully. "At this rate, you'll be out of intensive care soon."

Eduardo placed a hand on Andy's shoulder and told him that Detective Lisa Morales and Officer Santiago Cobos wanted to ask him a few questions about the crash.

Morales moved closer to the patient's bed. She said she wanted information that might help her investigate the crash. "Is that okay with you?"

Andy agreed.

"Please relate the activities that led up to you substituting for Stan Stevens as the balloon pilot," she said.

"It was a last-minute decision. Stan was called away on business and he hated to disappoint his son who was to fly that day. So I stepped up."

"You offered?" she asked.

"Stan asked me to take his place."

"Are you qualified to pilot in an event like this?" Morales asked.

"I'm licensed, if that's what you mean."

"Have you piloted in other mass ascensions?"

"Smaller ones, like Angel Fire and Taos Mountain, and medium-sized ones like Red Rock in Gallup and the White Sands Balloon and Music Festival."

"Do you own a hot-air balloon?" Morales asked.

"I've used loaners. Stan provides them."

"Are you always the pilot?" she asked.

"Stan and I have flown together many times over the years. We've shared a love of anything related to air and space travel. I'm a sleep researcher for the European Space Agency."

"What do you think caused the crash?"

Andy blinked. "Seeing the balloons around us was thrilling. The sky was alive with color." He stopped and became visibly upset. "There was this flash of light . . ."

Morales glanced at Eduardo. He held his hand up as if to ask her to wait until Andy was ready to talk again.

"The burner flame . . . it flared, hitting Kenny, and he fell. My wife, Cindy, rushed toward him and fell too. Next came a big flash of light and a loud sound." He held his index finger up as if to signal he needed a few seconds. "The next thing I remember is being in a room with bright lights. Doctors, nurses, maybe a dozen of them, were all around me. That's when I knew something had gone wrong. I recognized Eduardo's voice and knew I'd be okay."

Morales turned to Eduardo, asking if the burns on the patient's face were caused by the burner flare.

"That's correct," Eduardo said.

"Does Stan have any enemies that might have wanted to bring that balloon down?" Morales asked.

"He's bigger than life. He's into everything. He's successful." Andy stopped as if to gather his thoughts. "It'd be natural for him to have enemies."

"Can you name any?"

Andy stared across the room with a blank expression. "I can't think of any." He looked back at the detective. "If I remember someone, I'll have my sister call you."

"How far back does your friendship with Stan go?"

Andy shook his head slightly. "To our days at Stanford. He came from money. I met him through Cindy, my wife. I was dating her, and she had a class with him." He stopped abruptly. Tears formed in his eyes.

"Take your time," the investigator said with empathy.

Nikki handed him a tissue.

"My wife. She didn't survive the accident," Andy said, wiping his eyes. "We became friends with Stan and Carol, his girlfriend at that time. Even back then, he was into ballooning and communications. He's a big player in those fields now. So is Carol. Though they've never done business together."

"Do you think his old girlfriend could have sabotaged the balloon?"

"Carol's an ambitious woman, but to kill people . . ." Andy blinked several times, as if he were thinking. "I hope not."

"Would she cause the balloon to crash if she expected people to survive?" Morales asked.

"That's pure speculation. I don't know. Cindy and I lost contact with her after we left Stanford. She wanted nothing to do with Stan's old friends after he broke up with her."

"What about your chase crew?" Officer Cobos asked, stepping closer to Andy's bed.

Morales, who had conducted the interview until now, moved aside.

Andy looked tired. Eduardo asked them to wrap up their questions as soon as possible.

Andy cleared his throat. "I don't know any of them very well, but I'm aware the crew chief was a felon. White-collar crime. Nice guy, well educated, I think Gustavo was in finance and committed fraud. That's different from killing someone, though."

"Mr. Stevens knew that his crew chief was a felon. Is that correct?" Cobos asked.

"Yes," Andy responded. His eyelids began to droop.

"Only a few more questions," Morales said. "Did you see the man who came in your room last night?"

"Yes, for a few seconds."

"Did you recognize him?"

Andy's brow furrowed. "I didn't get a good look at him. He wore a hoodie and had a thick beard. He punched my brother-in-law in the face . . . see his bruise?"

Morales nodded. "Why do you think he came here?"

Andy sighed. "Maybe he thinks I know something. He came in with a syringe of something. I'm lucky Eduardo was here. Otherwise, he might have killed me."

"Do you have any idea what the intruder thinks you know that could incriminate someone?"

"I've thought about it, but no, I don't. It must be related to my friendship with Stan. But I don't know enough about his business to be a threat." Andy took a hand to the side of his head. "My memory is a bit foggy."

"Is there anything else you know that you should tell me?"

"Please get the person who caused this. My daughter's lost her mother. I've lost my wife." Andy closed his eyes.

# CHAPTER THIRTY

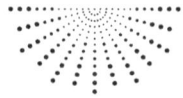

Nikki thanked both Detective Morales and Officer Cobos for interviewing her brother, and she was about to usher them out of the ICU ward when the officer turned to Eduardo.

"What happened to the syringe?"

"It's locked in the fridge, waiting for the FBI to pick it up. Said they'll be here later and send it to their lab," Eduardo said.

"You'll turn it over to us," Cobos said. "We'll get it to the lab and find out what's in it."

Eduardo walked to the nurses' station and asked the head nurse to unlock the box in the refrigerator containing the syringe and to release it to the officer. She followed Eduardo back to the room and asked the officer to sign for it.

Cobos thanked Eduardo and told him he'd inform the FBI that he'd taken the evidence to the lab. He also told Eduardo they'd interview him privately before they left.

"Why privately?" Eduardo asked. "You questioned my brother-in-law while we were present."

"That was best since he's your patient," Officer Cobos said. "Is there a private room we can use?"

"I think the sitting room is the only place. No one's there," Nikki said, looking out the doorway toward the small area beyond the nurses' station.

"We'd like to interview you after we talk with your husband," Morales told Nikki, "so please stick around."

After fifteen minutes, Eduardo returned to the room and told Nikki the police were ready to question her.

"Let's sit," Morales said in a commanding voice as Nikki strode up.

She opened the photo app on her mobile phone and selected a photo. Passing the phone to Nikki, she asked her what she saw.

"That's me. I was picking up the compact circuit board with the miniature camera lens."

"That's tampering with evidence," Morales said.

Nikki raised her eyebrows. "I gave that to you. It was outside the cordoned area. If I had not picked it up and turned it over to you, your people would not have found it."

Nikki wanted to ask the detective why she'd suddenly changed her mind about that piece, but she wouldn't get an answer. It was the police who were asking the questions, not her.

"Continue scrolling through the other pictures and stop if you see anything unusual," she said.

Nikki looked through ten pictures without seeing anything atypical. She handed the mobile back to the detective.

Morales brought up a video. "I want you to play this back two or three times and let me know what you see, if anything."

"Again, that's me. And Gustavo, the crew chief. The local news showed up with a complete camera crew and reporter to do a piece that ran on the national news."

Morales asked her to run it again. "Stop right there," she said, halfway into the video. "What are you doing there?"

"Asking the officer to get bystanders behind the yellow tape. They mobbed the place taking pictures, videos, and intruding upon the news reporters. I didn't want the evidence to be trampled," Nikki said. "But here's something else . . ."

"Yet, right here," Morales said, stopping the video at precisely the time when Nikki was waving at Gustavo to approach the balloon. "You're aiding and abetting the crew chief to sneak in and tamper with the evidence and take photos of the burner system."

"Have you interviewed Gustavo?" Nikki asked to deflect the questioning away from herself.

"Of course. He's the crew chief." Morales glared at Nikki. "I've done a few investigations before, you know."

Morales started the video again and stopped it at the point where the crew chief was taking photos.

"Did you get copies of those pictures he took of the burner and the valve?" Nikki asked, trying again to deflect away from herself.

The detective sighed. "Yes, I did."

"Please back the video up," Nikki said. "There, stop. I recognize that face, that man."

Morales looked straight at Nikki. "What man?"

Nikki pointed to a bystander. "That's Derek Brown. He's the contract engineer that works for Stan. He's the same fellow Carol Peters hired to help her with drone designs."

"What about him?"

"He's the guy that ran to the balloon shortly after the crash. The one in the picture I shared with you."

Morales seemed perplexed.

"The picture of the man's backside. He was running away and that's all I caught in the photo. There you can see him from the side, and you can tell it's the same guy. But here he's watching. It's creepy, like the killer who returns to the scene of his crime."

"Do you think he was covering something up?"

"That's the way it seems to me," Nikki said, "but I can't prove anything. I returned to the field that night. I'd wanted to see the area of the crash without people around. The strange thing is that Derek was there. I asked him a few questions and he was very nervous."

"Did you ask him what he was doing?"

Nikki nodded. "He was waiting for Stan, and indeed Stan drove up a few minutes later."

"Thanks for the information," Morales said. "Now leave the investigation to us."

"If it were your family, you would try to find answers too," Nikki said, trying to keep her annoyance from showing too much. "I told you I'll search for evidence, interview people, run my own investigation. I told you that on the field."

"We don't need novices messing up our evidence," Morales said, her voice testy.

Nikki gazed at her in amazement, thinking the only novice here was the police detective. "Wasn't it only this morning you said you were closing this investigation? For lack of evidence?"

"Ladies," Officer Cobos said, "we have a crime to solve. Let's put our energy toward that instead of fighting."

"So what do you suggest?" Nikki asked, staring at the officer.

"To start, I'm ordering twenty-four-hour police protection of your brother's room."

"It's intensive care," Nikki blurted. "I don't know if the hospital will allow police here."

"We'll work it out," Cobos said.

"Can we go over your initial assessment of sabotage?" Morales tapped her pen on her notebook. "What made you think this was done on purpose?"

Nikki glanced at Officer Cobos and focused back on Detective Morales. "It was the drone I saw. It moved so fast. The way the sun was shining, and it was small, I wasn't sure I'd seen anything. Two things happened that confirmed a drone had indeed flown next to my brother's balloon."

"Can you explain?" Cobos asked.

"An eyewitness by the name of Celia Hernandez told me she'd seen it. She'd been standing directly below my brother's balloon when the drone flew close to it. If the balloon had come down in a straight line, she said it would have hit her. I moved to that spot to have a look. But I told all this to Detective Morales on Saturday, and she interviewed the woman too," Nikki said.

"Right after the accident, what made you move to that area outside the yellow tape?" Cobos asked.

"To search for debris that might give us clues about what went wrong."

"And that's when you found the compact circuit board?" Morales asked.

Nikki nodded. "The piece of evidence that you should send to a lab. They might determine who manufactured it. Or some information about the drone itself."

"Do you know that Stan's company manufactures drones and weather equipment that contain cameras of all sizes?" Morales asked.

"Of course, I do," Nikki said. "His former girlfriend, Carol Peters, also manufactures all that equipment. As I've told you, she hired Derek Brown, Stan's contract engineer, to design drones and communication devices for her."

"You've done your homework," Morales said. "What else have you investigated?"

Nikki bit her lip, thinking she could not fess up to everything she'd done. She did not reveal she'd been in contact with the reporter, Maxine Sanchez.

"I've interviewed Carol," Nikki admitted.

"What did you learn?" Morales asked.

"That she and Stan planned to get married after they finished their studies at Stanford, but Stan broke it off," Nikki said.

"Interesting," Morales said. "Did you learn anything else?"

"Only that she plans to overtake Stan's company in sales in the next five years," Nikki said. "Oh, and she knew where Andy is hospitalized."

The detective's eyelashes flickered briefly. "That was probably on the news."

Officer Cobos thanked Nikki and asked her to be in touch if she learned of anything that would help their investigation.

# CHAPTER THIRTY-ONE

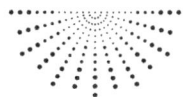

Nikki watched Morales and Officer Cobos step inside the elevator. When the officer had questioned her, it sparked a memory about pending patents on the technology that Stan had presumably offered to the Chinese government. Nikki remembered something Maxine had said when she'd first called her to solicit her help. Nikki had not revealed it, thinking she wanted to follow up before she informed the police. As soon as the elevator doors closed, she called Charlotte.

Without any small talk, Nikki immediately asked her research guru to dig into the pending patents on a breakthrough communication discovery that, in Maxine's words, was a game changer.

"Probably filed by Stan Stevens's parent company, Omega Satellites," Nikki added to make sure Charlotte could go directly into her research without wasting time finding the name of the legal entity.

Nikki could hear the keyboard clicking as Charlotte input a few items into her computer.

"I'll get on this right away," Charlotte said. "Anything else?"

"That's my priority," Nikki said, "but when you get a chance, I'd like for you to check on Derek Brown again. He's handled special research projects for Stan, and he's done work for Carol Peters's company, Drones over Mars. See if there could be any overlapping proprietary issues that hold clues to Carol's technology that may be innovations from Stan's company. I hate to think that Derek might be unlawfully giving out tech secrets."

To Nikki, the sounds from Charlotte's keyboard were a familiar jingle, a tune she often heard when she asked her to perform research.

"Got it in my notes," Charlotte said. "How is everything else?"

"An intruder came into Andy's room last night and may have meant to kill him."

Charlotte gasped.

"Eduardo has slept on the sofa in Andy's room since the surgery. He fought off the intruder and now he's sporting a shiner where the guy hit him. I shudder to think what might have happened if Eduardo had not been there."

"That's dangerous," Charlotte said. "What about taking Andy somewhere else? Like Miami."

"Andy's in ICU and can't be moved yet. The police assigned a guard that'll arrive later. That should help."

Charlotte told Nikki she'd start her research to help them get home as soon as Andy could be moved.

"And there's something else," Charlotte said. "Six months ago, Stan took out an insurance policy on his son . . ."

"What?" Nikki interjected.

"It's not a huge amount for a man who owns a company like Omega," Charlotte said. "A hundred thousand."

"Hmm, I'll ask him about it next time I speak with him." Nikki thanked her and asked her to update Floyd on the latest developments.

---

Nikki dialed Stan's business partner, Mark Edwards. Amazed that he answered, she identified herself and asked to meet with him.

"Where are you right now?" Mark asked.

"At the university hospital with my brother, but I can meet you at any coffee shop in this city within a half hour," she said. "Name your place."

"The same one where you met with Stan."

"The Blackbird Coffee House?" Nikki asked to confirm.

"Yes, in half an hour." Mark hung up without saying another word.

She dashed to Andy's room to pick up her purse and to inform Eduardo she was off to meet Stan's business partner.

Eduardo grabbed her arm as she turned to leave. "How about a kiss?"

"Come closer," Nikki said. "I'm flustered. I've been trying to speak with this man, and I need to catch up with him before he changes his mind or leaves town."

Eduardo put his arms around his wife and gazed into her eyes. "Who told me that anxiety kills creativity? Relax a little and use your creativity to unravel this case. And don't forget the resources you have available, including the police. You *will* find the culprits. I'm sure of it."

Nikki smiled. She kissed Eduardo on the lips. She touched his skin next to the bruise. "Does it hurt?"

"Not much," he said.

"I love you," she said, breaking away from the embrace and striding down the hall to the elevator.

# CHAPTER THIRTY-TWO

With an urge to speed out of the parking lot, Nikki could hear Eduardo's advice echoing in her mind. She took it slowly and eased the car into the street. She'd get on the interstate, take the Old Town exit, and be at the coffee shop in no time. No need to rush.

Nikki parked the rental and walked to the front entrance.

She had googled Mark and knew what he looked like. A man, mid-forties and wearing a Stetson, sat on a bistro stool by the counter. Other than the hat, he resembled the photos she'd seen on social media. He stood and walked toward her, making her think he'd looked her up online too. He looked rugged and handsome, wearing a casual red-and-yellow shirt worn loose over jeans. His cowboy hat and boots completed the look. Given what she'd seen on social media, she'd expected more polish. Then again, this was New Mexico, not Manhattan or Hollywood.

"Nikki," the man said, "I'm Mark. Let's find a place outside."

She followed him to the same table where she'd sat with Stan a couple of days earlier. Not knowing why, she felt uneasy, as if someone was watching them. The patio was empty except for two women, deep in conversation, at the far end. She chose a seat where she had a view of the door.

"Sorry I didn't get back to you after Stan asked me to meet with you. I left town on business and returned last night." Mark removed his hat and placed it on the table.

"You're aware of the balloon accident where Stan's son and my sister-in-law both died. I'm trying to piece things together to figure out what caused the balloon to crash, and I'd like to ask you a few questions."

"I don't know what I can add," he said and smiled as if to apologize.

"The evening before the Balloon Fiesta opening, Stan was called out of town. Why?"

Mark looked stunned. "I thought you'd discussed that with Stan."

"I asked him if there was any truth to the rumor that he'd been called out of town about inappropriate sales of his weather balloon technology."

"What did Stan say?" Mark asked.

Nikki took a deep breath. "He denied it."

A server interrupted them to take their order. Nikki asked for a coffee mocha and fidgeted with her nails as Mark asked about the house specialties. Then she looked around the patio. No one seemed to be looking their way.

Mark settled for a cottonwood tea latte and an assortment of sweet and savory empanadas. Nikki suppressed a smile. A tea latte did not fit the cowboy attire he was wearing. A locally brewed beer would have completed the image much better.

"Back to Stan," she said. "What urgent matter made him leave on a trip the evening before the fiesta opened?"

Mark shrugged. "I assume it was for business, but honestly, I don't know. Stan called me from DC on Saturday, after the police notified him about his son's death. He was so shaken by the accident that he asked me to fly back with him. He made a stopover in Denver to pick me up. He talked about Kenny and his own childhood, but we never discussed the trip to DC."

"You're a minority partner, are you not?" Nikki asked.

Mark nodded. "Yeah, I own slightly less than five percent of Omega Satellites."

The server brought their orders and Nikki reached for her coffee. "The accident . . . it doesn't seem like an accident. Do you know why someone might cause the balloon to crash?"

"What makes you think that?" Mark shifted in his seat as if he felt uncomfortable.

"According to Stan, the balloon was in top condition. Plus, the weather was good that morning. It shouldn't have caught fire or crashed. If I knew why Stan was in DC, I might be one step closer to knowing if there was sabotage."

"I don't think I can help you. I'm not involved in day-to-day operations."

"Do you know Carol Peters?" Nikki asked.

"Of course I do. I tried to make an investment in her company, but she's difficult to deal with. I understand why Stan broke off with her years ago. She's a bright lady and she's ambitious and out to prove to Stan that she's smarter, better, more successful than he is."

"Why don't you invest more with Stan?"

"He started Omega Satellites and is rightfully proud of owning almost all of it. He'd buy me out in a second, but he doesn't want to sell to anyone. And it's a large private company. If he ever lists on the stock exchange, I'll be a buyer." Mark picked up an empanada and took a bite.

"What type of work are you in?" Nikki asked.

"You might say that I'm an attorney." Mark shifted in his chair and stretched his legs. Gazing at Nikki, he said, "do you realize how boring an attorney's work is?"

"No more boring than being a CPA," she responded.

"Is that your line of work?"

"It used to be," Nikki said. "Do you know if someone was out to get Omega's latest technology? At any cost."

"They've created the most innovative technology in the field. I can see where someone would want to steal it, but so far as wanting to kill Stan, well, that's unimaginable to me." Mark ran his index finger across the brim of his hat to remove empanada crumbs that had fallen on it. He glanced at Nikki with a quizzical expression. "Would anyone want to hurt your brother or his wife?"

"Andy and my sister-in-law were last-minute substitutes. No one would have known they'd be flying."

"I disagree. There's the chase crew." Mark took the last bite of his empanada and looked at Nikki again. "Then there's Stan himself."

Nikki's head jerked up. "Kenny was in that balloon. Stan would not have hurt his son."

"Just saying," Mark said with pursed lips.

"You can't be serious!" Nikki felt her face getting warm.

"Ambition knows no bounds," Mark said.

# CHAPTER THIRTY-THREE

On the way to the hotel, Nikki's phone buzzed. Eduardo told her an officer had arrived at the hospital room. The administration had agreed to let the police carry out twelve-hour shifts to guard Andy twenty-four hours a day until the hospital released him.

"That's wonderful," Nikki said. "You'll be free to return to the hotel. I can't wait to have you in my bed again."

"I'm looking forward to that," Eduardo said, "and getting back to serious business, how did your interview with Mark go?"

"He was elusive. He hinted Stan might have crashed his own balloon. When I objected to that thought, he then asked if Andy and Cindy had enemies who wanted to eliminate them."

"I wonder how Stan would react to his business partner making such an accusation," Eduardo said, "though to be fair, you asked the same questions."

"True," Nikki said. "As I think about his responses, I didn't find anything out about him at all. I learned more from googling him than meeting with him."

"Changing the subject," Eduardo said, "Floyd called to ask about Andy. He was concerned about the intruder and correctly pointed out that we won't know if it was an attempt on his life until the lab identifies what was in the syringe."

"Yes, but the intruder's behavior indicates he was planning something bad," Nikki said, pulling into the hotel property. "When will I see you?"

"This evening. Andy's making remarkable progress, though I'm still administering antiseizure medication. I'll stay with him the rest of the day."

Nikki ended the call, thanking her husband for his love and support.

---

Nikki sent Keiko a text to inform her she was on her way up to the room. When Keiko opened the door, colored Lego pieces were scattered all around the low coffee table.

"Legos? Really?" Nikki asked. "I thought they were for older kids."

"These are Kiddy Legos," Keiko said. "Plus, I'm helping Olivia put them together."

Keiko had ordered lunch for herself and Olivia. Two stainless steel covers were over plates on the table. Keiko removed them to reveal chicken sandwiches under one and slices of chocolate cake under the other. Olivia dropped the Lego piece she was holding and moved toward the cake. Keiko placed the cake on the dresser and Nikki smiled with delight.

"I think I'll call room service," Nikki said. She picked up the hotel phone and ordered a tuna fish sandwich, a cup of coffee, and a piece of chocolate cake.

Olivia picked up a red Lego and handed it to Nikki.

"We were in the process of making a red barn for the cow and horse that Olivia colored in the coloring book I bought her on Saturday. Then I cut them out so we can place them in the barn we're about to build," Keiko said.

Nikki glanced at the brown squiggly lines Olivia had drawn on the horse. She thought the whole idea was wonderful, especially since Keiko could continue to entertain Olivia and that would free her up to work on the case.

Except that Olivia thought her aunt had returned to play with her.

"Tia Ki, Tia Ki," Olivia said, running to her aunt and dropping Lego pieces on the desk where Nikki had her computer. "Ake barn, barn." She slapped her little fist on the pile of colored Lego pieces. "Barn, barn."

Nikki's eyes filled with tears. She wanted to sit and play with her niece, but she felt pressured to uncover who had taken Olivia's mother away from them. The child's determined personality reminded her of Robbie at that age and the little girl's smile melted Nikki's heart, just as her son's had.

She took a tissue, wiped away her tears, and walked Olivia to the other room. She took her mobile with her. She wanted to make a video of Olivia building a barn from Lego pieces to show Andy.

Nikki joined Keiko and Olivia on the floor, and the three of them built the barn.

# CHAPTER THIRTY-FOUR

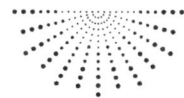

Olivia looked tired, and Keiko put her down for a nap. It was surprising the toddler fell asleep so easily. Nikki took advantage of the quiet and went to her room to work, closing the door between the two rooms to prevent the child from interrupting her.

Nikki had thought it was unusual that she had not heard from Cindy's parents, especially since the father had mentioned they would fly in to obtain their daughter's remains. But her remains would be given to Andy, her husband, not her parents. And what about Olivia? Didn't they want to see their granddaughter? She thought of calling the Smiths but decided to make use of her quiet time and call Floyd for an update on the FBI colleague he'd asked to assist them. She paced as she waited for him to pick up.

"I was about to call you," Floyd said when he answered his mobile. "The police in Albuquerque reported the results on the syringe to the FBI."

"What did they say?" Nikki asked.

"A lethal dose of fentanyl."

The room began spinning around Nikki. She stumbled toward the bed.

"Nikki, are you there?" Floyd asked.

"Yes," she mumbled. "I'm trying to understand why someone set out to crash the balloon, killing Cindy, and now they're after my brother. Could it be that Sammy Amaya's kidnapping case is coming back to haunt us?"

"That's my take," Floyd said, "but I spoke with Clive Underwood. You remember Clive, our CIA friend, don't you?"

"Of course I do," Nikki said.

"Clive's of the opinion there are several possibilities," Floyd said. "I asked him to look into this situation. When he investigated a bit, he found Stan owns several patents on technologies that could be used in spying. It could compromise national security if the technology fell into the wrong hands. That perked up Clive's interest. Foreign governments and competitors could steal Omega's innovations, especially if China has purchased from them in the past. Clive's going to research the company's recent patent applications."

"I've already asked Charlotte to do that," Nikki said. "But why go after Andy? He wouldn't know enough about Stan's inventions for someone to attempt to kill him."

"Maybe Stan has shared critical information with him," Floyd said.

"But wouldn't they be out to get Stan?"

"Maybe that was the reason the balloon crashed. They thought they were getting Stan."

"But it's Andy and Cindy they've gone after. Why?"

"Clive told me that an Albuquerque police detective subpoenaed the surveillance videos at the hospital. The assailant that went into Andy's room is captured in two videos, but they haven't identified the man."

Nikki sighed. "That detective, a woman by the way, was ready to close the case this morning."

"What changed her mind?"

"I think it was when I told her about the intruder in Andy's room."

Floyd coughed. "I'm going to fly in and help out."

"Thanks, but that's not necessary," Nikki said. "Stay at the office to take care of our clients. Besides the police detective is already having fits that others, like me, are investigating."

"Fine," Floyd said, "I'll stay here on the condition that you move to a different hotel. The one you're currently in does not allow enough escape routes if you should need a speedy getaway."

"I'll research other locations," Nikki said, agreeing with her boss's assessment. She heard banging on the door between her room and Keiko's. Olivia was obviously awake and ready to play again.

"Charlotte's already done that," Floyd said, coughing again. "It's the Crowne Plaza near the intersection of I-40 and I-25, giving numerous escape routes and a direct line to the airport, if that should become necessary."

"I don't think we'll need to escape to the airport."

"You never know," Floyd said. "Charlotte has already made the reservations. Two connecting rooms, like you have now."

"Eduardo will be staying at the hotel tonight. The police have placed a guard at Andy's hospital room."

Floyd was pleased to hear that bit of news and reminded Nikki to call if she needed anything.

Nikki sent Eduardo a text saying she would move everyone to the Crowne Plaza, have dinner with Keiko and Olivia, and drive by the hospital to pick him up. She'd show Andy the video she'd taken of Olivia. Then she realized Andy would be sleeping by the time she arrived at the hospital. She sent it to her brother's phone so he could see it as soon as possible.

# CHAPTER THIRTY-FIVE

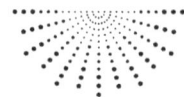

The food service worker delivered dinner to Andy's room. Eduardo glanced at the tray holding Andy's chicken-vegetable soup and a slice of toast as well as his own chicken dinner. Andy's soft diet looked more appetizing than the order of chicken and rice smothered in gravy.

Eduardo lifted the back of the bed into a high Fowler position, removing the pillow to make sure Andy's neck was fully extended. He checked the leg compression machines before moving the overbed table within easy reach for Andy to eat.

"I'll be returning to the hotel, now that there's a guard with you," Eduardo said, taking his own plate off the tray. "I'll leave after we've eaten, and you've drifted off to sleep. If you need me during the night for any reason at all, tell the nurse to call me. She has my contact information."

Andy put the soup spoon down and looked at Eduardo. "I'm afraid. What if that man comes back?"

"That's why the officer is outside your room. To protect you."

"He has to sleep too. He can't be awake all night," Andy protested, looking out the window into the hall where the guard sat.

"His replacement will arrive later, and he'll stay right here in the room with you."

"What'll happen to Olivia if I die?" Andy was shaking his head.

"You're not going to die," Eduardo assured him.

"What if I did? Her mother's gone. Who would take care of my little girl?"

Eduardo understood his brother-in-law's concern. "Nikki and I would raise her, but please understand that you're safe. No one will touch you."

"Why did that man try to kill me?"

Eduardo thought about how much he should say. "I think the accident was caused by someone trying to get rid of Stan."

"If they were after him, why did that man come to knock me out?"

Andy had a point. If Stan was the target, why come after Andy? More importantly, it showed that Andy's mind was trying to solve the puzzle they all wanted to decipher.

"Who called Stan away the night before the fiesta's opening?" Eduardo asked, thinking out loud.

"It was his anniversary," Andy said.

Eduardo, chewing a piece of tough chicken, didn't understand what he heard and asked Andy to explain.

"Stan forgot his anniversary was Saturday. Melissa had left Friday afternoon. She called him when she arrived in New York, in tears, saying he didn't love her anymore, reprimanding him for not going to New York with her to celebrate. Stan dropped everything and flew to be with her."

"New York?" Eduardo repeated, worried about his brother-in-law's memory. "Wasn't he meeting a client in DC?"

"That's what Stan wanted people to believe, but he went to New York." Andy nodded. "Yes, New York. Melissa took the nanny and the children with her. She was doing a photo shoot for *Vogue* over the weekend."

"Why did he lie about his trip?"

"For Kenny's sake. Stan didn't want his son to know it was Melissa who'd caused him to miss the mass ascension. It would've disappointed Kenny even more."

"What else were you covering for Stan?" Eduardo asked, putting his dinner plate aside.

"Not much else. His life's complicated. His business is demanding, his three ex-wives are always asking for money, Melissa is super jealous and controlling, and he didn't want Kenny even more upset with him for missing the opening of the balloon fiesta."

Debating whether to tell Andy that Kenny had also died in the crash, he thought he might as well set the record straight. "Kenny was killed when the balloon came down."

Andy stared at his brother-in-law. His hand went to his mouth in shock. He tried to say something, but the words didn't materialize. His eyelids fluttered. His body twitched and trembled.

Eduardo moved closer, afraid Andy was having a seizure. "I'm sorry for the bad news."

Andy rolled his head to one side. "Cindy . . . Cindy's gone. This is all too much." He closed his eyes and tears rolled down his face. "How am I going to raise Olivia? She needs her mother. I need my beautiful wife."

Eduardo assured him that he and Nikki would help in whatever way was needed with Olivia. Slowly, Andy regained a semblance of calm.

The conversation passed without Andy experiencing a full-blown seizure. Eduardo decided, given Andy's overall reaction, that he should remain in the hospital one more night in case his brother-in-law took a turn for the worse. After all, Andy was still on painkillers, antibiotics, and antiseizure medications.

Eduardo called Nikki after Andy went to sleep.

"Your brother suffered a very minor seizure about an hour ago. I told him about Kenny. That brought memories of Cindy. He cried and expressed concern about raising Olivia on his own."

"Should you stay another night at the hospital?" Nikki asked.

"You read my mind, my darling clairvoyant wife. Speaking of clairvoyancy, Andy said Stan's trip was to New York, not DC."

"He must be hallucinating," Nikki said. "He was the one who told us it was a business trip to DC."

"Hmm, I'm not so sure. He told me Saturday was Stan's wedding anniversary. Melissa was doing a photo shoot in New York, and she was upset her husband had forgotten their anniversary, so Stan immediately arranged to join her."

"I thought antiseizure meds cause memory issues."

"That's correct, but in this case, you can double-check," Eduardo said. "Why don't you call Stan and find out."

# CHAPTER THIRTY-SIX

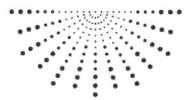

Nikki checked in at the Crowne Plaza. She'd seen Floyd's point in having better getaway routes. She smiled, thinking that criminals established their getaways in advance, so obviously the good guys must too.

After settling Keiko and Olivia into their new suite of rooms, she glanced at her watch, checking that it wasn't too late to call Stan. Given how upset he'd been when she met with him, she'd probably end up leaving a voice message. She was surprised when he answered. He apologized for not staying in touch, but he'd been busy with arrangements for Kenny's celebration of life as well as tracking down the police to get the crashed balloon for testing.

"I've meant to visit Andy," Stan said, sounding embarrassed. "How's he coming along?"

"He's struggling with Cindy's death," Nikki said, thinking whether she should mention the attempt on her brother's life. "Has the police department released the balloon to you?"

"If it's okay with you," Stan said, his voice sounding distant over the phone. "I'd like to meet you at Blackbird Coffee in twenty minutes."

Nikki agreed. She told Keiko where she was headed and grabbed her purse from the shelf in the closet on her way out. The coffee house was a bit further from this hotel, but she was sure she could make it at the appointed time.

Nikki parked the rental next to a green Mercedes Benz SUV. The door opened and Stan got out.

"Thanks for coming in person," he said. "I did not want to discuss details over the phone. Call me paranoid."

"Understood," Nikki said. "I prefer a face-to-face meeting as well."

They hit the remote lock buttons on their respective cars and walked to the shop, ordered coffee, and sat at a quiet corner table where they had privacy.

Stan wore glasses with thick dark frames. He removed them and put them in his shirt pocket. "Getting old, I need them for driving," he said. "You wanted to know if the police have released my balloon."

Nikki nodded.

"Not yet," he said. "The National Transportation Safety Board hired an expert to evaluate the burner, the valve, and the charred parts of the gondola and the envelope. I don't know when they'll release it to me."

"I'd understood the NTSB had already declared the accident was caused by pilot error," Nikki said.

"The police said they found a couple of items needing more investigation, so they called the agency back. Then my son's autopsy revealed deep burns, so they want to test the burner system. It may have caused the accident."

Nikki wondered if Lisa Morales had in fact retracted everything when she learned of the intruder in Andy's room, or if she had lied to Nikki about having closed the case.

"When the police interviewed Andy, he mentioned the burner had flared and then there had been a minor explosion," she said.

"Interesting," Stan said, staring blankly, "because that'd be consistent with Kenny's bad burns. You know, they all had classes on how to survive a hot-air balloon crash. Unfortunately, it didn't help them. Damn, I wish I hadn't left town."

"You can't blame yourself." Nikki took a deep breath. "Where did you actually fly to on Friday night?" she asked, looking straight into Stan's eyes.

He looked away and pounded his fist on the table. Nearby patrons turned and stared but quickly reengaged in their own conversations.

"You didn't go to DC, did you?" she asked.

"It was my anniversary. Melissa was angry that I'd forgotten it. I changed plans to make my wife happy. That's when I asked Andy to take my place as pilot, and he asked if Cindy could come along. You know she loved ballooning."

"So you flew to New York?"

Clamping his lips tight, Stan nodded. "Andy told you, didn't he? No one else knew. He promised not to tell Cindy. And I didn't let my wife know I was coming either. Wanted to surprise her."

"Now, I need to tell you something," Nikki said, almost whispering. "Someone tried to kill my brother last night."

Stan's eyes widened. "What? That can't be."

"Ask the detective working on the case," Nikki said. "Either you're in danger yourself, or you're trying to get rid of Andy."

"You can't be serious. My son was also in that balloon."

"But you'd taken out life insurance on your son," Nikki said.

Looking stunned, Stan stared at her. "I took it out and named Juanita the beneficiary. It was an inexpensive policy through my company."

He threw money on the table and left.

# CHAPTER THIRTY-SEVEN

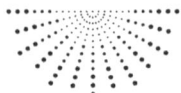

Nikki awakened as the first light of dawn was filtering around the edges of the curtains. She planned to leave for the hospital before Keiko and Olivia woke up. After getting dressed, she scribbled a note to Keiko letting her know she was joining Eduardo and Andy.

Once she arrived at the hospital, she stopped at the cafeteria to grab breakfast before taking the elevator to Andy's room. Eduardo seemed overjoyed to see her.

"Thanks for the fresh change of clothes. I need them," he said, taking the bag. He kissed her on the lips. "Staying in the hospital is wearing on me."

"You looked overjoyed when you saw me carrying the fresh clothes."

Eduardo laughed. "You're the one who brings me joy. Though I admit having clean clothes is nice." He glanced at Andy. "He was hungry this morning. It's a good sign. We'll both be out of here soon. Dr. Kahn came by, and he agrees with me that Andy will be good to go to a regular ward in a day or two."

Andy was sitting in the high position Eduardo had cranked his bed into. Now that he'd finished eating scrambled eggs and toast, he rested both of his arms on the overbed table. He asked about his daughter.

Nikki took Andy's hand in hers. "Your recovery is great. Of course, you have an extraordinary surgeon." She turned to Eduardo. "Can Andy have his mobile phone back? I sent him a cute video of Olivia building a barn from Legos. She colored a horse too."

Eduardo nodded. He grabbed the mobile from a drawer in the nightstand and handed it to his brother-in-law.

Andy remembered his phone's password, but his fingers fumbled and he had to input the email password three times before the app opened. He watched the video and started to cry.

"I'm sorry," Nikki said. "I didn't mean for it to make you sad." Tears clouded her eyes as she watched Andy.

"It's Cindy . . . I can't believe she's gone." Andy wiped his eyes with an edge of the sheet.

Nikki handed him a couple of tissues and placed his mobile back in the drawer.

A nurse came in and spoke quietly with Eduardo.

"Would you like to see Stan?" Eduardo asked, approaching Andy's bed. "He's downstairs. I can give him permission to come up for ten minutes, but only if you want to see him."

Andy nodded, wiping his tears. "There's something I need to tell him, but I don't remember what it is. Maybe I'll remember when I see him."

The nurse left to call the visitor.

When Stan arrived, Andy burst into tears again.

A solemn-faced Stan walked to the foot of the bed. He seemed shocked to see stitches across Andy's partially shaven head. Stan looked lost.

"I'm sorry about Cindy," Stan mumbled. "And my Kenny. It's so tragic and I feel responsible. I'm so sorry." Tears cascaded down his face.

Andy shook his head as he tried to regain his composure. "It . . . it's not your fault," he stammered.

Turning to Eduardo, Stan introduced himself and thanked him for allowing him to visit his friend in the ICU. He acknowledged Nikki but barely looked at her.

She felt awkward. The situation between her and Stan was tense. Especially with her blunt questioning from the night before. Yet she realized her brother needed to see Stan. Painful as it was for them, they needed to talk about the loved ones they'd lost. It would help both men in their emotional healing process. Andy and Stan had been good friends for a long time. She wasn't giving Stan a pass on the crash, but she couldn't see how he'd possibly have such an emotional visit with Andy if he had caused it.

"There's something I want to tell you," Andy said, looking straight at Stan. "The launch went fine. When we were in the air, we could see other balloons, the Sandias, the west mesa, and downtown. It was all so beautiful. Then something strange happened to the burner."

"Like what?" Stan asked.

"It was weird. The flame flared for no reason. It hit Kenny and knocked him down. I remember he yelled. Cindy screamed, moved to help Kenny, and then she fell too. I quickly adjusted the valve to keep the burner system from exploding. Then there was a huge flash of light, almost like lightning had struck the balloon. A loud noise . . . a loud noise was the last thing I heard before I awakened here in the hospital."

Stan looked at Andy's bandaged hands. "Did your hands get burned?"

"Yes, but they don't hurt," Andy said.

"That's because you're on painkillers," Eduardo explained.

"I'm sure the police are having their expert check the burner for malfunction," Stan said. "Do you remember anything else?"

"For some reason I remember there was something important I should tell you, but I can't recall what it is. There was a thought in my mind the minute I woke up from the anesthesia. But it's evaporated."

"If it's important, it'll come back to you," Stan said. "I have an important issue to clear up. Your sister thinks I may have caused the accident." Stan's eyes narrowed and he stared at Nikki. "There's no way I would ever do that. Not even to my worst enemy."

"I know," Andy said, glancing at Nikki. "My sister doesn't know you. She's investigating what caused this awful accident to happen. When you get to know each other, you'll see she's a great person."

"Yeah," Stan said, nodding.

Eduardo told Stan the ten minutes were up.

"Call me if you need anything." Stan turned to leave. "Get well soon, Buddy. Olivia needs you."

# CHAPTER THIRTY-EIGHT

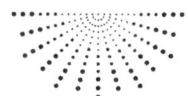

Nikki's phone buzzed and she stepped into the bathroom in Andy's room to take the call. Charlotte, who was always upbeat, sounded somber when she asked Nikki how things were going.

"Andy's recovering well. Olivia is great, and I'm thankful Keiko is with us to take care of her. And Eduardo, well, my husband is amazing. I'm the one feeling a lot of pressure. As far as the investigation is concerned, I don't have anything to report. It seems as if I'm running in circles."

"I don't know if this information will help you or not. What I do know is that you're not going to like it," Charlotte said. "My husband helped me trace the embedded numbers and dates on the compact circuit board. The board's design followed the layout used in military drones, which narrows the number of manufacturers. We also located a partial identifying code on the lens. I must remind you that we're working from photos, not the fragment itself, so we could be wrong."

"Just give me what you've found," Nikki said, sighing.

"Omega Satellites made the drone. The fragment matches up perfectly to their suppliers and their designs."

Nikki reached out for the wall to hold herself up. "The owner, Stan Stevens, just left a few minutes ago. He came to visit my brother, and he told Andy he had nothing to do with the crash."

"Even if Omega manufactured the drone that brought the balloon down, it doesn't mean that Stevens had anything to do with it," Charlotte said.

"True," Nikki said. "It makes it harder, though, for me to think of him as being innocent."

"What have the police told you?"

"Not much, so I'll have to call the detective and pry information out of her. It would help if she shared data with me, but it's not her style. I think I've given her a few bits that were essential to the investigation."

"Don't take it personally," Charlotte said. "Good or bad, the detective is doing her job."

Before wrapping up the conversation, Nikki asked Charlotte to email the information she and Chuck, Charlotte's husband, had uncovered. "Send it without any trace back to you, Chuck, or Security Source," Nikki said, "as I will provide the file to the police detective."

When Nikki stepped back into Andy's room, her brother had fallen asleep.

Eduardo asked her to join him in the hallway. "What's happened? You're ashen white."

"It's the fragment of compact circuit board and lens. Stan's company made them."

"So the drone came from Omega Satellites." Eduardo raised his eyebrows. "Are you sure?"

"Not a hundred percent, but Charlotte and her husband investigated enough to make it fairly certain."

"Stan seemed to be telling the truth when he said he was innocent," Eduardo said.

"His company sells the equipment. Someone may have bought it and used it to bring the balloon down. He may be innocent. I swear I'll find the culprit. As far as I'm concerned, Stan is still a suspect." Nikki returned to the room. "If you don't mind, I'm going to visit Detective Morales. First I'll go to the hotel, check on Keiko and Olivia, and pick up my laptop."

Eduardo nodded. "I think you should. Maybe the detective will open up and talk with you."

"I need a hug before I leave," Nikki said, moving in to embrace him.

Eduardo wrapped his arms around her. "I will join you at the hotel tonight."

Nikki kissed him. "That's wonderful. Best news I've had in three days."

"Before you go," Eduardo said, "let me suggest that you look again at those videos the detective showed you."

Nikki looked confused.

"There's a possibility," Eduardo said, "that the entire drone crashed out on the field. The videos might show someone picking up the rest of it or pieces of it."

"That's why I miss you on the job. You always add so much to an investigation, my charming, wonderful Latin lover." Nikki looked over at her brother. "But I'm thankful you've returned to neurosurgery."

# CHAPTER THIRTY-NINE

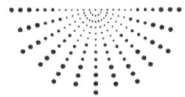

Nikki pulled into the parking lot of the police station on Cibola Loop. In the lobby, a friendly receptionist buzzed Detective Morales to let her know Ms. Garcia had arrived.

Morales looked up from her desk. "What brings you here?"

"Intel you might find useful," Nikki said. "In fact, I've brought my laptop in case you want a printed copy."

Morales checked her watch. "It's been three days and four hours since the accident. Let's see what you've got."

Nikki sat on the chair facing the desk.

"Oh, pardon me," Morales said with an edge of sarcasm. "Please make yourself comfortable."

Nikki smiled. "We should talk about the case first. Have you come up with any leads or suspects since we last spoke?"

"As I said, it's been three days and four hours." Morales glanced at her watch again. "Add two more minutes to that. Why don't you give me the data you think I need, and I'll review it."

Nikki, holding her laptop, looked at Morales. "It'd be far more useful for us to exchange data."

"You don't work for our police department."

"Consider me an informant," Nikki said. "To make sure my

information is useful to you, I need to know what's turned up on the burner system."

"Investigators from the National Transportation Safety Board have disassembled it to take a closer look at any malfunction."

"Has the fragment I picked up been sent to a lab?"

"It's being looked at internally. Beyond that, I can't say anything."

"Could you tell me what names are on your suspect list?"

Morales looked impatient. "Where's this going?"

"As I said, I have information you might find useful." Nikki narrowed her eyes. "I need to know where the investigation stands, so I can get essential data for you."

"Just give me your stuff, whatever it is." Morales shifted in her chair, as if she might stand.

"I will," Nikki said. "As soon as we discuss suspects."

"We don't have suspects at this point. I'll tell you who I've spoken to. Besides you, your husband, and your brother, I've talked to Carol Peters, Stan Stevens, and his wife. I've also interviewed Derek Brown, Gustavo Marquez, Brad Wood, Celia Hernandez, and Stan's first wife, the mother of the young man who died."

"Do you have any leads on the man who entered my brother's room?"

Morales shook her head. "We've looked at the security cameras on that street and in the parking lot. We see a tall man wearing a hoodie, but the cameras did not pick up his face. I can assure you we'll do our best to find him."

"Finding that person is key. Didn't the surveillance videos pick anyone up getting in or out of a car?"

"Not at all. He must have scouted out the camera locations pretty carefully and parked in an area without cameras."

"Have you tried the INTERPOL database?"

"Hmm, that might be an option," Morales said.

"And the syringe had a lethal dose of fentanyl in it," Nikki said, watching Morales's face for any reaction.

The detective's eyes narrowed. "How did you find out about that?"

"I can't disclose my source at this point. That's why I'm an excellent informant. I can dig stuff up."

"What else do you want to discuss?" Morales asked.

"I'd like to look at all your pictures and videos again. Maybe I could detect something else."

Morales turned her monitor around for Nikki to view.

It took almost thirty minutes to go through the videos and the pictures, but Nikki did not find anything she had not already seen.

"If you get any more videos from witnesses, let me know and I'll take a look at them," Nikki said. "In fact, have the police chief ask people to send him videos of the crash next time he's interviewed on TV."

"What are you looking for?"

"Anything out of the ordinary."

Morales did not seem convinced, but she didn't pursue it.

Nikki asked if she could print the file she wanted to give her.

Morales suggested that Nikki email the file to her instead. "First, tell me what it is."

"Information about the circuit board, like its design, which is used in military drones. In the file, you'll find a partial identifying code on the lens. Nothing your lab can't discover on its own, yet here it's all spelled out. Your lab can verify the data."

"What else do you know?" Morales asked.

"That it's likely Stan's company made the drone."

The detective's jaw dropped. "You think Stan did this?"

"That I can't say, but it seems appropriate to consider him a person of interest."

Morales blew through pursed lips, as if to whistle. "When I spoke to Juanita Rodriguez, his first wife, she said Stan would be incapable of doing such a thing. I can only imagine that either the perpetrator purchased the drone, or an insider did it to incriminate Stan."

Nikki put her laptop on the desk and leaned in. "It's a different way to investigate the case. The military design limits who could have access to the drone. A government agent, a contractor, or an employee."

Morales nodded. She stared blankly across the room.

"You need Stan's help," Nikki said. "He needs to scour his records for people and organizations with access to that drone."

The detective looked at Nikki. "This conversation has been very useful. I'll redirect my efforts."

"Stan took out an insurance policy on his son about six months ago," Nikki said. "Named Juanita as the beneficiary."

Morales's head jerked up. "I'll discuss that with Juanita."

"I've been told you're busy with cartel issues, drugs, and people smuggling. Once you get a list of people to investigate or interview, let me help you. I can find more information for you."

Morales nodded. "So close to the border, we've always had the drug problem, but human trafficking is the big issue these days. We don't have the staff to handle it all."

Nikki smiled. "That's why I can help with the balloon crash."

Morales leaned over her desk toward Nikki and spoke softly. "I agree, with one condition. You must talk only with me about your findings, and don't mention to anyone that you're providing information to me."

"Thanks. Call when you have something." Nikki picked up her laptop and stood to leave.

# CHAPTER FORTY

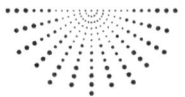

Driving back to the hotel, Nikki saw Smith's Grocery Store. It reminded her she'd not heard from Helen or Harold Smith, Cindy's parents. They were mourning their daughter and probably did not want to contact Nikki. Cindy's father had been angry when she spoke to him, a natural reaction under the circumstances, yet she wanted to reach out to them. Surely they'd want to visit Olivia.

Nikki pulled into the grocery store's parking lot and proceeded to call the Smiths. She smiled, recalling the TV series *The Lincoln Lawyer*. The attorney used his Lincoln as an office, even sleeping in it overnight. Nikki's rental car had become her branch office. Her smile evaporated when Harold Smith answered.

After identifying herself, Nikki was at a loss for words.

"I know who you are," he said. "What do you want?"

"Can I help you and Helen in any way? Also, if you've arrived in Albuquerque, I thought you'd like to visit with Olivia."

"Leave us alone." Harold ended the call.

Did Harold really think Andy had placed their daughter in harm's way? Didn't they know Cindy loved adventure? Were they unaware that Cindy was happy in her marriage? Then a terrible thought struck Nikki. What if Cindy had not been as content with her marriage as she'd let on. What if she'd told her parents that she was miserable? It would not be the first time a spouse had pretended to be satisfied when the truth was just the opposite. Nikki recalled Cindy saying that she loved New Mexico and her life and the research she and Andy did together, that they never went on vacation because everything Cindy loved was right there—her husband, their daughter, their work, and their home.

Nikki pulled back onto the street, telling herself to remain positive despite the misfortune. She'd promised Cindy to take care of Olivia if Andy could not. And that was a good reason for keeping her spirits up.

Nikki arrived at the hotel and notified Keiko she'd be up in a couple of minutes. Why not take Keiko and Olivia shopping for more art supplies? Besides, it was lunchtime. Keiko would probably enjoy eating somewhere other than the hotel.

When Nikki knocked on the door, Keiko opened it with Olivia in her arms and handed her to Nikki.

"Tia Ki, Tia Ki," Olivia chattered, planting a gooey kiss on Nikki's cheek. "Play, play now."

Nikki put her niece on the floor. The child ran to the bed and started using it as a trampoline. Nikki held Olivia's hands as she jumped and laughed.

"You've inherited your mother's love of adventure," Nikki said, picking her up and hugging her before putting her on the floor and taking her hand. "And your mother loved good food, so let's go out for lunch."

Keiko grabbed her purse and followed Nikki to the hallway.

"I saw a Japanese restaurant in the university area when we rode the motorcycles. Let's try it and we'll go shopping afterward," Nikki said, speaking to Keiko in Spanish.

Keiko's eyes lit up at the mention of Japanese food.

Nikki drove past the university area where they'd seen the pothole crew working. "Look, the potholes are fixed," she said. "After the accident happened, I forgot to tell you that the supervisor of the pothole crew, Gustavo Marquez, is the chief of Stan's chase crew."

"Interesting coincidence," Keiko said.

Nikki agreed. She thought of telling Keiko that Gustavo had served time in prison. Being accustomed to not revealing more information than necessary, she remained silent on the subject. Besides, it would only worry Keiko.

"You mentioned shopping," Keiko said. "Do you need something?"

"I thought you could use more art supplies for all the work you're doing with Olivia. It's like she has her own private kindergarten."

"She's a very bright child," Keiko said. "A fast learner. I don't want to think of the day when her father takes her back. I'm going to miss her a lot."

"And she'll miss you even more," Nikki said with a wink, "you're spoiling her."

Nikki's mobile buzzed. Hesitating a few seconds, Nikki answered Helen's call.

"I only have a couple of seconds," Helen whispered. "Forgive my husband's rudeness. He's having a hard time accepting what's happened. He's been in contact with the police in Albuquerque. They've told him our daughter's remains will be released on Friday. We fly in on Thursday. I want to see Olivia, even though it will be bittersweet. I hope I can get Harold to go with me to see our granddaughter."

Nikki offered to pick them up at the airport, but Helen said they'd already rented a car.

"Call me whenever it's convenient," Nikki said, "and I'll take Olivia to see you."

After ending the call, she pulled into the Japanese restaurant's parking lot.

"We're here," Nikki announced to Keiko. "Let's enjoy a good lunch before we shop for more art supplies for you and Olivia to use."

# CHAPTER FORTY-ONE

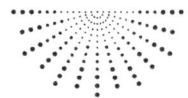

That evening, Eduardo arrived at the hotel room in time for dinner. Before taking Keiko and Olivia with them to the restaurant, he updated Nikki on her brother's condition.

They enjoyed a leisurely dinner, or as leisurely as a family with an eighteen-month-old can have. Keiko asked Eduardo about the bruise on his face. He touched it and said he'd recover soon enough.

"Just like a man," Keiko said. "Men will tough it out."

Upon their return to the room, Keiko wished them a good night and said Olivia would not bother them since she'd be asleep in no time. She closed the connecting door between their rooms.

Eduardo looked around the suite. "Nice. Much more space than the other room." He sat on the bed and gave it a bounce. It would do.

"Each room is bigger, but the walls are not soundproof. I can hear Olivia when she cries or makes noise," Nikki said.

"Now tell me what you found out from the detective."

"Not much," Nikki said. "I did convince her to let me be her informant."

"That's good progress," Eduardo said. "She needs to tell you stuff so you can follow up."

Nikki smiled, looking pleased with herself. "That's why I did it. I looked at the videos and photos again, as you suggested. Nothing I hadn't already noticed. The problem is that clues in them might go over my head, like people I don't know."

Eduardo nodded and stroked his chin. He was overdue for a shave. "Did you catch that Andy can't remember something he wants to tell Stan?"

"Whatever it is, I hope it comes to him," Nikki said. "It could provide a clue. Is it his injury or the surgery causing the memory lapse?"

Eduardo shrugged. "The anesthesia could have made it worse, but the bump he got when the balloon hit the ground is the most likely reason."

"I wonder if showing him the videos or the pictures would help his recall," Nikki said.

"It could. My only concern is the toll it might take on him to review pictures from the event. You know, like seeing Cindy. I don't want him to fall into depression."

"You're right," Nikki said. "Let's wait until he's recovered a bit more."

"On the other hand," Eduardo said, "we should let him view them before the balloon fiesta ends. Some of those people will leave town, making it harder for you to speak with them."

"It's the end of day three. We have six more days."

Nikki's ringing mobile interrupted their conversation.

"Hi, Max, what's up?"

Maxine asked if they could get together and go over new developments.

Nikki agreed to meet for drinks at the hotel bar at nine p.m.

Eduardo turned on the television when Nikki finished her call. The news was on, and the police chief was coming to the podium.

The camera focused on a reporter. "Can you tell us what the police have found about the fatal balloon crash?"

The chief adjusted the microphone. "We're looking into possible criminal activity, but it's too early to tell if this was an intentionally planned accident or merely equipment failure."

The camera panned back to the reporter. "Do you have any suspects?"

"Not at this time," the chief said, "but that's a good question. I'd like to ask the viewing public to send us videos and pictures of anything near the crash site on Saturday." He provided the email address.

Nikki gave Eduardo a thumbs-up and whispered that she'd asked the detective to have the police chief make that plea.

The reporter asked if such public videos were legitimate to use in a possible crime.

"The answer is yes," the chief said. "The evidence is also admissible in the courts if the videos meet certain legal standards. If anyone saw something suspicious, give me a call." He repeated the email for sending videos and pictures and added the phone number for verbal reports.

Eduardo turned away from the TV to face Nikki. "Looks as if you're already impacting the process." He suspected the chief asked the public to submit their videos so they could make sure there was a crime before more assets were assigned.

Nikki nodded, smiling. "Thanks. I love it when you compliment me."

She looked at her watch.

"Time to get downstairs to meet your reporter friend?" Eduardo asked.

She nodded.

"If you don't mind, I'll wait in the lobby while you have your meeting."

"It's fine," Nikki said. "Just pretend you don't know me. I've told her I'll keep everything confidential."

Eduardo nodded in agreement.

# CHAPTER FORTY-TWO

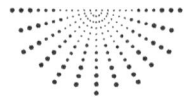

A few minutes early for the meeting with Maxine, Nikki stepped out of the elevator with Eduardo. She looked around the lobby. Not seeing the reporter, she headed toward the bar. Not spotting her there either, Nikki returned to the lobby.

She didn't have long to wait. Maxine sauntered in, looking as if she didn't have a care in the world. She saw Nikki and waved.

The women were entering the bar when someone shouted Nikki's name. They both turned.

"Nikki Garcia, that's you, right?" A tall, striking young woman was marching toward them.

"Ay, Dios mío," Maxine said, "That's Melissa Stevens."

"What can I do for you?" Nikki asked in a calm voice.

"You've accused my husband of shooting down his own balloon. What kind of damned bitch would say a stupid thing like that? Don't you know his son died in that crash?" Her voice rose with every word.

Guests in the lobby had turned to watch the commotion. Patrons in the bar came out to see what was happening.

Eduardo rushed over. Nikki held her hand up to keep him from approaching too closely.

"I'm a private investigator," Nikki said to calm the woman.

"I don't care what you are. No damn bitch will call my husband a murderer." Melissa was red-faced and appeared to be hyperventilating.

"I never accused him of killing anyone," Nikki said. "All I've done is ask questions."

Melissa lunged for Nikki. Maxine stepped between them. Melissa's tall, bony frame bumped into Maxine and knocked her over.

"See what you made me do?" Melissa shouted at Nikki. She threw a punch. Nikki blocked Melissa's punch, caught her arm, and applied an L-wrist technique to control the hysterical woman.

Eduardo helped Maxine stand up.

Right behind him, the hotel manager and a bellman rushed over.

"Ma'am, please step into my office where we can talk calmly," the manager said to Melissa.

They took Melissa by the arms. She spat at the manager.

"I didn't want to call the police, but now I will," he said, wiping his face with his free hand. With a nod, he told the bellman to make the call.

"Don't call the police," Melissa shrieked. "I'll go to your office."

"Ma'am, you can't come in here and verbally abuse or physically attack our guests." Turning to Maxine, he asked, "Are you okay?"

Maxine nodded. "I'm fine."

"That woman there," Melissa jutted her chin toward Nikki, "is making false accusations about my husband."

"There are better ways to resolve an issue. We're going to my office until the police arrive," the manager said. "I'd like for all of you to remain here in case the police want to interview you."

"You can't bring the police into this," Melissa said in a quieter yet demanding tone. "Don't you know who I am?"

"In my office you can explain who you are and why you're here." The manager led her away.

Nikki introduced Eduardo to Maxine.

She thanked him for helping her get off the floor.

"You took a nasty fall," Eduardo said. "Are you okay?"

"I think so." Maxine rubbed her left hip. Turning to Nikki, she asked if they could still meet.

"That's why I'm here," Nikki said.

Eduardo offered to stay in the lobby and let them know when the police arrived.

"Where did you learn to subdue someone like that?" Maxine asked as the two women walked into the bar.

"The elbow-wrist technique?" Nikki rubbed her own wrist. "From special training in martial arts."

"Impressive," Maxine said, taking a seat at the bar. "I wanted a glass of wine but with the police coming, I don't want alcohol on my breath."

Maxine ordered a club soda and Nikki a virgin Bloody Mary.

"How did Melissa know I was here?" Nikki asked, taking a seat next to Maxine.

"That's my fault," Maxine said. "I interviewed her before coming here. I was running late, and I ended the meeting with her saying I had an appointment with you. I'm sorry. She must have followed me."

Nikki couldn't believe that an experienced reporter would make such a critical error.

"I thought we'd compare notes and see what we've discovered," Maxine said.

"Max, we each agreed to complete discretion. Yet you led Melissa right to my hotel. How can I trust you?"

Maxine nodded. "I understand. I'm sorry. Let me share what I've discovered. You're under no obligation to tell me anything. If my findings prove useful, maybe you can trust me again."

The bartender put their drinks in front of them. "Now I don't want you ladies to get inebriated," he joked.

Max reached for her club soda. "I met with another contact, one from my days researching the Mexican cartels."

Nikki's spine prickled, thinking of Sammy Amaya's enemies. Could that be it? Could the cartel still be out to get Sammy, the CIA spy, through his good friend Andy? Her brother had helped Sammy, but she and Eduardo had too. Were they all in danger?

"He mentioned cartels are buying drones these days to do their dirty work along the Mexican border. If they want to eliminate someone, they do it with a drone. If they want to transport drugs over the border, they do it with a drone."

"Are you suggesting a drone was used to bring down the balloon?" Nikki had not disclosed that detail to Maxine.

"That's what an eyewitness claimed," the reporter said.

"What eyewitness?" Nikki asked.

"A woman who watched the whole enchilada as the balloon crashed," Maxine said.

"Getting back to your contact, did he say who the cartel boss wanted to kill?" Nikki asked.

"He was only surmising. He assumed the cartel would want to get rid of Stan Stevens. After all, he invented the technology the cartels might find useful. There could be a connection between the cartel and buyers from China or North Korea wanting to purchase drones from Stevens." As she spoke, Maxine seemed to study Nikki's reaction.

"I need your contact's name so I can investigate this assumption," Nikki said.

"I can't disclose my source," Maxine responded.

"In that case, I'll have to stop working with you." Nikki pushed her drink away and picked up her purse. "You gave my location away to Melissa, but you can't give me a name I need to pursue this investigation?"

"Okay, okay, I get it," Maxine said. "My contact is Ramon Estrada. For God's sake, don't disclose his name to anyone."

"Is he the one that helped you get the goods on the Mexican cartel boss your work put behind bars?"

Maxine nodded. "One and the same."

Eduardo approached them, saying the police had arrived and wanted to question them about the altercation in the lobby.

Maxine limped toward the hotel manager's office. "Look, I'm sorry about Melissa. I should have been more careful."

Nikki recognized the officer.

Santiago Cobos glanced up and smiled. "Come in and sit down. I just have a few questions."

The officer started by introducing himself as if he'd never met Nikki or Maxine.

"Do either one of you want to file a complaint against Melissa Stevens?"

"I don't think it's necessary," Maxine said.

"The hotel manager explained to me that the fall caused you enough pain that you're limping, and Dr. Duarte recommends that you get checked by a doctor," Officer Cobos said. "Now I'm asking you, Ms. Sanchez, if your limp came from the fall you took when Ms. Stevens knocked you to the floor?"

Maxine nodded, adding that she was knocked down by Ms. Stevens when she moved to protect Ms. Garcia.

The officer questioned Nikki, asking if she wanted to file a complaint or a restraining order.

"I would ask Ms. Stevens to refrain from behaving in such an aggressive manner. If she wants to speak to me, I'll be happy to do so in a civilized fashion. If she agrees to that, I won't need to file."

The officer asked Melissa if she could refrain from such aggressive behavior against the other two women.

Melissa nodded.

"I need a verbal answer," the officer said.

"I won't cause any trouble," Melissa said, looking at the floor.

Officer Cobos gazed at Melissa and explained that he'd write up a report to record the incident. "To avoid future legal action, no more outbursts like you had here tonight." He told everyone they were free to leave.

# CHAPTER FORTY-THREE

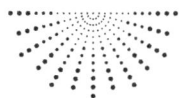

Nikki and Eduardo sat in the hotel restaurant, enjoying breakfast and discussing the Melissa Stevens incident. Keiko and Olivia were upstairs eating breakfast in the suite. Nikki's mobile phone buzzed.

"Good morning, Detective Morales," Nikki said. "What can I do for you today?"

The detective informed Nikki that a couple of videos had come in overnight after the chief's request. She asked Nikki to visit the police station to review them.

Pouring syrup on her pancakes, Nikki agreed that she'd be there within an hour.

She glanced at her husband. "I need to see Detective Morales at the police station. They got more videos after the chief's televised request. Do you want to relax around the hotel till I return?"

"My time is better spent going to see Andy. I'll take an Uber. Call if you need me." Eduardo took a bite of his vegetable omelet and stared across the room as he ate it. "I still don't get what was behind Melissa's appearance here last night."

Nikki shrugged. "I understand she's very controlling and jealous of Stan. She's young and spoiled."

"It doesn't make sense to appear on the scene, yell, and behave the way she did," Eduardo said. "I wonder if Stan knows what his wife did?"

Nikki placed her fork and knife across her plate. "Maybe we'll find out her motive, or maybe she's just a little unstable."

"Stan's about sixteen years older than her. She must have married him for his money," Eduardo said.

"Hmm," Nikki said, "do you suppose she's hiding something by diverting my attention?"

"I'd think she doesn't know much about Stan's business." Eduardo signaled the server to bring the check. He took his mobile out and selected an Uber.

Nikki stood and hugged Eduardo. "I'll call Floyd before I see the detective to share what Maxine told me last night about her informant."

Nikki hated to leave the hotel without checking on Keiko and Olivia, but she was anxious to review the videos at the police station. She called Keiko to let her know her plans for the day. She promised to return as soon as she could. She walked to the rental and before getting in, she hit Floyd's number.

When he answered, he asked about Andy's progress.

"He's better but he's still in intensive care. They should be moving him to a regular room soon."

"What about the investigation?" Floyd asked.

"It's getting to me. The balloon fiesta will end on Sunday. That gives me today plus four more days to work. After that, it'll be difficult to interview people. Key players, like Stan Stevens and Carol Peters, will leave. I don't even know what'll happen to secondary ones like Derek Brown or the chase crew members."

"Nikki, you'll get it done. I know you," Floyd said.

"I need your help on an informant the reporter gave me. It's a guy that gave her the scoop that took down one of the cartel bosses who is now in prison."

"I'll be happy to help," Floyd said, "but why don't you speak directly with Clive. He said he'd find a way to fly into Albuquerque if we need him."

"That's great, but maybe you can also have Charlotte check the guy out."

Floyd asked for the informant's name.

"Ramon Estrada. Lives in a place called Placitas, north of Albuquerque."

"I'll see what we can find on him. I can also ask some of my FBI friends. In the meantime, I recommend you call Clive."

Nikki thanked him and said she'd be on it.

She glanced at her watch before dialing Clive.

"How's Andy doing?" Clive asked without saying hello first. "Floyd has kept me informed. Cindy was so vibrant. I can't imagine she's gone."

Nikki felt a fresh wave of sadness over Cindy's death. She thanked Clive and moved to the next topic before she broke down. "I haven't unraveled who caused this accident and I'm running out of time."

Before she could say more, Clive interrupted her. "From what Floyd's told me, you've uncovered a lot already. Don't worry, we'll get the perps. How can I help?"

Nikki took a deep breath to keep her emotions in control. "Floyd told me you thought a possible motive for the crash is the technology used in the weather balloons and drones manufactured by Omega Satellites."

"Could be," Clive said.

"Late yesterday I had a conversation with a reporter that's investigating the crash. She has an informant from her days of reporting on drug cartels who suggested that one of the Mexican cartels wants Stan's technology to build their own drones. His take was that a cartel boss approached Stan to get the latest drones, and the deal didn't get done. So the cartel retaliated."

"Did the reporter say her informant knew that or was merely speculating?"

"I think it was speculation, but I convinced her to give me her contact's name. I thought you might check him out," Nikki said.

"She gave you her contact's name? Doesn't believe in confidentiality, does she?"

"I sort of forced her hand," Nikki said. "I thought if you checked him out, I could contact him."

"Let me do it," Clive said. "The man can't be trustworthy if he's a snitch on the cartels. Plus, that frees you to investigate other leads."

Nikki thanked him, but Clive said he had something else to discuss.

"I've analyzed worldwide patents on Stan's latest innovation. There's a company in Europe that's recently been granted patents on very similar, if not the same, technology."

"Could it be one of Stan's companies?" Nikki asked.

"My gut tells me no."

"I'll ask Stan if he recently obtained patents in Europe," Nikki said. "Which country?"

"Not sure yet, possibly Germany. The problem is that the entity appears to be a shell company. I'll need more time to dig. I'll be in touch."

"Why don't you ask Charlotte from my office to help you with the research. I'll tell her you'll contact her."

"Let her know I'll call her in half an hour," Clive said. "Take care."

Nikki sent Charlotte a text, asking her to assist Clive with the patent issue. She added that Clive would call her.

Charlotte responded that she'd be happy to work on it with Clive.

Nikki unlocked the rental to get in. She hesitated. Her motherly instincts set in. She couldn't possibly leave without giving Olivia another hug. She locked the car again and sent a text to Keiko saying she was on her way up to see them before she set off to work.

# CHAPTER FORTY-FOUR

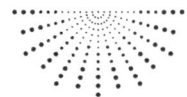

The receptionist at the police station recognized Nikki. "Detective Morales is expecting you. You can go straight to her office."

Morales, sitting on the front of her desk, waved Nikki into the chair next to her. She brought a video up on her computer.

Taking a seat, Nikki rested her elbows on the desk and leaned in to study the video. A pang hit her chest when she saw Cindy standing next to the balloon gondola, holding Olivia in her arms. She had to concentrate on the work she had to do, not on the emotional side. Though she admitted to herself that Cindy looked very happy holding her daughter and participating in an activity she loved. The video panned upward, catching the balloon's envelope as it fully inflated. The view panned downward and out, showing Gustavo and the volunteers holding the ropes to keep the balloon from flying away. The video faded and Morales opened the next one.

"This one is much longer," Morales said.

The opening angle showed three balloons in the air shortly after launching. One balloon was much closer to the camera. Nikki recognized it as taking off shortly before the one Cindy and Andy were going to pilot. In fact, the zebra had waited until that one had drifted southward before he gave the okay for Andy's to lift off. The video then panned toward the ground. Kenny, Andy, and Cindy were ready for flight and the video followed them as the turquoise-colored balloon rose gracefully into the air. A closeup of the globe logo with the bold lettering of the slogan, Connecting the World, felt like a stab in Nikki's heart. As the balloon drifted further up, she saw a shiny object fly in.

"There, stop the video," Nikki said.

Morales gazed at Nikki as if she were waiting for a revelation that could solve the mystery.

"A drone. Did you see it?" Nikki asked.

Morales backed the video up and watched as Nikki pointed at the tiny object that flew in and adjusted its speed to hover next to the balloon. Shortly after, a fire erupted inside the gondola.

Nikki slumped in the chair, closing her eyes. "I cannot watch the rest."

"I understand," Morales said, angling the computer so Nikki could not see the screen.

Nikki sat in silence, trying to keep her composure. Thoughts of losing Robbie, her son, raced through her mind. So did the thoughts of losing her parents in that car accident when she was a teenager. Mostly, Olivia was on her mind. Olivia was just a toddler and would grow up not knowing her mother. It'd be important to tell her stories about Cindy.

"This confirms what you and Celia Hernandez witnessed on Saturday," Morales said when she finished watching the video. "Was there anything else that you noticed?"

Nikki shook her head and wiped her tears away.

"I'm sorry," Morales said.

"It's difficult for me to watch, but we must find the perpetrators. Tell me what's on the rest of it," Nikki said.

"Once the balloon started deflating, the drone flew away. There's no doubt it caused the accident. After that, the balloon starts falling. The recording ends right before the crash. The guy who took it started running with the video still on, but it only shows the ground as he ran."

"I can watch it now," Nikki said, sitting up straight. "Let me see the last part of the video."

Morales ran the portion showing the drone flying in, hovering near the balloon, and speeding away after the balloon began falling out of the sky.

# CHAPTER FORTY-FIVE

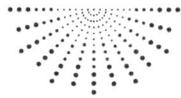

Wondering how her brother was doing today, Nikki dialed Eduardo.

"How's it going with Andy?"

"He'll be moved to a regular ward tomorrow if all goes well today," Eduardo said. "Anything new on the investigation?"

"The detective showed me a couple of videos. I'm disappointed they didn't show much other than to confirm that a drone caused the crash."

"Proving there was a drone involved is a lot," Eduardo said.

"It's all moving at such a slow pace," Nikki complained.

He asked her what she expected after only four days of investigations. "Let's be thankful Andy is recovering so well."

"The police dragged their feet in the beginning, not believing this was sabotage," she said. "I know the detective is convinced now."

"Give it a little time," he said. "When will I see you?"

"I'm driving to the hospital now."

Eduardo suggested she concentrate on her driving. Within fifteen minutes, she had parked.

When Nikki passed the receptionist's area in the lobby, she noticed the vase of flowers Keiko had arranged. The receptionist smiled and waved at Nikki.

"I hope your brother is better," the receptionist called out.

Nikki thanked her.

In the elevator, Nikki took a deep breath.

---

Eduardo saw Nikki and smiled. He took her in his arms.

"I'm so happy to see you," he said.

"You're the most wonderful husband in the world. Thank you for everything."

"I don't know what you're referring to, but I appreciate the sentiment." He kissed her gently.

"You're taking such good care of Andy. You don't know how much this means to me." Nikki turned to look at her brother.

"I took the drain tube out this morning," Eduardo said. "And the nurse took him walking in the hall for fifteen minutes."

She approached the bed. Andy looked up at her.

"I want this brain fog to go away," he said, looking dazed. "I know there's something important I need to tell Stan, and I can't remember what it is."

"Is it something about the crash?" Eduardo asked.

"I wish I knew," Andy said.

"When did you first have this thought?" Eduardo asked.

"Like as soon as I came out of the anesthesia."

"Is it about the balloon itself?" Eduardo asked. "Or could it be about Kenny?"

Andy seemed to be thinking. "Hmm, it could be either one. It makes sense that it could be both."

"Maybe when you go off the painkillers, you can think more clearly," Eduardo said.

"Then take me off of them now," Andy requested.

"Soon," Eduardo said. "You've had brain surgery. And a bad injury to your head before that, so it'll take a little while before your memory is fully working again. As your doctor, I'd ask you not to think about it. That'll relax you and may help you remember what it is when you least expect it."

Nikki moved to the foot of the bed and asked Andy if he wanted his feet rubbed.

"That would be nice." He put his legs over the sheet so she could reach his feet.

Within five minutes, Andy was asleep. She stopped the foot massage.

"Will he recover his memory in full?" Nikki asked, sounding concerned.

"Only time will tell," Eduardo replied. "Before you arrived, he asked if he'd be able to take care of Olivia. I assured him he'll be a great dad."

Nikki inhaled slowly and glanced up at her husband with sad eyes.

"Don't give up," he said, moving her into his embrace. He felt the rise and fall of her breathing, slow and deliberate breaths until she relaxed in his arms. This was the first time he'd seen Nikki unwind since the accident.

A nurse came in to check on Andy. Eduardo asked her to come back in half an hour. He wanted Andy to sleep for the time being.

"I spoke with Clive," Nikki said, breaking away from the embrace. "He thinks Stan's technology may have been stolen and has now been patented in Europe."

Eduardo listened to Nikki's explanation of the European patents. "Is Clive certain the patents were granted on Stan's technology?"

"It appears that way, but it's not proven yet. I've asked Charlotte to help Clive. In fact, I'd already asked her to investigate Omega's patents, so she should have a head start."

"What makes him think the technology was stolen?" he asked.

"He didn't specify, but he must have leads or info that make him suspect it. Otherwise, he wouldn't waste his time."

"What about asking Charlotte to check into Melissa's past?" Eduardo suggested.

"You don't think Melissa is responsible for the crash, do you?"

"After her behavior last night, I think you need to look into her. That was so bizarre."

"Could she be on drugs?" Nikki asked.

Eduardo shook his head. "Her eyes seemed normal when I looked at her. Yet she behaved that way for a reason. I'm not psychoanalyzing her, but it seemed like an emotional outburst. My guess is this is not an isolated incident."

"I'd like to talk with Stan again," Nikki said.

"Why?" Eduardo asked. "None of your conversations with him have gone well."

"The patents in Europe. Perhaps the shell company belongs to him and that would save Clive some work."

"Maybe I can meet with Stan," Eduardo said.

"Great idea. Why didn't I think of that?" Nikki gave him a bright smile.

# CHAPTER FORTY-SIX

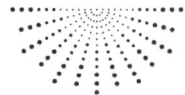

Eduardo stopped for a cup of coffee at the counter of the Blackbird Coffee House before joining Stan on the patio. It was the same place Nikki had met with the balloon owner. Stan either liked this place or didn't know of a handier location, which seemed unlikely since he'd spent a lot of time in this area.

"Thanks for meeting with me on such short notice," Eduardo said.

"I don't have much to do right now." Stan tapped his fingers on the table and looked across the patio. "I'm waiting for the medical examiner to release my son's body. Kenny's mother and I are planning his celebration of life. This is the hardest thing I've ever had to do."

"Do you think the police will uncover what happened?"

Stan looked somber. "I'd like to think it was human error, but the facts seem to point to sabotage."

Eduardo took a sip of his coffee. It was much better than what he could get at the hospital. He allowed Stan a few seconds to dwell on his thoughts.

"I guess you have questions, or you wouldn't be here." Stan looked across the patio again. "I'm originally from Texas. My dad was in the petroleum exploration business. As a teenager, I thought Texas was boring. The land was so flat. I had a motorcycle, and I'd ride into New

Mexico. Almost as soon as I crossed the state line, the countryside turned gorgeous. Once I had the money, I bought a place in Santa Fe. The more I traveled the state, the more I loved it. The balloon crash has changed that. I can hardly wait to get out of here. Every time I see the Sandia Mountains, I feel angry about what happened. I find it hard to breathe, hard to get out of bed."

"The crash was not your fault," Eduardo said.

"It was definitely my fault." Stan tightened his lips. "I wanted to surprise Melissa on our anniversary. Quite honestly, I'd forgotten about it until she called. She was upset that I wasn't going to New York to be with her. That's when I changed plans." He looked as if he'd break down at any point. "Without telling her, I called my pilot, and we set off late Friday night, arriving Saturday morning."

Eduardo was unsure whether he should continue to listen or if he should change the subject.

"You didn't come here to see a grown man cry," Stan said, as if reading Eduardo's mind. He reached for a napkin to blow his nose.

"As a medical doctor, I'd encourage you to find a way to release the stress you're under. And forgive yourself. Living with guilt will sap your energy and your ability to grieve in a healthy manner."

Stan nodded and wiped his nose with the napkin. "If I'd been here, Cindy would not have been in the balloon. She'd still be alive. Andy would not be in the hospital."

"I have a question," Eduardo said, changing the subject.

Stan looked down, like a child being reprimanded.

Eduardo cleared his throat. "Have you patented your latest technology in Germany?"

"Patents in Germany?" Stan's jaw dropped. "I have worldwide patents on my products. Why?"

"Do you have shell companies in Europe that register your innovations?" Eduardo asked, rephrasing the question. "As you know, Nikki is a private investigator. She works with a former CIA operative. Together, they uncover a lot of information. They found recently issued patents that could be your technology."

"My umbrella company, Omega Satellites, holds all my patents," Stan said. "I'll have to call my attorney on this. Is there specific data you can give me?"

"She's not certain yet, but there's a possibility your patents may have been stolen," Eduardo said.

Stan explained that Omega had been working on a new line of high-performance weather balloons with integrated surveillance. The products would be far more advanced than anything currently on the market. "Two government agencies already stated they could use this latest surveillance technology. The nature of the products leaves me open for copycats, but I'm not aware of anyone stealing the latest innovations."

"You should look into it."

"My patent attorney is excellent. I'll share his contact info and Nikki can have a chat with him. He'll want to know what she's found." Stan opened his mobile phone and sent the data.

"Nikki's coworker will be the one to contact your attorney. His name is Clive. He's a national security specialist."

"I'll notify my attorney," Stan said.

Eduardo thought Stan was rather nonchalant about the possibility his patents were stolen. Thinking about Melissa's vicious attack on Nikki the night before, he mulled over an indirect way to find out if Stan knew anything about it.

"Why do you always pick this coffee shop to meet with us?"

Stan looked surprised. "It's close to your hotel in Old Town."

"Oh, I thought your wife might have mentioned we're at the hotel where the interstates cross."

Stan frowned. "Melissa? How does she even know where you're staying?"

"Last night, she followed a reporter, Maxine Sanchez, to our new hotel. Melissa turned up to question Nikki."

"When did this happen?" Stan's brows furrowed.

Eduardo was surprised. Stan showed more anger at this than the news of stolen technology.

"Sorry," Eduardo said, "I thought you knew. It happened last night."

Stan rolled his eyes. "Melissa. Oh, Melissa. What have you done now?" he said, as if talking to himself. Then he glanced at Eduardo, adding, "She never mentioned it."

Eduardo gestured not to worry about it.

"Can I visit Andy again?" Stan asked.

"Come by anytime. He'll be moved to a regular ward tomorrow. After he's released, we'll take him and Olivia to Miami to stay with us until he fully recovers."

"I can loan you my jet to take you. It's an Embraer Phenom 300. Very comfortable. Let me know when you need it."

"Thanks," Eduardo said. "I'll mention it to Andy."

# CHAPTER FORTY-SEVEN

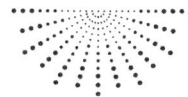

Eduardo opened the door to the room. He felt a smile spread across his face when he saw Olivia riding Nikki's back. Olivia's arms pressed tight around Nikki's shoulders and her little legs wrapped around Nikki's waist, as if she were riding on a pony.

"Looks like fun," Eduardo said. He took her off Nikki's back, hummed a waltz, and danced across the floor exaggerating the movements, much to his niece's delight. Olivia giggled and giggled. After a few minutes he asked Keiko to care for her since he needed to speak with Nikki.

When Keiko took her, Olivia cried. She wasn't ready to stop the play. Eduardo told Olivia he'd be back, and they'd dance again.

Eduardo closed the door to their room. "The meeting with Stan went extremely well."

"He wasn't aggressive?" Nikki asked.

"Quite the contrary. He was helpful. And he didn't know anything about Melissa coming here last night."

"Did you mention that she behaved abominably?"

Eduardo shook his head. "I merely told him she'd followed the reporter to our hotel. The important part of my meeting is that he didn't suspect his technology had been stolen."

"Interesting," Nikki said. "So you discussed it?"

"He gave me his patent attorney's number and said you could call him. I told him it would be one of your colleagues who'd contact him."

"Did you give him Floyd's name?" Nikki asked.

"No, Clive's. That's who'd be investigating, right?"

"Yes, but at this point, he's doing this as a favor to Floyd. There may be a case here that the CIA will take over. That is, if it involves unsanctioned sales to foreign countries. And Clive wouldn't waste his time if he didn't agree."

"I get it. You and Floyd sort of act as CIA informants."

"I didn't say that," Nikki said, with a sparkle in her eyes.

Nikki's phone buzzed. It was Clive. He was downstairs and asked if they could speak. When she told him she'd be right down, he suggested meeting in her room, if possible, to keep from being seen together.

In a couple of minutes, they heard a knock. Eduardo looked through the peephole and opened the door.

Clive came in, closed the door, and gave Eduardo a hug. Turning toward Nikki, he enveloped her in a hug too, telling them both that it was good to see them.

Nikki said she'd order coffee, but Clive said he was short on time and preferred to talk over an issue and be on his way. He had other business in New Mexico besides the balloon investigation.

"At this point, I don't know if the CIA will be involved. It all depends on whether there's a threat to national security," he said. "If there isn't, then I've just done Floyd a favor."

They sat in the seating area in the corner of their room.

"I spoke with the reporter's informant," Clive said. "He wasn't happy at first, thinking that Ms. Sanchez had given his information to me. I told him the information had come to me from Europe where a company was preparing to build drones for the cartels. I hope he believed me."

"Do you believe China, the cartels, or both are connected to the balloon crash?" Nikki asked.

"I wouldn't be here if I didn't think so," Clive said, looking at Eduardo and then turning back to Nikki. "I'm also here to ask you to leave the investigation to me. You could put yourself in grave danger."

Eduardo scoffed. "I think Nikki's already in significant danger. Her brother's in the hospital. They know who we are and can come after us at any moment."

"Neither you nor Nikki need to be actively involved in this." Clive scratched his chin thoughtfully.

"Hmm, I met with the owner of the balloon, Stan Stevens, this morning," Eduardo said. "I asked if he knew that his technology may have been stolen and registered in Germany by a shell company."

"How did he respond?" Clive asked.

"He seemed surprised and gave me his patent attorney's number," Eduardo said, shrugging. "I was going to send you that info later today."

"I'll take it now and call the guy this afternoon. I'll ask him to review what I've uncovered," Clive said. "Did you give Stan my name?"

"Only your first name," Eduardo said, forwarding Stan's number from his phone.

Nikki, looking concerned, interrupted. "You know that I'm extremely careful. I'd ask you to keep me in the loop. Floyd too. That way, I can continue to help."

"The cartels are unforgiving, Nikki," Clive said.

"But as Eduardo told you, they already know who we are."

Clive looked at the floor. "Yeah, you're correct. But I don't want you to meet with the reporter. I'll do it from now on. She's obviously not careful enough with the intel she gathers. Or the sources she obtains it from."

"Yet there's a cartel chief serving time thanks to her reporting," Nikki said.

"Precisely because she's caused problems for the cartel, I want you to stay miles away from that woman." Clive looked straight at Nikki. "You hear me?"

Nikki nodded.

"Good," Clive said. He turned to Eduardo. "And that goes for you too."

Eduardo cleared his throat. "I'm not actually working for Floyd anymore. I've returned to practicing medicine."

"I knew you had, but I thought you were still somewhat involved as a consultant for certain cases."

"May I ask about the shell company?" Nikki asked.

Clive nodded.

"Have you discovered the true owners?"

"The owners are probably not in Europe, as best I can tell. The directors are front people, set there to obscure the real owners. But I'll find out," Clive said. "And Charlotte has been helpful in tracing some of the banking transactions."

"She's excellent at following money flows," Nikki said. "So Security Source is doing a bit of research for you. That means I can continue to investigate, even if you've tied my hands in some areas."

Clive agreed, admonishing Nikki to be careful. Reminding them he had other business to do, he said goodbye.

After Clive left, Eduardo told Nikki he had to get to the hospital. "Stan said he was going to visit Andy, and I must be there if he does. But first, I promised Olivia I'd dance a waltz with her. I don't want to break my promise."

# CHAPTER FORTY-EIGHT

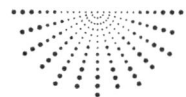

Eduardo reviewed the results of the CT scan he'd ordered on Andy. It all looked good. He personally checked Andy's vital signs and asked the nurse to forward the test results to Dr. Kahn.

"Looks as if you can get out of ICU soon. I'll keep you here one more night."

A second nurse came into the room and told Eduardo that Stan Stevens was downstairs, asking to see the patient.

"Tell him to come up."

When Stan approached the door to Andy's room, the officer stopped him until Eduardo gave him permission to enter.

Andy seemed happy to see his friend.

"How are you feeling?" Stan asked.

Andy stretched his bandaged hand out in greeting. "Much better. I'll be moved to a regular ward tomorrow so I shouldn't be here much longer."

"That's great news," Stan said. "Your brother-in-law said they'll take you and Olivia to Miami until you fully recover. I've offered my plane."

"You don't need to do that," Andy said.

"Look, it'll be far more comfortable than flying on a commercial airline." Stan glanced at Eduardo. "And you'll have your doctor right next to you."

"I'd have that on a commercial flight too."

"I'm not going to argue. But my jet can land at your brother-in-law's command and a commercial flight will not do that. I'll let the doc decide which way to fly you to Florida. By the way, I think you'll be happy to know that your sister's investigation is helping my company. She's discovered that my patents may have been stolen."

Eduardo turned his attention to Stan's conversation. He'd admonish him not to be throwing that information around.

"Patents . . . patents?" Andy repeated. A frown formed on his brow. His eyes focused on Stan. "That's it. I remember now."

"What are you talking about?" Stan asked.

"The party on Friday night. After you left, I heard something you need to know. I tried to call but it went into voicemail, and I wasn't going to leave a message. And well, you know the accident happened the next morning."

Stan gazed at his friend, a quizzical expression showing his confusion over Andy's statement. "I'm not following you. Can you explain?"

"It's the first thing that popped into my mind after my surgery," Andy said, stretching his legs on the bed.

Unsure if Andy was fully coherent, Eduardo stepped in closer.

"At the party, Carol went outside. She stood under a large cottonwood, talking on the phone." Andy paused as if to gather his thoughts.

Stan tapped his fingers on his leg, trying perhaps to keep his impatience in check.

"She didn't know I'd walked up behind her. I can't quote her exactly, but the gist of her conversation was that she'd received notification that the patents had been registered. In Europe, I believe. She mentioned you by name." Andy paused. "Hmm, she said Omega, that Omega's patents were still pending on that technology."

Stan still looked confused. "Do you know what technology she was talking about?"

"Omega's latest innovation. She said by the time you found out that someone had beaten you at your own game, she'd be laughing all the way to the bank."

"Did she specifically mention she'd stolen the technology?" Eduardo asked.

"I don't remember," Andy said. He looked straight at Stan. "In any case, I thought it was important that you knew she was messing with you."

Stan looked stunned. "That doesn't mean she stole the technology from my company. Maybe she's been working on similar stuff and got there first."

"We spoke about your patents when we met for coffee," Eduardo said. "Carol may be a silent owner of the shell company that's registered the products. She may be operating through it."

"Carol's ambitious and selfish, but to steal technology, I don't know if she'd be so dubious. Especially since it's illegal and she can get caught," Stan said, staring across the room. "I've never thought of Carol as evil."

"For your own safety," Eduardo said, "I'd strongly recommend that you not speak about the stolen technology or the patents to anyone until we know more."

Stan nodded, but his thoughts seemed far away. "I'm so sorry for all that's happened. If someone's stolen my innovations and caused Kenny and Cindy's deaths, I will get them, even if I spend every penny I have." He patted Andy's shoulder. "I'm glad your memory is working better, Buddy."

Eduardo escorted Stan to the elevator. "I'll update Nikki about Carol and the patent registrations. She'll take it up with Clive. In the meantime, keep this between your attorney and Clive, when he contacts you."

# CHAPTER FORTY-NINE

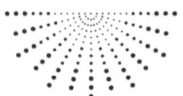

When Nikki arrived at the hospital, Eduardo told her that Andy remembered the incident he'd wanted to convey to Stan.

She was appalled that Carol Peters had apparently bragged about registering Stan's technology. Her mind raced and she wondered if the outcome of the mass ascension would have been different on Saturday if her brother had acted more decisively after overhearing Carol. If only he'd notified Stan that night of what was happening. But what could Stan have done? Nothing in Carol's phone conversation could possibly have alerted anyone of a plan to sabotage the balloon.

"Keep in mind," Eduardo urged his wife, "that everyone is innocent until proven guilty. There could be a genuine misunderstanding about what Andy overheard."

"I'll call Clive and update him," Nikki said. He didn't answer so she left voicemail. Five minutes later her mobile buzzed.

She motioned to Eduardo that she'd step into the hall. Nikki answered with trepidation, knowing it'd be difficult to speak with Clive about the woman she'd interviewed, a woman who had impressed her in a positive way.

"I called," Nikki said, "because my brother remembers what happened the night before the balloon crash. It's information that might help you."

Clive said he was listening.

"Carol Peters, the owner of Drones over Mars, competes head-to-head with Stan. My brother overheard her claim to have patented Stan's innovation. She may have stolen the technology and used it to develop something similar. Or maybe she stole the technology outright and applied for the patents."

"Is she in business with Stan?" Clive asked.

"Not at all. They'd been engaged when they were students at Stanford, but they never married. Stan called it off. When I interviewed her, she indicated her business would overtake Stan's in a matter of five years or less."

Clive asked where Nikki had met with her.

"She's in Albuquerque until the Balloon Fiesta ends this Sunday. One of her balloons is racing all week. It was also in the mass ascension."

"Does she fly hot-air balloons?" Clive asked.

"She does, but she told me she doesn't care for piloting in the mass ascension. It's too chaotic for her taste. Instead, she sipped a mimosa as she watched the balloons from the patio of her boutique hotel in the North Valley."

"Do you think she's the mastermind behind the crash?"

"I can't say," Nikki responded, "but it seems she knows far more than she shared with me."

"Changing the subject, has Charlotte contacted you?"

Nikki told him she had not heard from her research guru.

"She's good. Really good. She traced the shell company to Luxembourg, not Germany."

"That makes sense," Nikki said, "since their corporate regulations are lax, yet they have strict privacy laws."

Clive coughed. "If Carol owns the shell, they have a front person. Her name does not appear on the registration."

"Plus, they'd have to validate a European patent in every country separately if they want to protect it throughout the European Union," Nikki said.

"But listen," Clive said, "I've got to go. I'll interview Carol and get in touch with you if I discover something."

No sooner had Nikki ended the call than Lisa Morales, the police detective, called asking if she could review another video the police department had received. Nikki said she'd be there in thirty minutes.

---

Nikki hated getting caught in traffic. Wasting time felt like an affront to her work ethic. Worse yet, balloons filled the sky above her. She felt a stab in her heart as she watched them drifting by. What would have been a beautiful sight before the accident was now a painful one.

Having come to a complete stop on I-25, she decided to put Charlotte on the speaker phone. That would keep her mind off the hot-air balloons.

"I was about to call to update you on my latest research," Charlotte said.

"Clive might have advanced some of your findings, but you know how guys are. They provide bare bones, and I want the full picture. Get your brushes moving and describe every detail," Nikki said.

"The shell company holds a Luxembourg registration. It's been in business for three years, if you can say that kind of entity is an active business."

"Hmm, about the time Carol may have discovered Stan had innovative technology worth stealing," Nikki said. "Who are the owners?"

"Two men. They live in Europe, but I need to verify what citizenship they hold. Looks like at least one is American, but I need to investigate further to know for sure."

"Traffic is starting to move," Nikki said. "Call when you find out who they are."

As Nikki drove to her appointment, she focused on this job, a job Security Source was not getting paid for. Floyd was always willing for her to work pro bono whenever necessary. It built goodwill. Besides, he received great cooperation from his former colleagues at the CIA, and contacts at the FBI too. He was happy to reciprocate. And as Eduardo had mentioned, Security Source often provided intel that the Agency found useful.

The receptionist at the police station welcomed Nikki like an old friend and told her to go down the hall to Detective Morales's office.

Morales was talking on the phone and Nikki waved and moved a few steps away until the detective finished.

Once she was free, Morales greeted Nikki. "We received a new video last night. I hope it'll shed some light on the case."

Nikki sat in front of the desk, placed her elbows on the desktop and held her chin between fisted hands. Morales positioned her monitor so they could both see it.

As soon as the video started, Nikki knew one of the crew members must have taken it. If not a crew member, it was filmed by someone very near their balloon before it launched.

"This was angled right at our balloon. Do you have the name of the person who sent it?"

Morales shook her head. "It was anonymous."

As the video panned out, Nikki saw her brother stride toward a nearby balloon. "Stop, right there, and back up slightly," she said.

Morales stopped the video, and she ran a little bit at a time until Nikki asked her to stop it again.

"Carol Peters lied to us," Nikki said.

"I totally missed Carol being there," Morales said, looking at Carol's image in the video. "She'd told me she was at her hotel during the mass ascension."

"Yes, sipping mimosas at six in the morning. I didn't know her at that point. I interviewed her a day or two after the accident. I remember Andy looking angry as he returned to his balloon. Now I realize it was because he'd been talking with her." Nikki pointed to Carol standing between two guys.

"Angry? Do you know why?" Morales asked.

"Told me there was something he had to tell Stan. That's the connection," Nikki said, thinking aloud.

Morales frowned. "What connection?"

"Whatever exchange Andy and Carol had right before the balloon launch might be the reason an intruder was sent to my brother's room." The words tumbled out of Nikki's mouth in frustration.

"I'm not following . . ." Morales said.

"Andy must have clashed with her about what he'd overheard her say on the phone the night before. She claimed her company had registered

Stan's latest innovations in Europe. That happened at the crew party the night before the mass ascension."

Morales blinked, her lash extensions fluttering. She looked confused.

"My brother recovered a memory about an incident involving Carol."

"You hadn't told me." Morales sounded put off.

"I only found out about it today and I would have called to tell you, but you called me first. You might want to talk with Andy about it."

"Yes, I'll go over there now that we're finished here," Morales said, turning her computer and monitor off and grabbing her purse.

"There's one more item you need to know about," Nikki said.

Morales put her purse on the desk.

"Maxine Sanchez, the reporter, came to see me last night. She gave me the name of one of her informants. Someone from her days investigating Mexican drug cartels."

"So Max believes the cartels are involved?" Morales asked, raising her eyebrows.

"It appears that way, yes," Nikki said. "You know cartels are using drones to transport drugs, knock communications offline, jam law enforcement surveillance, and even to kill people."

"Looks as if I'll have to talk to Max, but your brother is my priority right now." Morales grabbed her purse again. "I'll see you at the hospital."

# CHAPTER FIFTY

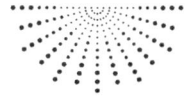

Eduardo met Detective Morales outside the intensive care unit and escorted her to Andy's room. The officer on duty outside the room recognized Morales and stood to greet her.

"Nikki will arrive shortly," Eduardo said. "She stopped by the hotel to check on our niece."

Morales nodded. She strode to Andy's bed and asked how he felt.

"Anxious to get out of here so I can take care of my little girl," he said. "Have you had a break in the case?"

She nodded halfway. "Let's wait until your sister gets here. In the meantime, tell me about Carol Peters claiming she registered patents on Stan's innovations."

Andy straightened up in bed. "At the crew party the night before—"

Morales interrupted him, asking if all the crew members and volunteers had attended.

"No, this was a private party. About forty people were in attendance. It was at a restaurant near the river, the Rio Grande. A bigger party would have been too chaotic. Stan hosted it."

"Who attended?" Morales asked.

"The owners and volunteers from four balloons. Stan's crew, Carol's group, and two other balloonists, Stan's customers from out of town."

"Can you name specific people?" Morales asked, opening her notes app.

"Gustavo Marquez, Kenny and his mother, Juanita Rodriguez, a guy who works with Stan, Derek something."

"Maybe Derek Brown," Morales suggested.

Andy nodded. "That's right."

"Why would Carol, a direct competitor, be there?" Morales asked.

"Stan's a nice guy. The fiesta is supposed to be a friendly gathering of balloon enthusiasts from all over the world." Andy shrugged. "Maybe he's extending Carol a hand of friendship."

"Is there any chance they recently went into a partnership? Or that her company has agreed to manufacture and market his products?"

"To my knowledge, there's nothing like that," Andy said. "You should ask Stan to make certain."

"If Stan was the host, why was Carol talking on the phone about getting the patents herself?"

Andy looked around the room as if he were uncomfortable.

"If you don't know the answer, I'm sure the detective will understand," Eduardo said.

"It's not that. It's because Stan's not here that I hate to answer."

"We can call Stan to come in, if you wish," Morales suggested.

"I discussed it with him this morning," Andy said. "It's probably okay if I tell you. It's difficult to talk about the fiesta because I lost my wife. Also, you should interview Stan."

Morales assured him that she had spoken to Stan, and she would be in contact with him until this case was solved.

Eduardo poured a glass of water for his brother-in-law. He offered to bring the detective a cup of coffee.

She declined the coffee but asked Andy to tell her what he'd overheard at the party.

Andy cleared his throat. "Carol went outside. She was standing under a large cottonwood, and I went out to check on her. I heard her talking on her mobile phone, so I stayed back."

"Did she know you were there?"

Andy shook his head. "Once I heard what she was talking about, I didn't like it. She was laughing that she'd beaten Stan at his own game."

"They're competitors, are they not?" Morales asked.

"Yes, but they've been friends, at least sort of friends, for years. What she implied on the phone was that she'd obtained his technology through dubious channels. And with the patents her company had just received, Stan would think she had created innovations like his."

"Did you notify Stan?"

"He'd left the party about an hour earlier to fly to New York. Right before leaving, he asked me to sub for him at the mass ascension."

"Sub?" Morales asked.

"To be the lead pilot on his balloon."

"So Stan had left before you overheard Carol talking about the patents," Morales said.

"That's correct. When I called to tell him, I thought I might catch him at the airport, or maybe even talk to him on the plane, but he didn't answer."

"What happened next?" Morales asked.

"When he didn't answer, I decided to wait until after the mass ascension the next day. After all, there wasn't much he could do overnight. Then the crash happened. When I awakened from the anesthesia, I knew there was something I needed to relay to Stan, but I couldn't remember what it was."

"When did you recall it?"

"This morning, when Stan came to visit," Andy said.

Nikki walked in, interrupting the conversation. She greeted everyone.

The detective's phone buzzed. She excused herself to take it in the hall.

Eduardo hugged Nikki. The police were finally making progress.

Morales looked tired or concerned or frustrated when she returned, though she'd only been gone for five minutes.

Eduardo announced again that he'd go for coffee and wanted to know how many takers he had.

"Wait," Morales commanded. "I need to speak with both of you outside."

Eduardo turned to Andy. "We'll be right back."

"Bad news." Morales glanced at Nikki and then shifted her gaze to Eduardo. "Maxine Sanchez, the reporter, has been killed."

Nikki gasped.

"What happened?" Eduardo asked.

"She was sideswiped in a hit and run. A large truck, according to bystanders on the street."

"Could it have been on purpose?" Eduardo asked, a chill running down his spine as he thought of the dangers his family faced.

"Too early to tell," Morales said. Her lashes seemed to weigh heavily on her eyelids. "Under the circumstances, I'd call it suspicious."

"Someone didn't want her to talk," Eduardo said.

The police detective agreed.

"Are there surveillance cameras on the street where she was hit?" Nikki asked.

"I've asked my assistant to check into it," Morales said. "We need to speak about your safety. Did the reporter know you're working with me?"

"Absolutely not," Nikki said. "I'm afraid that Max was not able to keep her information as confidential as she should have."

Morales frowned. "What do you mean?"

Nikki explained that the last time she met with Maxine, the reporter had been followed to the hotel by Melissa Stevens.

"Describe the incident in more detail, please," Morales asked.

"Max had interviewed Melissa shortly before she was to get together with me. Apparently, Max was running late, and she mentioned to Melissa that she had to end the meeting with her because she had an appointment with me. Melissa then followed Max to the hotel."

"Why would Melissa do that?" Morales looked confused.

"She wanted to fight me for questioning her husband."

"Ahh, it's worse than that," Eduardo said, "Melissa lunged at Nikki and Maxine jumped in to protect Nikki. Unfortunately, Melissa hit the reporter and knocked her to the floor."

"That's weird," Morales said.

"Officer Santiago Cobos was called but no charges were filed," Eduardo said. "He did write a report of the incident. You can check with him."

Morales bit her lower lip. She looked at the floor. "I was going to call Maxine for an interview. I guess I'm a bit late." She turned to Nikki. "Now, I need the name of Maxine's contact."

"Ramon Estrada," Nikki said. "He lives in Placitas."

## CHAPTER FIFTY-ONE

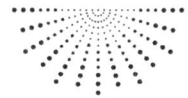

"Clive," Nikki said, "I have bad news." She paused for a second before telling him that Maxine had been killed earlier that day.

"Sorry to hear that. What happened?"

"A large truck in a hit and run," Nikki said. "Under the circumstances, the police detective is calling it suspicious."

"I'll run a check on Ramon Estrada," Clive said. "I want to make sure he's still alive."

"Could he have ordered the hit on Maxine?" Nikki asked.

"Probably not, but who knows," he responded.

"I gave his name to the police detective. I think she may follow up with him."

"And let her do the investigation. Do you hear me?"

"Yep, I hear you," Nikki said.

Clive cleared his throat. "I'm meeting with Carol Peters late today. If I learn something useful, I'll call you."

No sooner had Nikki ended the call than her phone buzzed again.

"This is Gustavo," a male voice said. "I'm in the lobby. Can you come down?"

"Lobby? Which lobby?"

"At the Crowne Plaza," he responded. "Isn't this where you're staying?"

Nikki swallowed hard. "I'll be right down."

Gustavo was pacing in the lobby when Nikki stepped out of the elevator. She joined him and they took seats in the coffee shop.

"How did you know where we're staying?" Nikki asked.

"Melissa told me."

"Oh, I didn't know the two of you were friends."

"I've been working with Stan and Melissa to plan the vigil. She asked if I would give you the details. That's when she mentioned you'd changed hotels. Is that a problem?"

"Not at all." Nikki focused on keeping her surprise in check.

"Stan's set up the permit, logistics, emergency services, and music for the vigil."

"Music?" Nikki sounded surprised. "That'll bring the crowds."

Gustavo nodded. "Stan's gone all out. Even purchased candles."

"Candles?" Nikki gasped. "Isn't that dangerous on a dry field?"

He shook his head. "Battery-operated. Safer than open flames in a crowd."

"Good." Maybe Stan was more thoughtful than she'd assumed.

"We'd like you to say a few words about Cindy. I know it's a lot to ask," Gustavo said. "Stan will speak about his son."

Nikki took a deep breath and closed her eyes, wondering what she'd say in front of a crowd. If she accepted, she'd want to make it meaningful, yet the thought of speaking in front of a crowd while carrying the weight of Cindy's loss made her chest tighten.

She looked at Gustavo. "I don't want to make it about grief alone. Cindy would want us to remember the adventure and the joy of ballooning. To remember the joy of life."

Gustavo thanked her. "Do you want us to send a limousine to pick you and Eduardo up at the hotel?"

"Limousine?" she repeated. "Oh, good grief, no. Thanks."

"The vigil will be held Friday evening at the launch field," Gustavo said. "The ceremony will start after the special shape balloon event at the opposite end of the field."

"The Sandias will be beautiful at sunset," Nikki said. "Very meaningful."

"We'll have a moment of silence, then the speakers, followed by the candle-lighting ceremony. There's a designated area for people to leave flowers or notes."

"Are you expecting a big turnout?" she asked.

"Yeah, a lot of pilots and crew want to be there. Balloon fans will attend. The fiesta organizers are fully backing it, and the media will probably cover it too."

Nikki thought for a second. "Is Maxine Sanchez, the reporter who was investigating the crash, also going to be honored at the vigil?"

Gustavo looked away. "Her name came up, but Stan said that we're honoring the ones killed in the balloon crash."

"What about security?"

"We've already talked to local law enforcement. They'll provide police officers and we're keeping a perimeter clear in case we need ambulances or police cars."

Nikki gasped. "Are you expecting trouble?"

"Any big gathering like this needs to plan for the unexpected. Emotions can run high, people could pass out. We must be prepared."

Nikki thought of Cindy's parents. They'd be in town by Friday. She'd mention the vigil to them, though she doubted the Smiths would attend.

"My other crew is going to help me build a stage and set up the loudspeakers."

"Your pothole crew?" Nikki asked.

"I prefer to call them my highway crew." Gustavo smiled.

"Sorry," she said, "I didn't mean it in an offensive way. I was visualizing the way I saw them working the day we rented the bikes."

"No offense taken." Gustavo made a hand gesture as if brushing the comment aside. "Can you think of anything we haven't considered?"

"You seem to have it all planned out," Nikki said, "but if I can pitch in, let me know."

Gustavo thanked her. He paused for a second and then asked if Nikki had anything to discuss on the investigation.

"It's in the hands of the police," she said.

"If you learn anything, give me a call," Gustavo said.

Nikki looked into his eyes. "Thanks for helping to set this up."

Gustavo gave her a curt smile. "I wish it were a victory celebration instead of a vigil."

# CHAPTER FIFTY-TWO

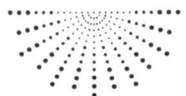

Nikki's heart felt heavy as she kissed Eduardo before he headed to the hospital. She was painfully aware the balloon fiesta would soon end. Witnesses and suspects alike would leave town. The police would not find the culprit in time.

She wanted to see Olivia and knocked on Keiko's door. Keiko, radiant and smiling, invited her into the room. Olivia was still sleeping.

"Let her sleep. I'll come back later," Nikki whispered. She stepped back into her room.

She dialed Clive's number.

"What's up?" he asked.

"Just checking on your interview with Carol." Nikki sat down at the desk.

"She's a charmer," Clive said. "That always scares me."

"Did she reveal anything?" Nikki asked, turning the desk lamp on.

"Not really. Said she'd gone to the launch field for a brief discussion with her pilot and crew chief on the morning of the mass ascension. Apparently, the two men had quarreled, and the chief was threatening to walk away."

"Did she say why?"

"That the chief didn't like the way the pilot was treating him," Clive said.

"Did you ask her about Andy talking to her that morning?" She heard something clatter on the other end of the line.

Clive took a few seconds to answer. "Sorry. Spilled a glass of water, and I'm cleaning it up."

"Shall I call back later?"

"No, you're good," Clive said. "Carol claimed that she and Andy attended Stanford together and Andy had gone over to say hello."

"Did you know a vigil is being held Friday night at the balloon park?" Nikki asked.

"I hadn't heard. Are you planning to attend?"

"I've been asked to say a few words to honor Cindy."

"Remember to look around the crowd," Clive said. "I'm in Denver on assignment or I'd go too."

Nikki fidgeted with a pen on the desk. "I'll be looking, in case the perpetrator returns to the crime scene. It might attract a lot of people since the crash and the deaths of two pilots have been all over the news."

"Stay safe," Clive reminded her before ending the call.

Nikki opened her laptop to check emails. Charlotte had sent information on the Luxembourg company, but there was nothing in the report that Nikki didn't already know.

She asked Charlotte to work her magic and locate photos of the two people who presumably owned the shell company and to dig further into their backgrounds, maybe even checking the INTERPOL database.

Nikki spent the next hour catching up on administrative items she'd ignored since arriving in Albuquerque.

Keiko knocked on the connecting door. Nikki closed her computer and opened the door.

"Tia Ki, Tia Ki," Olivia said, showing her a squiggly line drawing.

"What is it?" Nikki asked.

Olivia pointed to one grouping of lines. "Horse."

"What a beautiful horse," Nikki said.

Olivia giggled and ran back to her room. She returned with another drawing. "Dog," she said, handing the sheet of paper to her aunt.

Nikki smiled at Keiko. "Why don't we drive to Old Town and visit the San Felipe de Neri church? I could use a break. I don't want to leave town without seeing the interior."

The thick adobe walls of San Felipe de Neri are constructed in a traditional cruciform style. Nikki read aloud from a plaque indicating this was the second church to occupy this spot, after the original one from 1706 collapsed during severe rainstorms in 1792. They stepped inside.

Wooden vigas, or beams, on the interior of the church supported the nave's roof. The interior decoration was sparse, compared to Mexican churches Nikki had seen, yet she found its simplicity to be quite profound in a spiritual sense. Maybe it gave her a respite from the investigation. Or maybe it provided her with a moment to meditate on Cindy's life. What she'd want to say at the vigil.

She asked Keiko to stand on the other side. With a quizzical look, Keiko moved to the opposite wall, taking Olivia with her. Nikki whispered that they were now experiencing the whisper gallery inside the historic church.

Wide-eyed, Keiko responded that the acoustics were marvelous. Olivia glanced around, perplexed that she heard her aunt's voice but couldn't see her. Nikki felt her heart melt at Olivia's reaction.

Keiko took Olivia across the street to the kiosk in the park to keep her busy. Nikki knelt at the altar to pray for her brother's recovery. Andy would be moved to a regular room today. She knew that placed him closer to being released from the hospital.

When Nikki completed her prayers, she went into the bright sunlight outside the church. She stepped off the curb to cross the street to the kiosk. That's when she saw a BMW, parallel parked, pull out into the street. Nikki knew that car. It had been at Carol's casita the day she met the woman. She watched and confirmed that Carol was the driver.

Nikki looked toward the park. Reassured that Keiko and Olivia were safe, she wondered if Carol had been following them. Did she pull away because she saw Nikki?

# CHAPTER FIFTY-THREE

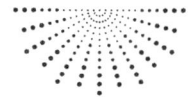

Nikki's phone buzzed and she saw it was the police detective.

"Can you come to my office?" Morales asked.

Nikki was hesitant and glanced at her watch. "Yes, in forty minutes, after I take Keiko and my niece back to the hotel."

Keiko sang softly to Olivia as Nikki drove, possibly to keep the child from disturbing Nikki's thoughts. It was a simple lullaby in Spanish, one that Nikki had never heard. By the time they arrived at the Crowne Plaza, Olivia had fallen asleep.

"Just leave me at the front door," Keiko said. "I'll manage with Olivia, and you can continue to your appointment."

"Thanks," Nikki said, looking around the parking lot to make sure she didn't spot Carol's BMW. "Call if you need me."

Nikki pulled away as soon as Keiko, carrying the sleeping Olivia, walked into the hotel. On the way to the police station, she wondered why Morales had called. Had she changed her mind about having Nikki help her? Maybe she was so overworked that she appreciated the assistance Nikki provided. Or she felt comfortable discussing the case with another woman. Might it be that Nikki had won her over by providing a couple of good leads? Whatever the reasons, Nikki was thankful to be a little closer to the investigation. She parked her car and went into the police department on Cibola Loop.

Morales was talking with the receptionist and stopped her conversation upon seeing Nikki enter the lobby. "Thanks for coming over so promptly."

With a head gesture, Morales motioned for Nikki to follow her down the hall.

Closing the door behind them, she asked Nikki to take a seat. She pulled an electronic folder up on her computer.

"I had an interview with Melissa. You know that she and Stan own a beautiful spread in Santa Fe, but she offered to drive to Albuquerque so I wouldn't need to go there. They have a condo here, a luxurious one, in the Tanoan section of town."

Nikki wasn't sure where this conversation was going.

"I got there almost an hour early, so I parked. Thought I'd make phone calls until the appointment time. Then I saw Gustavo Marquez and Derek Brown come out of the building, followed by Melissa, holding a child's hand. About three years old. Hers, I assume."

"You do know that a vigil is being held tomorrow night at the balloon park, right?"

Morales nodded.

"They probably got together to discuss the program," Nikki said. "Stan is paying for music and other incidentals, like the candles. Gustavo and his workers from the asphalt repair company are setting up the stage and the audio system."

"The weird thing is that Gustavo climbed in his truck and drove off." Morales opened the file on her computer, revealing several digital photos, showing the three people she had witnessed.

"Derek and Melissa continued to talk. When Derek left, he got into a small SUV half a block away. The driver was Brad Wood, the guy I'd dismissed as not having a role in all of this."

Nikki wasn't sure there was anything suspicious about these people getting together, since Stan and Gustavo were working on the details for the vigil. She sensed that Morales felt differently.

"Why did you dismiss Brad Wood?" Nikki asked.

"He had no access to the balloon until the morning of the mass ascension. I confirmed that with Stan and Gustavo when I interviewed them. And there were too many others around during the ascension."

"I'll be on the lookout at the vigil tomorrow night," Nikki said. "Will you be there?"

Morales nodded. "A lot of ballooning enthusiasts will attend. Could number in the thousands, so I'm not sure we'll discover much. Is your husband going with you?"

"For sure. We'll arrive early because I've been asked to say a few words about Cindy."

The police detective stood and opened a cabinet behind her, taking out a couple of Kevlar vests and placing them on a chair next to Nikki. "You and Eduardo must wear these. I'll also double up on security at the hospital for your brother."

"Thanks," Nikki said, unable to say anything else for fear she'd break down.

"You're not planning to take your niece or nanny with you, are you?"

"They'll stay at the hotel, but Keiko is a close family friend, not a nanny." Nikki thought about security for a few seconds. "I hadn't considered they'd be in more danger than usual. They should be safe at the hotel, shouldn't they?"

"I can't justify an officer to guard them," Morales said. "I seriously doubt they're in danger. I mean, someone had motive to kill your brother, but I doubt anyone would have motive to harm your niece. Or your friend."

Nikki wondered if anyone would use Olivia to hurt Andy. She'd been worried about kidnapping. She'd even talked to Keiko about security. As the days passed without further attacks on Andy, or even herself or Eduardo, Nikki had ceased to worry about someone trying to snatch Olivia. But then she'd seen Carol this morning.

"Carol Peters," Nikki said, "was at the park when I took my niece and Keiko to the church in Old Town."

Morales blinked.

"It made me uneasy," Nikki said. "Like she was following us. And if so, why?"

"Was she shopping?"

Nikki shrugged. "She pulled away from the curb in front of the church when I started to cross the street. My niece and Keiko were in the park waiting for me."

"Did she see you?"

"I don't know for sure."

"Did she talk to them?"

"I didn't ask Keiko, but she would have told me if someone had approached them."

"Like I said, I can't justify security detail for them, but I can recommend a private firm where you can hire a guard for the evening."

"I'm overreacting," Nikki said. "It's probably a coincidence. Old Town's a major tourist spot."

"Getting back to why I called you here, I thought you could talk to each one of these people," Morales motioned to the picture open on her computer.

"To ask why they got together?" Nikki asked.

"That's right," the detective said, looking at Nikki. "If you don't mind."

"I'll call Gustavo and ask if I can stop by to see him to discuss the vigil."

"There's something else," Morales said. "The lab investigators sent me a report stating that the valve on the burner system looked as if it had been tampered with. Then when the drone caused the explosion, the valve was further damaged."

"Interesting. Any suspects?" Nikki asked.

"Not at this point." Morales frowned. "Changing the subject, I want to check out Ramon Estrada's place. Do you mind taking a ride up to Placitas with me?"

Nikki knew that Clive wanted her to stay away from Estrada. Nikki had not met the man. She was curious about him but ambivalent about the request.

"Like going into his house?" Nikki asked.

"If I have to, yes."

"With a warrant?" Nikki asked.

Morales shook her head. "I'll knock on his door. If no one answers, I'll see if I can get in. Make sure he's still alive."

"When do you want to do this?"

"How about right now?"

"And what do you expect me to do?" Nikki asked.

"Basically, keep me company. If Estrada is at home, I'll ask if he knows that Maxine Sanchez was killed."

"That could be dangerous," Nikki said, "if he's involved in cartel business."

Morales seemed lost in thought for a few seconds. "My guess is that he plays both sides—gives info out on the cartel leaders but also has a connection with them that puts him in a position to obtain critical intel."

"You only want me along for the company?" Nikki asked.

"Yup. Just ride with me. In case anything happens to me, call the police, an ambulance, or whatever's needed."

Nikki raised her eyebrows. "Really?"

"Nothing's going to happen," Morales said with a smile. "Shall we go?"

# CHAPTER FIFTY-FOUR

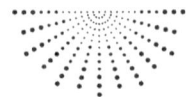

Eduardo had ordered a late lunch for Andy and himself. Andy ate solid food today for the first time. Not a lot, but Eduardo was pleased with his brother-in-law's progress. He approached Andy's bed.

"We'd like for you and Olivia to live with us in Miami Beach until you recover."

Andy looked uncomfortable. "What if I never recover fully?"

"You're doing so well that it should only take about three more months," Eduardo said.

Andy blinked. "Thanks. I hate to be a burden, but it's the best situation for Olivia and me. If I didn't have her, I wouldn't bother you."

"It's not a bother," Eduardo said. "That's what families are for."

The hospital's head neurosurgeon, Dr. Khan, came in followed by Dr. Patel, the intern.

"Good morning," he said, glancing at Andy. "You're looking much better." He took a notebook computer from Dr. Patel and reviewed Andy's charts. "Keep this up and you'll be ready to leave us in a few days."

"Can you say when?" Andy asked.

Dr. Kahn looked at Eduardo.

"Probably Sunday," Eduardo said.

"The last day of the fiesta," Andy said with a sigh.

"It's great that you're aware of the dates. I'd like to recommend a rehab hospital where you can continue your therapy for a couple of weeks," Dr. Kahn said, looking from Andy to Eduardo.

"My wife and I are taking him to Florida with us. I'll hire a therapist to come to the house and work with him," Eduardo said.

"How will you get him to Florida?"

"By airplane," Eduardo responded. "Given that his progress has been solid, I think he can safely travel ten days after the surgery. He shows no signs of residual swelling, and his oxygen levels are stable. That said, we need to take every precaution: compression stockings, an oximeter, and supplemental oxygen."

"In that case," Dr. Kahn said, "I'll evaluate the patient on Monday morning to make sure he's up to a four-hour flight plus all the time at the airport. If all looks good, I can release him at noon that day."

Eduardo nodded. He did not mention the possibility of a private jet, which would diminish the security lines and make the process much smoother. He thanked both Kahn and Patel.

"I'm glad the surgery was so successful," Dr. Kahn said, preparing to leave the room. "If I need help in the future, I might call you."

"Call anytime. You know where to find me," Eduardo said.

"Thanks, I will."

Once they were alone, Eduardo emphasized to Andy that he was doing so well, even Dr. Kahn was impressed. "Now the question is whether you want to fly to Florida in a private plane or a commercial one?"

"Stan's jet sounds good to me. It'd be more comfortable. Even though we've been friends for years, I've never flown in his plane."

"I'll call and tell Stan we'll take up his offer," Eduardo said. "We'll avoid the crowded checkpoints and gates. That'll work well for us. You'll be in a wheelchair, and the private terminal will make it all easier."

Andy gave him a thumbs up and thanked Eduardo for taking care of him.

"There's one more item. Your sister called and said there's a candlelight vigil for Cindy and Kenny tomorrow night. The police will provide an extra guard during that time."

"Why?"

"Just to make sure you're safe," Eduardo said.

# CHAPTER FIFTY-FIVE

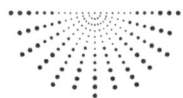

Morales sped past a sign welcoming them to Sandoval County.

"We're no longer in Bernalillo County," Nikki said, surprised. "Isn't this out of your jurisdiction?"

"Yes, but we're not going to arrest anyone. Of course, I could deputize you, if we need to." Morales laughed.

Nikki wondered what her motive was. A sense of unease settled on her. It had not occurred to her that Morales might be a dirty cop. She chastised herself for not considering this possibility or analyzing the danger before going with Morales to visit a cartel contact in an isolated location.

Nikki glanced at her watch. "Eduardo will be expecting me soon. I'll text him that we'll catch up later." She texted him where she and Morales were headed and the reason they were going.

She asked herself why she had not thought about the dirty cop risk before now. After all, Morales was about to close the crash investigation until Nikki reported the intruder to Andy's room. But she had provided police protection to Andy after that incident. Nikki's mind felt like a caged animal again.

Realizing that she was so close to the case, Nikki knew she was not thinking objectively. She didn't want to think ill of Morales.

If the detective was up to no good, at least Nikki still had the baby Glock hidden in her purse.

The GPS took them right up to a rather humble house on the outskirts of Placitas.

"Hardly looks like the place where a narco associate would live," Morales said. "I'll go further up and park. Keep your phone handy in case I need help."

Morales turned the car around and parked so that Nikki could keep an eye on her as she approached Estrada's house.

"Do you carry a gun?" Nikki asked.

Morales tapped her jacket at her waist.

Nikki watched as the detective walked down the slight incline to Estrada's house and knocked on the front door.

A screen door swung open, and an older gentleman, gray-haired and round-shouldered, stepped out. He looked up and down the street. He and Morales spoke for a minute or two. She held something out, probably her badge, for him to see. The two of them talked again, and he looked toward the parked car.

Morales held her phone to her ear.

Nikki jumped when her phone buzzed.

"Estrada wants you to join us."

Nikki held her breath. "Why?"

"He doesn't want you to be up there by yourself."

Angry with herself about going against Clive's advice, she knew she'd had a choice. Her determination to find the perp or perps that caused the crash had clouded her judgement. Nikki opened the secret compartment of her purse to make her gun more readily available. She reluctantly got out of the car.

The screen door squeaked as Estrada opened it for the women. Once inside, the interior of the little house was immaculate. Still feeling uneasy, Nikki evaluated where she might take cover if bullets flew.

"Please sit," the man said. He pointed to a set of monitors embedded in a cabinet on the wall. An accordion-style sliding door that could enclose the cabinet was open to one side. "I doubt anyone followed you here, but if they did, we'll know before they arrive."

Morales glanced at Nikki and then turned to Estrada. "We're here about the accident that killed Maxine Sanchez."

Estrada looked at his hands before he responded, saying that he didn't know anything about it.

"You must have some ideas who might have wanted to kill Maxine," Morales said.

Estrada nodded. "The drug kingpin, Vasquez, might have ordered it. He's serving time in part because of her investigative reporting."

"Is his organization still active?"

"His son, Vasquez Medina, has taken over. He's in Mexico, but he operates in this country."

"Hmm, you think Maxine's death is a simple vendetta?"

"More than likely, from what you've told me—a hit and run in a big truck—that would be my guess."

"How are you connected to the Vasquez cartel?" Morales asked.

Estrada looked at her. "They killed my son."

"I'm sorry to hear that," Morales said. 'When?"

Estrada rubbed his hands. "Eight months ago."

Morales appeared to be perplexed. "I've worked on cases involving the Vasquez cartel, but I don't recall anything about this killing."

"It was never reported as a murder. It was also made to look like an accident. My son was riding a motorcycle and a truck hit him." His voice trailed off to a whisper. "I received a phone call after it happened that if I caused any trouble, I would regret it. They know I have a daughter and grandchildren."

"Why did they kill your son?" Morales asked.

"Juan was a computer whiz. A genius. But he didn't complete his degree. He was bored at the university, he knew more than his professors. Without a degree, he had trouble getting the job he wanted. He jumped around for years with different companies. Somehow the jefe's son, Vasquez Medina, heard of him and offered him a job. First, Juan set up a whole computer system for them."

Nikki wondered if Juan had set up his father's security system.

"With the advent of drones, Vasquez Medina asked Juan to build some for them. It was an exciting project for Juan." Estrada paused, emotion evident in his tone.

"Go on," Morales urged.

The man looked around the room. "Despite Juan's ability, Vasquez Medina was not happy with the slow progress. Juan had been building drones for several years, but he sold them to photographers and other enthusiasts. They didn't have the capabilities Vasquez Medina wanted. The cartel bought one off the black market for Juan to use as a model to copy. Juan told me it was like an advanced spy machine."

"The cartels have been using advanced drones to circumvent police communications and other uses," Morales said, moving to the edge of her seat and leaning in toward Estrada.

"Not as advanced as what they were asking Juan to build. They contacted several companies specializing in drones. Then someone from one company offered to sell drones to them."

"Could that have been Stan Stevens?" Nikki regretted the words as soon as she said them. This was the detective's interview, not hers.

Estrada stretched his fingers and glanced at his hands again. "I don't know. I never knew the name of the person or the company who offered to sell them, but later they reneged on the deal. Another cartel was offering more money is what I heard. That other cartel sent a negotiator who posed as a Brazilian government purchasing agent."

"When did that happen?" Morales asked, her voice cracking with energy.

"Maybe a year ago, maybe longer. Vasquez Medina accused Juan of messing up the deal and told him to produce something equivalent. My son realized the drones would not only have spying capabilities, but they would also kill people. He couldn't do that."

"That's when they killed your son?"

"Not quite. But Juan realized he was in danger. He knew that his refusal to build a drone capable of killing people would put me and my daughter in danger as well." Estrada gestured to the monitors. "Juan put additional security in for me. My daughter, Juan's sister, moved out of state. She didn't want her children at risk. She invited me to go with them, but I couldn't leave Juan here alone."

A buzzing sound alerted them to motion on the monitors. All three glanced up. A pickup truck headed toward the house. Nikki was able to discern the lettering on the passenger door: Potholes and More, Gustavo's road repair company. It stopped at the front door. Gustavo, carrying a bag, got out.

## CHAPTER FIFTY-SIX

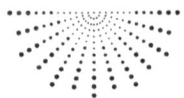

Eduardo dialed Stan and passed the phone to his brother-in-law. He thought it would be best if Andy himself asked to use the private plane.

After greeting his friend, Andy told him he was on speaker with Eduardo. "Can we borrow your plane and pilot on Monday around noon to fly to Miami?"

"You bet," Stan said. "I'll send a car to take you and your family to the airport. Eduardo, let me know what equipment you need."

"Supplemental oxygen for Andy," Eduardo said, jumping into the conversation. "Your plane may already be equipped with it."

Stan confirmed the Embraer had supplemental oxygen. He added that he'd coordinate with Nikki on the schedule.

"We'll be in touch," Andy said, thanking his friend and ending the call.

Eduardo asked Andy how he felt about leaving the hospital.

"I can hardly wait to see Olivia. It's been so long." Andy closed his eyes as if saying a prayer.

"I know you're eager to leave, but don't forget you've spent a lot of time in bed, and you will be weak," Eduardo cautioned. "If anything happens, I'll take care of you."

"I'll be fine. After all, I've been walking around the ward," Andy said. "What about Cindy's ashes? I can't go to Florida without them."

"The hospital has recommended a mobile notary service that will come to the room. You can give me a limited power of attorney, and I'll pick the ashes up for you."

---

Estrada opened the door and invited Gustavo in. The crew chief was surprised when he saw Nikki and the police detective in the small living room.

Nikki stood to greet him. He awkwardly asked about Andy's progress.

"He's in a regular room now, in case you want to visit and see for yourself."

"What brings you here?" Morales asked, apparently not wanting to be left out of the conversation. Without standing she shook hands with Gustavo.

"Thought I'd check on my friend here and bring him a homemade pumpkin pie. Juan and I went to school together." Gustavo took the paper bag off and set the pie on the kitchen table.

"I love your mother's pie," Estrada said. Studying the two women, he asked if they wanted a slice.

"That'd be great," Morales said, standing to help serve.

Nikki sat down again, thinking that there were already too many cooks in the kitchen. With only four people in the living and kitchen area, the house felt crowded.

Gustavo sliced the pie, Estrada got dishes and forks out, and Morales served everyone a piece.

"It's my turn to ask you what you're doing here," Gustavo said, taking a bite of pie.

"They came to check on me after what happened to Maxine, the reporter," Estrada said.

Nikki suppressed a gasp at Estrada's honesty.

Gustavo shook his head. "That was not an accident. Someone ordered her killed."

"Who?" Morales asked.

Gustavo shrugged. "Vasquez Medina."

"Isn't he in Mexico?" Morales asked.

"Yes, but his reach is wide," he said, "you should know that." Turning to Estrada, he added, "the accident was not far from where Juan was killed. From descriptions I've heard of the truck, it might have been the same one."

Morales leaned forward. "The vehicle used in Juan's accident also caused Maxine's hit and run?"

"That's right," Gustavo said, describing the truck. "Changing the subject, tomorrow night's vigil is all organized from our end of it. The crowd will move to the vigil once the special shape balloon event finishes. Is the police department ready?"

"We're always prepared," Morales said. "With a little luck, I'm hoping for clues about the balloon crash."

"I'd like to request that you not investigate Juan's hit and run. Just let it be. I have a daughter and grandchildren to think of," Estrada said, putting his plate on a side table.

"You know that I can't promise that." Morales picked up the empty dessert plates and took them to the kitchen. "I need to get back to the office."

"Do you know who tried to harm Andy Garcia?" Gustavo asked.

Morales shook her head. "Not unless you give me some intel."

"I don't know," Gustavo said, "but I'd look at the cartel."

"What makes you say that?" Nikki squirmed, surprised.

"No reason, other than it would make sense."

"I don't get the connection," Morales said.

"Just seems that the cartel is responsible for all these deaths and attempted assassinations—Juan, Maxine, maybe Kenny and Cindy, though I think the last two were in the wrong place at the wrong time. So maybe they went after Andy at the hospital." Gustavo turned to Estrada and asked what he thought.

"You might be correct," the older gentleman said.

"I'll take that into consideration." Morales turned to Gustavo, frowning. "How did you know someone tried to harm Andy?"

"Melissa mentioned it," he replied.

Morales glanced at her watch and repeated that she had to get to the office. She thanked the two men.

The detective and Nikki left the little house. As they walked up the hill toward the car, Morales said she was surprised about the connection between the crew chief and Estrada.

"Apparently, Gustavo and Juan were friends growing up." Nikki gazed at the vegetation on the hilly landscape. Pinyon and juniper were familiar, but she saw a small tree she'd never noticed before.

"What kind of tree is that?" Nikki pointed to one near the road.

"Placitas wild cherry. The locals make an interesting wine from it," Morales said. "Back to the topic at hand, I wonder who recommended Juan to the cartel."

"Probably word of mouth, but who knows," Nikki said. "Seeing Gustavo reminded me of the pictures he took of the valve and the burner system after the crash. Did the lab ever look for fingerprints on the actual valve?"

"For sure," Morales said. "They didn't recover any. The flames probably eliminated any evidence."

Nikki glanced at Morales. "Why did you mention finding clues about the crash at the vigil?"

"To make Gustavo squirm if he had any part in it."

# CHAPTER FIFTY-SEVEN

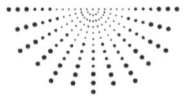

Nikki spent much of the day in the hotel room, researching suspects on the computer, calling Charlotte, and comparing notes.

"Let's go over Brad Wood's information again," Nikki said.

"Okay, Brad Wood. Auto mechanic. He graduated from high school in Albuquerque, never attended college."

"Can you find if he worked at the Denver auto dealership with Gustavo?" Nikki asked.

"Brad never lived in Denver. Manuel Quezada was Gustavo's accomplice in the fraud case."

"Just double-checking," Nikki said. She thanked Charlotte and told her she'd call back if she needed further information.

She was checking out, as Morales had requested, why Melissa, Derek, Gustavo, and Brad would have been at Melissa's condo. Nikki was convinced they were merely planning the vigil. And if there were something more sinister these people were up to, maybe it would become apparent at the vigil.

If she didn't keep herself busy, Nikki thought she'd go mad. At that, her stomach churned in anticipation of the vigil. She went over the remarks she'd prepared and felt satisfied her sister-in-law would approve of what she would say.

Remembering that Cindy's parents would be in town, she called Helen Smith.

After a bit of small talk, Nikki invited them to the vigil.

"I doubt Harold will want to attend. Besides, going to the field where our daughter died will be too hard," Helen said.

"I hope you're planning to see Olivia while you're in town," Nikki said.

"If Harold is up to it, I'll call Saturday morning and perhaps we can stop by your hotel on the way to the airport. But I doubt it. Harold's very upset. You're probably aware that the coroner will not release Cindy's remains to us. Told us only Andy can claim them."

"I heard that," Nikki said, trying to sound sympathetic. "I hope you will come to visit Olivia on Saturday."

Nikki spent several hours with Olivia. She wanted to give Keiko a break, though Keiko insisted she loved taking care of the active toddler. If nothing else, it gave Nikki a better understanding of Keiko's patience and talent for dealing with the rambunctious little girl. It was exhausting.

When Eduardo arrived at the hotel, he was carrying a container with Cindy's ashes. He told Nikki he'd place the urn in his suitcase.

She nodded and pointed at the Kevlar vests on the bed. "Detective Morales specials. We're to wear them tonight."

He raised an eyebrow. "What's the chance we'll need them?"

"They're uncomfortable, but a bullet would be far worse," Nikki said.

They put them on, under their clothes.

"Hmm," Eduardo said, looking at Nikki. "My bride has gained a little weight." He embraced her.

She pinched his ribs but found the Kevlar didn't squeeze.

He grabbed her hands and kissed them, but she could tell he was anxious to arrive at the park before the crowd moved from the special shape balloon event to the launch field for the vigil.

"How are you feeling about the vigil?" he asked.

She leaned her head against his shoulder. "I want life to get back to normal," she whispered. "I want to be back on our turf."

"Me too," he said. "I've missed you. It has been stressful, the accident, the nights at the hospital, Keiko and Olivia in the next room. It's all been too much. Considering everything, Andy's doing great."

"Will you mind having this bunch at our house in Miami Beach?" she asked.

"Not at all. The house is much more convenient, and besides, our bedroom is on the second floor. We'll have the privacy we need." He chuckled, winking at her. "I can hardly wait."

"Time to go," Nikki said, breaking away from his embrace. She knocked on the connecting door.

"Call or text me if anything comes up," she said when Keiko opened the door. "I hate to ask you to remain in the hotel, but that's the safest place to be while we're at the park this evening."

"Go and honor Cindy," Keiko said. "We'll be fine."

---

The special shape balloons were still launching when Nikki and Eduardo arrived at the field. Nikki had read that ten countries were participating in the special shape flights. Wanting to share these balloons with Olivia and Keiko, she took pictures. Eduardo put his arms around her as the last balloons lifted into the air. The sight delighted them, and they laughed at the various shapes—the cow, the stagecoach, the blue parrot, a fish aquarium painted on the envelope with a turtle straddling the top of it, and an oversized human brain, all floating into the air.

Once the final balloon, a sunflower wearing sunglasses, lifted off, they walked to where the vigil would take place. The stage had been set up with the Sandia Mountains as the backdrop. Nikki could only imagine how majestic the mountains would be at sunset. Gustavo and Brad were arranging chairs in the VIP seating.

Gustavo welcomed them. "With the special shapes over with, can the two of you help make sure that the VIP seats are not taken by fans looking for a place to park their butts?"

Eduardo laughed. "I'll do my best."

"Those bleachers," Gustavo said, pointing to five large portable bleachers, "are for folks who really do need to sit, yet are not VIP guests."

Beyond the bleachers were food trucks offering New Mexico fare. Four smaller ones had free water and soda pop. About ten taxis lined the side of the road by the field. Not far behind them, a row of porta-potties was set up.

Derek Brown, Stan's good friend and innovation consultant, sauntered over and asked if he could help. Gustavo told him to watch for the musicians and take them to the stage where they could set up.

Two trucks with Potholes and More on their doors drove up. Gustavo instructed the drivers to park on each side of the bank of bleachers.

"My men are going to hand out candles," he said to Nikki, "mostly by letting people grab their own from open boxes on the truck beds."

The musicians arrived. Nikki watched Derek lead them to the large stage that had been built for this event. They set up: an octet with string instruments, a clarinet, and a horn. Soon they were rehearsing Vivaldi's *Four Seasons*.

Nikki nudged Eduardo. "Have you read the Bible verses on the electronic signs at each end of the stage?" She took photos to show Andy after he recovered a bit more.

The one on the right side had Cindy Smith Garcia's name followed by the verse that Eduardo read aloud: "Jesus said to her, 'I am the resurrection and the life. The one who believes in me will live, even though they die; and whoever lives by believing in me will never die.' *John* 11:25–26."

Nikki's voice broke as she read the verse quoted under Kenny Stevens's name: "To everything there is a season, and a time for every purpose under heaven: A time to be born and a time to die. *Ecclesiastes* 3:1–2."

Nikki adjusted the Kevlar vest under her blouse. It was cutting into her ribs. She watched people drifting over from the other side of the park. Some took spots on the bleachers, others grabbed water or sodas. Most walked to the trucks to pick up candles.

Mounted police patrolled, police cars had parked in an empty area not far from the road, and an ambulance waited in case of an emergency. Detective Morales strode from one officer to another as if she were a general, commanding her troops.

"Tomorrow is the last full day of the Fiesta, and the police are not even close to making an arrest." Nikki faced Eduardo with sadness.

"Maybe the police know more than we do," he said.

"After yesterday's strange visit to Estrada in Placitas, I doubt it."

"Tonight, let's honor Cindy and Kenny," Eduardo suggested.

Analyzing the entire setup, Nikki stepped closer to her husband and whispered. "This will not be a solemn event. It's going to be a circus. I wish I'd declined to speak."

"Let's see how it goes," he said in a reassuring tone.

Two limos drove up. The chauffeurs opened the doors to let out about ten people.

Stan and Melissa were the first to step out.

"What happened to our limo?" Eduardo asked, laughing.

"I told Gustavo we'd drive ourselves."

"Well, doesn't that lady appear to be important," Eduardo said, watching two women exit another limo.

"That's Carol Peters," Nikki said. "Looks like she has Kenny's mother, Juanita, with her."

Stan crossed in front of the VIP section to join Nikki and Eduardo.

"Looks like everything is set up," Stan said, rubbing his hands together in a nervous gesture.

The VIP section had filled up, only leaving the reserved spots in the front row open. The bleachers were full, and the standing crowd overflowed into the field of parched, trampled grass.

"How many people are speaking tonight?" Nikki asked.

"Only a handful," Stan said, glancing at the entire field. "I want to make it more about the minute of silence and the music. Melissa and Derek will be masters of ceremony. I'll limit my remarks about Kenny. I don't want to break down."

Stan took a folded piece of paper and handed it to Nikki.

It was a program listing the speakers, the candle lighting, and the selection of music. It gave thanks to the Fiesta organizers and sponsors, those who had helped plan and coordinate the vigil, and the many who had expressed condolences to the families who lost loved ones.

Passing the program to Eduardo, Nikki focused on Stan. "May I ask a question?"

"Of course."

"Carol Peters may have stolen your technology and yet she's here as a VIP?"

Stan pursed his lips. "The police detective asked me to make sure she's included as a guest since she's an important sponsor of the balloon fiesta."

"I see," Nikki said, raising her eyebrows.

# CHAPTER FIFTY-EIGHT

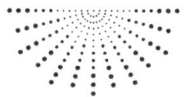

The sun was low in the sky and would soon cast its golden glow on the Sandia Mountains, transforming the rugged, muted gray of their peaks into pinkish-red watermelon hues. The loud hum of the crowd quieted as the musicians filled the air with Vivaldi's *Four Seasons*.

Nikki and Eduardo sat on the right side of the front row of the VIP section. Despite her worry that the vigil would turn into a circus spectacle, a solemn and spiritual feeling had settled upon the crowd. She wished the Smiths were in attendance.

Melissa and Derek were center stage, in front of the musicians. Dressed in a gold-colored lamé evening gown, Melissa looked every inch the *Vogue* model that she was. Holding a microphone in her hand, she welcomed everyone. Next, she thanked the VIP guests, including sponsors and politicians. She thanked her husband, his chase crew, and the volunteers from the company Potholes and More for putting such a fitting tribute together for the two victims of the balloon crash.

Derek, also holding a mic, welcomed Stan to the stage.

Stan's voice, thick with emotion, carried across the hushed crowd as he thanked the guests for attending.

"Kenny," he said, "was more than my son—he was my fearless ballooning companion. He had a love for the skies that matched my own.

From the time he was little, he participated in chase crews. As soon as his age allowed, he became a licensed hot-air balloon pilot. Though his time with us was far too short, he lived every moment with passion and wonder." Stan paused for a moment. "I can only hope he's soaring even higher now, where the winds never fade and the skies have no limits."

Stan thanked Juanita Rodriguez for being such a wonderful mother to their son, and Melissa for helping him through this sad time of his life. He finished by asking the crowd to read the *Ecclesiastes* verse with him.

Derek took the mic from Stan. "Now please welcome Nikki Garcia to the stage for a few words about her sister-in-law, Cindy Smith Garcia, who also died in the crash."

Nikki stepped forward. Taking the mic, she stood tall and swallowed hard.

"Cindy was a light in our lives," Nikki said in a strong voice laced with sorrow. "She was the kindest person I've ever known, and she made everyone feel welcome. She had a strength of character that carried her through life's challenges, and a love for her husband Andy and their daughter Olivia that was unwavering." Nikki paused for a deep inhale before continuing.

"She found joy in the simple moments: laughter around the dinner table, the warmth of family, and the adventure of new experiences, like piloting hot-air balloons. She would want ballooning enthusiasts to continue exploring the beauty and boundaries of this incredible sport. Cindy would tell you that ballooning is the safest sport in aviation, backed by statistics from the National Transportation Safety Board.

"Losing Cindy leaves a space in our hearts that can never be filled, but I take comfort in knowing that love does not end. I ask you to recite with me the verse from *John* 11:25–26 where Jesus said, 'I am the resurrection and the life. The one who believes in me will live, even though they die; and whoever lives by believing in me will never die.' Cindy's spirit lives on in all of us, in the love she gave and the memories her family and friends will cherish forever."

The crowd exploded into applause as Nikki left the stage.

Carol was standing by the stairs to the stage. Nikki had not seen Carol's name on the program, but perhaps, as a Fiesta sponsor, she'd been asked to say a few words. Glancing over her shoulder to see the stage, Nikki made her way to her seat next to Eduardo.

As Carol took the stage, Derek approached her. He seemed perplexed. She asked for the mic, and he handed it to her.

"I want to say a few words on behalf of Juanita Rodriguez, Kenny's grieving mother . . ."

Melissa rushed toward Carol and ordered her off the stage.

"I'll only take a minute," Carol protested.

Gasps and murmurs erupted from the crowd.

"You stole my husband's technology, and you have the hypocrisy to stand up here. Leave. Leave, right now." Melissa's voice boomed over the sound system, each word causing loud static.

Nikki cringed. Melissa was out of line. Even if Carol had stolen the technology, Melissa should not accuse her in public.

"Juanita asked me to say . . ."

"Get out of here!" Melissa insisted.

Two officers scrambled up the stairs. One of them took Carol's arm and helped her off the stage. The three spoke for a few seconds. Carol then walked behind the VIP section.

Derek turned to the musicians and waved his hand as if he were the conductor. On cue, they played "Amazing Grace."

Stan rushed up on stage, took Melissa's hand, and escorted her off.

As soon as the musicians finished, Derek introduced the pastor who would have the final word. He handed the mic to the pastor and exited the stage.

The dark blues of the eastern sky hugged the dusty rose and lavender hues of the Sandias. The scene was so dramatic that Nikki wasn't sure if anyone heard the pastor's farewell. Simple words could not compete with the final shifting of colors in the mountains, from the lively pinks to the darker magentas now enveloping the mountains.

The pastor's voice rose across the sound system. He asked for a minute of silence for the two deceased victims of the balloon accident.

When the pastor spoke again, it was to ask everyone to turn the candles on. One minute later, the musicians broke into a rendition of "Ave Maria."

Detective Morales stepped up as Nikki and Eduardo stood.

"Where's Carol?" Morales asked.

Nikki glanced at the other side of the VIP seats. Juanita was being escorted off by Stan, presumably to her limo, given the direction they were headed.

"In this crowd, it's impossible to tell," Nikki said, "but if we follow Juanita, Carol is sure to show up since they came together."

The three of them walked through the throng of people leaving the event and approached the limousine where Juanita was waiting.

Morales knocked on the car window and waited for Juanita to roll it down.

"I'm looking for Carol Peters. Do you know where she is?"

"I'm waiting too. After she came off the stage, she was visibly upset. She disappeared behind the bleachers. Next I saw Derek Brown with her. He seemed to be consoling her. They went that way," Juanita said, pointing toward the back of the field where the porta-potties and the parking lots were located.

"How long ago?" Morales asked.

Juanita looked at her watch. "About forty minutes ago. Before the music, while the pastor spoke."

"Do you know what kind of car Derek drives?" Morales asked.

Juanita shrugged. "No clue."

"I don't know either," Nikki said, "but in the pictures you showed me, Derek got into an SUV that Brad Wood was driving."

Morales took her mobile phone out. The field had a few lampposts scattered along the road, but the area where they stood was quite dark, except for the lights coming from vehicles leaving the park. Juanita opened the door and asked the detective to climb in so she could see her phone better.

Morales cussed when she found the pictures. "I didn't get the license plate." She used her phone to make a call. "I need for you to put out a 'be on the lookout alert', a BOLO, for a white Honda CR-V owned, or at least driven, by either Derek Brown or Brad Wood. If located, stop it, and call me."

She thanked Juanita and stepped out of the limo.

"I'll call Carol," Morales said, dialing a number.

When there was no answer, Morales informed Nikki she was going to do rounds with the police on patrol to see if they'd seen anything unusual. After that, she'd return to her office before heading home. "Call me if you need anything."

"Look over there," Nikki said. "It's Derek."

"Wait here," Morales told Nikki as she walked away.

Nikki watched as Morales and Derek spoke, but she was too far away to pick up the conversation or even body language.

After three or four minutes, Morales rejoined Nikki.

"Derek took Carol for a short walk to get her over the embarrassment of Melissa accosting her on stage. Then she left in a taxi."

"Interesting that she left without saying anything to Juanita," Nikki said. "We should tell her what happened, so she doesn't wait around for Carol."

Morales agreed. "Why don't you tell Juanita while I call off the BOLO."

# CHAPTER FIFTY-NINE

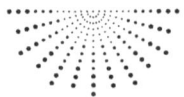

Nikki glanced at her watch as they arrived at the hotel parking lot. "Wild traffic." The drive from the vigil had taken them almost forty-five minutes. Keiko and Olivia might already be asleep.

Looking up at the windows of their hotel, she saw dim lights coming from Keiko's room. Maybe she was awake after all. She dialed Keiko to let her know they were on their way. No answer. She dialed again, thinking Keiko might be giving Olivia a bath before putting her in bed.

Still no answer.

"Quick, let's make sure everything's okay," she told Eduardo.

They dashed to the elevators. Impatient, Nikki punched the elevator button several times.

When it arrived, she jumped in. Eduardo was right behind her. As they stepped into their dimly lit hotel room, a strange unease settled over her. The air was still, unnaturally so. Eduardo flicked on the overhead light.

The connecting door was closed. Nikki threw it open.

The twin beds remained untouched, the pillows perfectly in place.

A chill ran down Nikki's spine. She dialed Keiko's number one more time. It sounded right in the room, under Keiko's bed.

Eduardo knelt and picked it up, turning it in his hands. The screen was shattered, the case bent. His jaw tightened. "This wasn't an accident."

"It's Carol," Nikki said, her heart pounding. "That's why she left early. That's why she didn't answer the phone when Morales called."

"Why do you think it's Carol?" Eduardo asked.

"She followed me to Old Town when I took Keiko and Olivia yesterday. She's spying on us. I'm afraid she wants to hurt Andy."

Nikki dialed the police detective.

"It's Nikki," she said, breathing hard. "Keiko and Olivia are missing. Their beds were not slept in, and Keiko's phone's been destroyed. I'm heading to Carol's boutique hotel in the North Valley. She's behind all this." She hung up before giving Morales a chance to respond.

Eduardo met her eyes, his expression dark with concern. He didn't need to say a word—he was going with her.

They were running out of time.

---

Carol did not answer the door. Nikki dialed her number, and her pulse pounded in her ears as she heard the phone's faint ring inside the pueblo-style casita.

"Something's terribly wrong," Nikki said, looking at Carol's BMW. "That's her car. Where is she? Where has she taken Olivia and Keiko?"

Eduardo's jaw tightened. He searched the immediate area around the front for clues. "There's a motorcycle here," he said. "Does she ride?"

"How would I know?" Nikki looked around desperately for something to break a window or the door. "We need to get inside that casita."

"I'm going around back," Eduardo said.

Nikki followed him, their footsteps crunching on the dry gravel. As they rounded the back corner, the sight before them sent a jolt of adrenaline through Nikki's veins.

Two hundred feet away, a massive balloon lay half-inflated, its nylon envelope glowing eerily orange in the darkness as the burner roared to life. The rhythmic blasts of gas echoed across the open space, drowning out the sounds of the night.

Through the din, she heard Olivia's terrified cries.

"Olivia!" she shouted and ran, panicked, toward the gondola.

Eduardo was right behind her, but before they closed the distance, a figure spun toward them from the balloon's gondola.

Derek. His face, half-lit by the flickering glow of the burner, was cold and determined.

Then the gun came up.

Nikki skidded to a stop. The metallic glint of the weapon froze her in place. Eduardo stopped beside her.

"Don't take another step," Derek warned, his voice calm, almost bored. His hand was steady on the gun.

Nikki's mind raced. She had to save her niece. And what had Derek done with Keiko?

The balloon's envelope rippled open as the hot air inflated it.

"Derek, put the gun down," Nikki said, praying the balloon would not rise into the air. "This isn't going to end well for you."

"It's going to end just fine." He smirked. "I'll get rid of all of you. I'll have the technology, the patents. Everything."

Desperate to find a way to take Derek down, Nikki looked around. A stake with a taut rope through it held the balloon to the ground. It was about three feet away. She shifted her weight ever so slightly, calculating her next move. She needed to distract the mad man, anything to close the gap between them, something to bring the man to the ground. She had an idea. It was reckless, but she had to save Olivia.

Nikki glanced briefly at Eduardo. With a small hand movement, she telegraphed that she was going to make a move.

Then, with a sharp breath, she lunged. Not toward Derek, but to the side, landing near the stake. She rolled on the ground in case he aimed for her.

Derek's hand shifted sharply in reaction to the unexpected movement. A shot rang out. A dull thump sounded when it hit the ground. His killer instinct kicked in, and he readjusted his aim.

That split second was all Eduardo needed. He charged forward, tackling Derek just as a second shot tore into the night.

# CHAPTER SIXTY

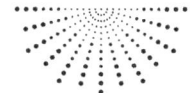

The gunshot split the night, a deafening crack that sent a shockwave of terror through Nikki.

"Eduardo!" she screamed, her heart pumping as if it would jump out of her ribcage.

On the ground, Eduardo and Derek were locked in a brutal fight. Derek had dropped the gun an arm's reach away. He stretched for it. Eduardo struggled to keep him from getting it.

Nikki's stomach twisted as she saw them battle. Who'd been hit? She started for the gun. But what if Derek untied the rope that tethered the balloon to the ground? She was torn. That balloon had to remain on the ground. Could she risk running to the propane burner to turn it off? In her terrified state, would she know which lever to turn?

She jumped toward the gondola.

At the same moment, Derek broke free. He kicked Eduardo in the groin and lunged for the stake anchoring the balloon. His fingers wrapped around the metal clasp that held the rope taut.

"Nooo!" Nikki shouted, turning in mid-air to face Derek.

With a violent yank, Derek loosened the rope. The balloon wobbled as if it had a mind of its own.

Eduardo scrambled to his feet and tackled Derek before he could fully release the tether. The two men rolled in the dust, their arms pounding and their legs kicking. The gun lay a few feet away and Nikki sprinted for it but had to veer off when the balloon's envelope billowed. The gondola moved, whipping the rope across the ground. Nikki grabbed the rope. It burned her palms, but she hung on.

"Hold it down!" Eduardo shouted, sweating to keep Derek from reaching the rope.

Nikki threw her full weight on the ground to keep the rope, and the balloon, from flying loose. The balloon tugged hard against her body. She didn't know how much longer she could hold on. Or how much longer Eduardo could contain Derek.

Olivia's terrified cries pierced the night air. And Nikki's heart.

Hold on, Nikki commanded herself. Hold on for Olivia's sake.

Eduardo shoved an elbow into Derek's chest, causing him to wheeze. But Derek fought on, like a wild man, and threw Eduardo off to the side.

Derek jumped to his feet and ran toward the gun.

Eduardo, right behind him, threw him to the ground. Derek reached for the gun, but Eduardo slammed his foot down on Derek's hand. Then, swinging his other leg out to knock the gun further away, Eduardo crashed to the ground.

At that instant, headlights flooded the yard.

Nikki, holding onto the rope, turned toward the headlights.

Lisa Morales hit the ground running, flanked by two uniformed officers, their Kevlar vests catching the glow of the balloon's burner and their service weapons at the ready.

"It's Derek," Nikki screamed. "He's kidnapped Olivia."

One officer tackled Derek from behind, driving a knee into his spine and pinning him hard against the dirt. The other officer kicked the gun even further away. Morales picked it up.

Nikki, still on the ground using her body to hold the balloon tether, yelled. "Help me keep the balloon from flying away."

The second officer headed to turn the burner off. He pulled the rip line, and the envelope began deflating, slowly. Nikki felt the rush of warm air escaping the envelope. There was no time for the officer to fully deflate it—that would have to wait. But the danger of the balloon flying away had been eliminated.

With the propane burner off, Morales helped Nikki get up.

Eduardo rolled aside, gasping for breath. Nikki knelt at his side, her sore hands skimming over his chest, searching for blood.

"Are you hit?" she choked out.

Eduardo coughed. "No, I'm fine, thanks to the Kevlar."

Relief crashed over her like a tidal wave, but then she heard Olivia's cries again.

Nikki jumped up. "Olivia, I'm coming!" Without hesitating, she sprinted the last few yards, leaping next to the gondola.

She expected to see Olivia, not the sight inside the gondola. In the flickering light of the headlights, three bodies lay motionless, bound, and gagged. A cold wave of horror washed over her. Were they . . . dead? "No," she whispered, shaking her head. "No, no, no. This can't be."

Olivia crawled over one of the bodies. Nikki's heart skipped several beats when she recognized Keiko's clothes. The child reached the side of the gondola and grabbed the wicker lining to stand and walk toward Nikki.

Nikki pulled her over the side of the gondola into her arms. The little girl clung to her, sobbing into her shoulder.

"It's okay," Nikki murmured, rocking her gently. She had to soothe Olivia before calling for help. "I'm here to take you home, sweetheart."

She tightened her hold on Olivia, shielding the little girl's face from the scene.

A flicker of movement! Keiko's leg stretched out ever so slightly.

Nikki gasped. "She's alive!" Turning toward Morales, she shouted, her voice raw with urgency, "I need help!"

The detective turned sharply from the spot where the officers were securing Derek with handcuffs.

"I've found three of his victims," Nikki cried out.

"Quick!" Morales commanded the officers. "Secure him in the van and get to the balloon."

An officer shoved Derek into the patrol van, locking him inside, while the others, including Eduardo, rushed toward the gondola. Nikki handed Olivia to her husband and climbed into the gondola.

Nikki dropped to her knees, her fingers working to remove the ropes binding Keiko's wrists. The rope burns she got from holding the balloon's tether made her clumsy, not able to loosen the straps holding Keiko. "Hang on," she murmured. "We'll get you out."

Keiko's eyes, wide with pain, met hers. She couldn't speak through the tape, but Nikki saw the relief in them.

Carol and Melissa lay just as tightly bound, groans their only communication. Earlier, the hissing sound of the burner must have drowned out their groaning.

The officers climbed into the gondola, flashlights on and knives slicing through the thick ropes.

"Careful," Eduardo said. "Don't cut their skin."

Keiko moaned as her arms came free, her fingers barely moving. Carol sagged forward, breathing heavily. Melissa, dazed, let her head relax, chin tucked toward her chest.

One of the officers peeled the tape from Keiko's mouth. She gasped, swallowing air greedily.

"We thought . . ." she coughed, her voice hoarse. "We thought he was going to kill us."

Nikki exhaled sharply. Back on solid ground, she took Olivia from Eduardo. The child's small arms clung tight around her neck. She kissed her niece's hair. "You're safe," she whispered. "Everyone is safe now."

Detective Morales crouched beside Carol, helping to remove the last restraints. "We'll get medics out here. Just hold on."

"Before we move them too far, I want to check their wrists, arms, and ankles. Then we'll walk them to the van where there's better light, and I can triage them," Eduardo said.

Nikki took a deep breath. The nightmare wasn't over. But at least for now they'd survived.

# CHAPTER SIXTY-ONE

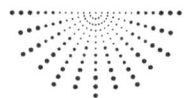

One of the officers opened the back of the patrol van so Eduardo could examine the victims before the EMTs arrived. Carol suggested the casita, offering the key to Eduardo.

"The van will work just fine. It's a quick exam," he said, thanking her.

The officer ordered Derek to sit at the very back. He read him his Miranda rights and told him he was under arrest. Then he took a seat to guard him.

Eduardo asked Nikki to bring Olivia. She saw Derek in the back of the van and started crying, so Eduardo took her to the cab and left the door open so he could have good lighting. He spoke gently to her, telling her everything was okay. Once she quieted down, he checked her and handed her to Nikki.

Eduardo called Keiko and asked her to sit on the floor of the van, between the open rear doors. He examined the lacerations on her wrists and ankles from the tight ropes. She followed his instructions, keeping her eyes focused on his index finger as he moved it left to right, then up and down. Keiko was very quiet during the examination, only talking when Eduardo asked questions. Perhaps she was so still since the detective, the officers, and Nikki were all anxiously staring at her.

"The EMTs will have alcohol and bandages for the lacerations. Other than that, you're doing well. Sit over there," Eduardo said, pointing to a bench at the back of the casita, "and make circles with your ankles and wrists to get the blood flowing again."

Carol's arms were covered in deep scratches, and they were bleeding.

"Fortunately, there's nothing serious about these," Eduardo said, "but they need to be disinfected when the EMTs get here, and you'll need to care for them daily, so they don't get infected."

"There is something seriously wrong with me, all right," Carol said.

Surprised, Eduardo asked what was wrong.

"It's called lack of common sense," she said.

"Common sense on what?" Morales asked.

"That idiot sitting in the back," Carol said, tilting her head toward Derek. "He convinced me to register patents on technology he stole from Stan."

"You were happy to do it. I didn't force you," Derek said. "Have you conveniently forgotten Luxembourg was your suggestion? That laws are lax there, so we'd get away with it?"

"That was before I knew you were a killer. And before I knew you'd promised to sell the product to a cartel."

The light from the van lit up Melissa's face. She was beet red. "You planned to kill my husband, didn't you?"

"How do you know?" Morales asked, looking straight at Melissa.

"You son of a bitch," Melissa shouted at Derek, ignoring the detective. "You deceived me."

Derek laughed out loud. "You didn't swear at me when I set up the app on your phone to spy on your husband."

"You dirty bastard," Melissa was shaking. "Before I left for New York, you asked me to take you into the garage to perform a quality check on the burner system. It's clear to me now, you tampered with the burner. You caused the balloon to crash." She turned to the detective. "He wanted to kill Stan."

Nikki was surprised that the police had allowed the shouting to continue, but maybe they thought the truth should come out regardless of who was present to hear it. Besides, Derek had been given his Miranda rights, so if he wanted to talk, it was his risk. He was smart enough to know what he was doing.

Morales climbed into the back of the van and sat next to Derek. "Was that your plan? To kill Stan?"

"He had it coming." Derek sneered. "That man never fulfilled his promise to make me a partner."

"So, you were going to kill him?" Morales repeated.

Derek fell silent.

"And you ordered Maxine Sanchez, the reporter killed, didn't you?" Morales asked.

"I want my lawyer," Derek whispered.

# CHAPTER SIXTY-TWO

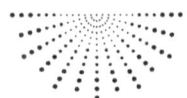

The EMTs arrived and Eduardo asked everyone to step over to the ambulance, except for Derek who remained handcuffed in the patrol van. They would examine him last, since he had not been bound.

Melissa asked the detective to call her husband. He would still be at the balloon field, helping to take everything down to prepare for the Saturday events.

"Derek offered to drive me home. Stan trusted him. My husband needs to know I'm being detained"—Melissa sniffled—"detained by the police for questioning. I have not done anything wrong except to let Derek into our garage. I didn't know he'd tamper with the burner."

Detective Morales asked one of the officers to call Stan Stevens. She pulled Nikki and Eduardo aside. "I'll let you take Keiko with you if you'll bring her in tomorrow for an interview."

"Thanks. What time do you want to see her?"

"Noonish," Morales said, with a nod to the others. "I'll be up most the night questioning this group."

"We're free to return to the hotel as soon as the EMTs clear Keiko. Is that right?" Eduardo asked. "I also want to check on Andy."

"I have two officers guarding him. He should be fine, but I'll check,"

Morales said. She took a few steps away to call the guards. She rejoined Eduardo. "Andy's fine."

Nikki, carrying Olivia, joined them.

Morales looked at Nikki for a few seconds and then at the ground. "I'm sorry I didn't send someone to protect Keiko and Olivia."

"You know," Eduardo said, "it's been a difficult time for our family. Despite everything, the vigil was a beautiful tribute to Cindy and Kenny." He glanced over his shoulder toward the van. "It looks like the culprit will be punished soon enough."

The detective thanked Nikki for all the help she'd provided. "Quite honestly, I could not have solved this case without you. Though there's still a lot waiting for us."

"What's next?" Eduardo asked.

"Formally charging Derek," she said. "I'll keep you abreast as we proceed. I'll still need to investigate the cartel side. Your guy Clive, who's determining if there's a national security issue involving the cartels, will need to decide whether he has a case or not. We'll see."

"Please keep us informed," Eduardo said.

"If it goes to trial, I may need both of you, and Keiko, to testify in court."

Eduardo nodded. "Just let us know."

The detective glanced at Nikki one more time. "We still have a few loose ends. We'll discuss them when I see you tomorrow."

"Sure," Nikki said.

The medical team released Keiko. She handed a prescription to Eduardo. "They said I should fill this and apply it to my wounds until they heal."

Eduardo opened the rental for his family to climb in.

Despite the soreness of her arms, Keiko asked if she could place Olivia in her car seat. "I'll sit in the back with her."

Once they were on the road, Keiko hummed a familiar lullaby and soon Olivia was asleep.

Eduardo asked Keiko what had happened.

"About fifteen minutes after you left for the vigil, someone knocked on the door. I looked through the peephole and saw a man wearing a zebra shirt. I thought he was looking for you, so I asked what he wanted.

"Said he had something to drop off for Andy Garcia. He held a package for me to see. I opened the door, and a gun came up into my face.

"He shoved me back into the room, grabbed Olivia, and told me to stomp on my mobile phone and throw it under the bed. With his gun pointed at Olivia, I did what he ordered. He handed Olivia to me and held the gun in his jacket pocket and said that if I did not obey, he'd shoot the child first, and then me."

Keiko coughed.

"He took us to that place you found us. At gunpoint, he got me out. I had Olivia in my arms. The balloon's gondola was tipped to one side, there in the back of the casita. He put Olivia in it while he gagged and bound me. My precious magomusume was so scared that she cried the whole time. Then he picked me up and dumped me in the gondola. He straightened it upright. Olivia stayed next to me, patting my face as if she understood I couldn't talk or move."

"What happened next?" Eduardo asked.

"It seemed as if we were there for hours. Then I heard a motorcycle. I couldn't see anything, but I heard a woman's voice. Friendly at first, and then our kidnapper must have turned on her because she screamed. He dragged her to the gondola and dropped her in with us. It was horrible. I couldn't speak, and by then, she had tape across her face too. She looked terrified."

"Do you know who it was?" Nikki asked.

"The older of the two women. The younger one was the last one he brought. But he left by truck, not on the motorcycle, to get her. Since the place is not too far from the balloon field, he brought the younger one shortly before the two of you arrived. She was harder to tie down."

"In what way?" Eduardo asked.

"The truck arrived. He must have had her gagged already and her hands tied, but I heard them running. He caught her, tied her ankles, dragged her to the balloon, and threw her in. At that point he laughed, said he'd take care of all of us soon, and I heard the burner system start. It provided light and I could see what was in the gondola. Then you arrived and saved us."

"I'm so sorry you went through this ordeal. Thank God you and Olivia are okay," Nikki said. "As well as the other two."

"Let's get on to more positive thoughts," Eduardo said. "We can't leave until Monday. We have the whole weekend here. I can take care of Olivia tomorrow so you and Keiko can relax. Maybe visit the museum or explore Old Town."

Nikki looked hesitant but turned to Keiko to ask if she was interested in the museum.

"Not really," she responded. "I'd like to stay with Olivia. She needs to recover from today's trauma."

"I agree," Nikki said. "Plus, we meet Morales at noon. Maybe in the future, after tonight's awful mess is forgotten, we can plan a motorcycle vacation on Route 66."

"Or we can all go to Spain and hike the Camino de Santiago," Eduardo suggested.

"Oh, I like that idea better," Nikki said.

# CHAPTER SIXTY-THREE

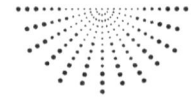

Nikki arrived with Keiko at the police station. The receptionist said the detective wanted to meet with Nikki first.

"Did you bring your niece and Keiko with you?" Morales asked upon seeing Nikki.

"Eduardo's taking care of Olivia. He didn't want people to think she was a suspect!" Nikki smiled. "And Keiko's in the lobby."

"I have to admit you were right about Derek when you took that picture of him after the crash." Morales waved for Nikki to take a seat.

"I suspected everyone at one point or another, even Stan," Nikki said with a sigh. "As the week passed, Carol seemed most likely to be the perpetrator. When my brother told us he'd overheard her conversation about patenting the technology stolen from Stan, I knew she was the culprit. That's why I rushed to her place when we found Keiko and Olivia missing."

"She's not squeaky clean, as you know. She'll face charges," Morales said, "but it's Derek who stole the technology. He also stole the drone from Stan's company and masterminded the whole scheme for his personal gain. He admitted that Stan was his target. He didn't know Stan was not flying the balloon until after the accident happened. Claims he would not have harmed anyone else if Stan had been killed."

"I doubt that's true," Nikki said.

"Why?"

"He told us when we first got to the casita last night that he'd get rid of all of us and he'd be king of the mountain, so to speak, owning the patents. I think he was planning to kill Carol too."

Morales sighed. "You might be correct. He admitted that he was going to fly the balloon over the west mesa, over those volcano wannabes out there, and throw his victims out of the balloon."

"He's a sick person," Nikki shuddered. "Only a monster could plan something so terrible. Must have thought he was invincible because he still had Andy, Eduardo, and me to get rid of."

"And Stan," Morales added.

"I always suspected the drone was stolen from Omega Satellites," Nikki said. "The perpetrator wanted the product codes on the equipment to make it appear Stan had crashed his own balloon."

"Like Stan was a madman committing suicide, or at least a reckless balloonist. I should have suspected Derek." Morales shook her head. "Derek has admitted to tampering with the valve, stealing the drone, and using it to bring the balloon down. He was angry that you saw him run across the field to readjust the valve after the balloon crashed."

"Did he send the person in to harm my brother?"

Morales nodded. "Your recommendation to search on the INTERPOL website paid off. I have a suspect. A fellow that's the registered agent for the shell company in Luxembourg."

"A foreigner?" Nikki, shocked by the news, sat up straighter in her chair. "My office manager did some research and thought the front people were American citizens."

"And she's right. He's a US citizen, living abroad. But he changed his name when he went to live in Luxembourg. He was a fugitive from the US, wanted for securities fraud."

Nikki shook her head. "That's unbelievable."

"There are ways to bring him to justice. It may take a little longer, but we'll charge him." Morales furrowed her brow. "After I found a match in the INTERPOL database, Derek confirmed it when I questioned him."

"What about Carol?" Nikki asked.

"Derek confessed to having an affair with her. He bragged about women falling for him and doing what he asked them to, like getting Melissa to let him into the garage of her Albuquerque condo while Stan was at his office. He'd convinced Carol to will the patents on the stolen technology to him. And he did the same for her. But his plan all along was to get rid of her and the patents would be solely his. The crimes were all premeditated."

Nikki's color drained from her face. "He might be a genius but he's too brash and arrogant about his abilities. I don't get why he needed Carol to participate in the patents."

"He needed Carol's money to get things set up in Luxembourg."

"Thought he could get away with murder, eh?"

"You got it," Morales said.

"What will Carol be charged with?"

"She's a coconspirator. She was into stealing Stan's technology and registering for patents in Europe. Her plan was to do it in a way that appeared as if she and Derek were the ones who got the technology first. Stan could have sued them once he found out, but they took the risk."

Nikki shook her head in disbelief.

"The profits from selling the drones would be split fifty-fifty," Morales continued. "But Carol presumably knew nothing about killing Stan or Derek's intention to supply drones to the cartel. He started the rumor about sales to China, but she was the one that told Maxine, the reporter, about it." Morales scribbled a couple of notes to herself on a pad of paper as she spoke.

"Unbelievable how criminals think they will never get caught. What about Maxine?" Nikki asked.

"Derek thought Maxine was on to him, so he had her killed."

"That suggests there's a connection between Derek and the Vasquez Medina cartel. It was probably the cartel that orchestrated the killing."

"I think so too," Morales said. "Derek will pay for his crimes. I'll make sure of it. I'll need you to testify for the prosecution when this case goes to trial."

"Absolutely. So will Eduardo and Keiko."

Morales was looking through the window of her office. "Derek told me that he planned to move to Luxembourg after he took care of his dirty business. Fortunately, we caught him." She turned toward Nikki. "Listen, I want to thank you for your help."

"Quite honestly, I didn't do much at all," Nikki said. "The hardest part was convincing you that I might supply you with good data."

They both laughed.

"I'm serious when I say that you contributed a lot," Morales said. "By the way, Carol said she did not see you by the church in Old Town. Said she went to pick up a piece of jewelry she had repaired. I thought you'd like to know where everything stands before you leave town."

Nikki bit her lower lip, still thinking about the case. "Derek was one of the MCs of the vigil. He pranced on that stage in front of the crowd like a hero. Given his performance, no one would suspect him. After all, he was a close friend of Stan's."

"Yeah," Morales said, "he was there to gloat that he'd get away with it all." She shook her head. "I'll never understand a criminal's motivation."

"You understand them pretty well. Otherwise, you would not be such a good detective." Nikki thanked her and stood to leave.

"Please send Keiko in."

---

Nikki said goodbye to the receptionist and asked her to tell Keiko she was waiting outside. She wanted to call Floyd and Charlotte.

When Charlotte picked up on the first ring, Nikki asked her to put Floyd on the call so all three of them could talk.

"Are you okay?" Charlotte asked, concern ringing in her voice.

"I have good news," Nikki responded.

Floyd joined the conversation.

"The police caught the guy responsible for bringing the balloon down. It's a bigger plot than I had imagined," Nikki said.

"Like cartels being involved?" Floyd asked.

"That's right," Nikki said. "How did you know?"

"Clive's kept in close contact. Says the cartel is posing a national security issue because of the drone capability Derek Brown may have already given them. Presumably, the shell company had a European manufacturer producing the drones already."

"I wonder if the police detective knows that?" Nikki asked.

"I don't know, but Clive will be in contact with her," Floyd said.

"She's asked Eduardo, Keiko, and me to testify at the trial."

"It'll take a while before they build a case," Floyd said. "The good part is that Clive kept you out of the part involving the cartel."

"Now that the arrests have been made, when will you come home?" Charlotte asked. "The office needs you in Miami."

"Glad you asked. Andy should be released from the hospital on Monday. We'll fly out that afternoon. I'll be happy to get back."

# CHAPTER SIXTY-FOUR

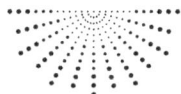

## ONE MONTH LATER

The scent of dashi, the rich, briny stock used in so many Japanese dishes, permeated the kitchen as Nikki and Keiko prepared Japanese omelets.

Before sitting down to breakfast, Nikki refilled Eduardo and Andy's coffee cups. Keiko carried cups of green tea for Nikki and herself. Steam curled from the cups as they gathered round the table, enjoying the quiet rhythm of their home after the chaos of Albuquerque.

Andy, still recovering from his surgery, sat comfortably with Olivia perched on his knee. She focused on drawing squiggly lines, which she called horses, on a blank sheet of newsprint. She drew with both hands, holding a black crayon in her right hand and a brown one in her left. She broke the tranquility in the room as she finished each drawing by smacking the palms of her hands on the table to imitate the clattering of hooves, as Keiko had shown her during their playtime in Albuquerque.

The kidnapping trauma seemed to be in the distant past, though not forgotten. What none of them would ever forget, Nikki knew, was the emptiness Cindy's absence left behind. Her joyous laughter, her presence, her very life, reduced to a mere memory.

Olivia finished another squiggly horse and made the hoof clattering sound on the table. Her laughter filled the room, and Nikki knew at that moment that both Andy and Olivia would be fine as they faced their new lives.

The group spoke quietly about nothing in particular as they savored the Japanese omelets. Andy mentioned his therapy sessions were progressing so well that his therapist thought he only needed a couple more weeks.

"I'll have a lot of work waiting for me when I return to New Mexico. But first, I'll take care of Cindy's ashes. She loved New Mexico so much that she told me that if anything ever happened, she wanted to have her ashes scattered in the mountains near Peñasco." Andy said. "We both agreed to that. It's in our wills."

"We'll fly out for the memorial service," Eduardo said.

"I got a phone call from Cindy's parents today," Andy said.

Nikki was surprised.

"Harold apologized for blaming me for Cindy's death. Said he was angry that she'd been taken so young. But they want to visit Olivia and me once we return to New Mexico. They will also fly out for the memorial service."

"I'm so glad to hear that Harold's come around," Nikki said.

"I also talked to my research fellows. Said they'd be happy to see me return. They've kept the animals fed and the research going, and as we move into the winter months, I'll let them handle most of the work with the bears. Hiring those two was a great decision."

"Don't leave until you're ready," Eduardo said. "Another month here should be good. You can't push it, you know."

Nikki glanced at her husband. Eduardo had been busy since their return to Miami Beach. He'd performed two brain surgeries in the last twenty-four hours at Mount Sinai Hospital.

"You should take a nap after we eat," Nikki said. "You could be called in again."

"I'm supposed to be off for the next two days," he said, stretching his arms above his head. "My patients are in good hands."

"Hmm, you've only had two hours of sleep. Maybe you're transforming into superman and don't need sleep," Nikki said. "Or you've found the elixir of youth."

"My sleep research might discover which," Andy said with a chuckle.

Keiko took the last of the breakfast dishes to the dishwasher.

"I want everyone to go outside," Nikki whispered, taking advantage of Keiko's absence from the table. "I have a surprise for her."

Once everyone gathered in the driveway, Nikki pressed the garage door remote. As it opened, a shiny red Kawasaki Ninja came into view.

Nikki put her arm around Keiko. "That's for you."

Keiko's jaw dropped. She looked at Nikki and signaled Eduardo to move closer. She embraced them both. "You two are my youshi, my adopted children."

"So I'm finally your youshi," Eduardo said with enthusiasm. "It's never too late."

"Can I ride it now?" she asked.

"Of course," Nikki said. "Your helmet is hanging from the handlebar."

It took Keiko no time to strap the helmet in place, climb into the seat, and start the motorcycle.

Olivia broke away from her father's hand and ran to Keiko, holding her arms up, begging her to put her on the bike.

"When you're older, my magomusume."

"Yes, when you're older," Andy said, taking Olivia's hand and stepping aside to let Keiko take the bike for a spin.

---

Eduardo opened the front door about an hour later when Keiko returned. She went through the house to open the garage door and put the motorcycle in. She returned to the living room to join the family.

"How did the ride go?" Eduardo asked.

"Wonderful. I'll like it even better when you and Nikki join me."

"Let's do that tomorrow," Eduardo said, yawning. He reached out for Nikki's hand. "Right now, I'm ready for a nap."

Nikki closed the door behind them as soon as they stepped into their bedroom. They fell into each other's arms, hungry to make love. Eduardo kissed her slowly, then passionately, playfully biting her neck, and unbuttoning her blouse. She responded with equal yearning.

"You *are* my superman," Nikki said between breaths.

Eduardo looked into her eyes. "In you, I've found the elixir of youth," he whispered.

# A NOTE FROM KATHRYN

Thank you for reading *Terror in Desert Skies*, the seventh novel in the **Nikki Garcia Mystery Series**.

If you enjoyed it, I would very much appreciate a review on Amazon, BookBub, and Goodreads so that other readers may also find Nikki's adventures.

**Newsletter**
If you would like to learn about my new releases, sales, and giveaways, please sign up for my newsletter at https://www.kathryn-lane.com

You can contact me by email me at KathrynLaneAuthor@gmail.com

**Social Media**
I invite you to follow me on:
Instagram: https://instagram.com/kathrynlaneauthor/
Facebook: https://www.facebook.com/kathrynlanewriter/
X: https://twitter.com/kathrynlane13

Thank you!
Kathryn Lane

# BOOKS BY KATHRYN LANE

**The Nikki Garcia Mystery Series**
*Waking Up in Medellin*
*Danger in the Coyote Zone*
*Revenge in Barcelona*
*Missing in Miami*
*Rage in the Wilderness*
*Murder in Monte Carlo*
*Terror in Desert Skies*

Audiobooks: The first six Nikki Garcia Mysteries are on Audiobooks
Box Set: The Nikki Garcia Mystery Series (A Trilogy)
Translated into Spanish: *Despertando en Medellín*

**Other Books by Kathryn Lane**
*Backyard Volcano (Short Stories)*
*Stolen Diary*
Spanish Translation: *Secretos Robados* (Publication – September-October 2025)

# AWARDS AND PRAISE FOR KATHRYN'S BOOKS

## WAKING UP IN MEDELLIN (NIKKI GARCIA MYSTERY #1)

***Waking Up in Medellin*** was named "Best Fiction Book of the Year—2017" by the Killer Nashville International Mystery Writers' Conference and won Killer Nashville's "Best Fiction—Adult Suspense—2017." It was also a finalist for the Roné Award.

## DANGER IN THE COYOTE ZONE (NIKKI GARCIA MYSTERY #2)

FIRST PLACE
AWARD WINNER

***Danger in the Coyote Zone*** won first place in the 2018 Action/Adventure Category of the Latino Books into Movies Award. It was named a finalist in both the 2018 Book Excellence Awards and the thriller category at the 2018 Killer Nashville International Mystery Writers' Conference.

## REVENGE IN BARCELONA (NIKKI GARCIA MYSTERY #3)

FIRST PLACE
AWARD WINNER

***Revenge in Barcelona*** won first place in the Latino Books into Movies—Latino themed TV series category 2020 and a silver medal in the Reader Views Literary Awards mystery category 2020. It was a finalist in the Eric Hoffer 2020 Book Awards, the Silver Falchion in suspense by Killer Nashville, the suspense category by Next Generation Book Awards, and the 2020 International Latino Book Awards. It was also awarded five stars by Readers' Favorite.

## MISSING IN MIAMI (NIKKI GARCIA MYSTERY #4)

FIRST PLACE AWARD WINNER

***Missing in Miami*** is the winner of the 2022 International Latino Book Awards, Best eBook Fiction. It received honorable mention in the 2022 International Latino Book Awards for best novel, mystery. It was noted as a distinguished favorite in the mystery category of the NYC Big Book Award and a finalist in Readers' Favorite, fiction-mystery-general.

## MURDER IN MONTE CARLO (NIKKI GARCIA MYSTERY #6)

Global Book Awards awarded ***Murder in Monte Carlo*** the silver medal in the Mystery - International category.

***Murder in Monte Carlo*** also received 5 stars from Readers' Favorite.

## STOLEN DIARY (FAMILY LIFE FICTION AND MYSTERY)

***Stolen Diary*** is the winner of the 2023 National Association of Independent Writers and Editors Book Awards Contest in the Genre Book category, and the winner of the 2023 National Indie Excellence Award for general fiction. It was also a finalist at the Killer Nashville International Mystery Writers' Conference in 2024.

## BACKYARD VOLCANO AND OTHER MYSTERIES OF THE HEART (SHORT STORY COLLECTION)

***Backyard Volcano and Other Mysteries of the Heart*** was named "Best Short Story Collection—2018" by the Killer Nashville International Mystery Writers' Conference.

# ACKNOWLEDGEMENTS

I am indebted to countless individuals, many of them from book clubs I visit, who ask for more Nikki Garcia adventures and request sequels to Jasmin's story. Their enthusiasm for my work motivates me to continue writing. The list is too long to include them all. Listed below are individuals who contributed directly to **Terror in Desert Skies**.

My incredible husband, Bob Hurt, who not only supports my writing but also happens to be my most enthusiastic fan.

I am grateful for my expert readers, also called Beta readers, Dr. Joseph Burckhardt, Andrew Mills, and Jorge Lane Terrazas. Their hard work in reviewing the manuscript and the feedback they offered make **Terror in Desert Skies** a better read.

I owe my gratitude to Dr. Lowell Mick White, who generously guided my early efforts to write and continues to offer advice on many of my writing projects.

I owe so much to my editor, Sandra A. Spicher. And special thanks to the cover designer, Zizi Iryaspraha Subiyarta, the book interior designer, Danielle Hartman Acee, and the designer of the Tortuga Publishing, LLC logo, Maureen Donelan.

To my readers, family, friends, and fans—I could not do it without you!

Thanks to all of you for accompanying Nikki on her journeys.

*Kathryn Lane*

# ABOUT THE AUTHOR

Photo by Mindy Harmon

Kathryn Lane writes mystery and suspense novels usually set in foreign countries. In her award-winning **Nikki Garcia Mystery Series**, her protagonist is a private investigator based in Miami who travels to various locations to investigate crime cases. Her latest novel, *Terror in Desert Skies*, is set in New Mexico.

*Stolen Diary*, about a math genius, is an award-winning novel of family life fiction and mystery. It is set in Mexico, the US, and Canada.

Kathryn grew up in a small town in northern Mexico and moved to a cattle station in the Outback of Australia when she married. After three-

and-a-half years in the Outback, she returned to Mexico and then moved to the US where she completed her Bachelor of Fine Arts degree and worked for a short period as a starving artist. To earn a living, she gave up the art world and enrolled in the MBA program at the University of New Mexico. She became a certified public accountant and worked for Johnson & Johnson in international finance.

Her enthusiasm for travel and her love of other cultures has been a great part of her life. She traveled extensively during her finance career, and since becoming a full-time writer, she travels for research purposes for her novels. Kathryn has now traveled to one hundred countries and counting.

Kathryn and her husband, Bob Hurt, live in Houston, Texas. If Kathryn is not traveling, writing, or researching, you might find her in the kitchen cooking up a storm.

amazon.com/-/e/B01D0J1YES
bookbub.com/authors/kathryn-lane
goodreads.com/kathrynlane
facebook.com/kathrynlanewriter
instagram.com/kathrynlaneauthor

Made in the USA
Coppell, TX
16 September 2025